In Due Time

a novel

by

Chaveevah Cheryl Banks Ferguson

In Due Time

NOTE: If this book was purchased without a cover, you should be aware that this book is stolen property. It was reported an "unsold and destroyed" to the publisher, and neither the author nor the publisher has received any payment for this "stripped book".

In Due Time

Published by A.J. Banks & Associates, Inc.
8282 East Outer Drive
Detroit, MI 48213-1386

ISBN: 0-97189-39-0-X
Library of Congress Catalog Card Number:

First Edition: (May 2002)

First mass market edition: November 2002

Printed in the United States of America

Photography & Cover Art by Lori Dale
Cover Models: Chantrice Vanarsdale and Lawrence Daniels

For my father, Phil Banks, Jr., lovingly known as "Pete"
[January 14, 1925-January 1, 2002]

You were strong, just, generous, and unabashedly proud of all your progeny and our accomplishments—both real and perceived. I'll never forget the pride in your eyes when I gave you my first, unedited, rough-draft of a manuscript; anyone would have thought you'd just received the first draft of a *New York Times* #1 best-seller. Thank you for instilling in me a belief that *anything* is possible. I love you, Daddy.

ACKNOWLEDGEMENTS

All thanks and praise to the Creator for the many blessings bestowed. Lord, place and keep my feet on a righteous path; never let me forget all You have done for me.

My mother, Emma L. Banks. Thanks, Ma, for your constant encouragement and love. Like Daddy, I love you for always making me feel that I could do anything.

My older brother, Al Banks. Thank you—your support, your confident [just-this-side of arrogant] Banks "can-do" spirit, and the fire you lit under me brought my words to these pages. Love you, Alfie!

Drs. Scharron Clayton and Jerry Domatob, thank you for providing much-needed technical advice, editing assistance, and constructive feedback. You saw what I could not.

Carolyn Banks and Phillip Banks, my big sister and younger brother, many thanks for your uplifting words and attentive ears. Being between you two has always been like a "sammich of love".

My sons and daughters, Tulani, Gadeeayl, Rishonah, Rabee, and Nia—thanks for "staying on my tail" and asking, "when are you gonna finish it?" and "what are you gonna do with your book?". Rishonah, a special thanks for always asking to read the new pages as I wrote them.

To Freddy McGregor, Steel Pulse, Bob Marley, and

all the other reggae artists whose music provided inspiration and meditation while I worked; 'nuff respect.

Enka Henderson, part of my Chi-town "posse" thanks for always saying "wait, y'all, let Chaveevah tell it!" it was you who made me realize I am a storyteller. Y'deedah Coleman, you left the posse and this earth way too soon, girl. Miss you.

Joshalyn "Rocki" Hickey, Pamela Campbell, Patricia Harris, Eular Harris, Lori Dale, Shelly Theroith, Tisch Jones, Chantrice Vanarsdale—thank you for being my Iowa posse: for laughing, crying, joking, supporting, encouraging, and kicking it with me. Y'all know how we do. Oh, and Lori? Girrrl, your cover art is all that and then some—Asante Sana.

To all the Banks-Barlow family and friends whose love, concern, and good-old-down-to-earth "realness" make me know I have a cherished place in this world. Thank you.

My husband, Jeffrey Ferguson—thank you for just *being*. You were patient as I spent untold hours at the computer writing, without complaint. You watched sports while I wrote; but you believed, sight unseen, that I *could* and *would* someday publish my work. You encouraged me when I wasn't feeling good about the process, and I will forever be thankful for your enthusiasm and love. I love you.

CHAPTER ONE

Tera awoke suddenly, as though she'd been yanked from her warm bed and tossed into a pool of ice water; it had happened again.

Familiar things in her bedroom came slowly into focus—the ceiling fan, the oak dresser, the armchair where she'd carelessly flung her clothes the night before—and she lay there for a few moments, breathing heavily as she got reoriented to her surroundings. She reached for the lamp on the night table, but not to turn it on; she just wanted to touch it, to feel its carved pottery designs. She ran her hands across the cool cotton sheets, the nubby chenille bedspread; it was as though she needed their solidity, their *realness* to prove to herself that she was really in her own bedroom. Tera wasn't afraid, but more than a little frustrated at what was happening to her.

For weeks, she'd had the same dream night after night. Each morning she'd feel herself wrenched from the peace and serenity of that dream; at first, she hadn't though much about it, but now she couldn't help but wonder what it all meant. Or if it meant anything. As she lay there in bed, her breathing slowing to normal, Tera remembered the dream in vivid detail. Nightly repetition had etched it deeply into her memory. Closing her eyes, she recalled the sensation of a light, cool breeze gently caressing her arms, raising gooseflesh.

She breathed the dense, humid air, felt the condensed moisture of morning dew on her bare feet as she slipped quietly across the damp grass. It was dark and still, so dark Tera could barely see her hand in front of her face, but she walked on soundlessly until she reached the meeting place. There was a field, broad and level, with an ancient oak seated squarely in the middle. In the dimness Tera could still make out the silhouette of the sheltering giant, and hurriedly moved closer to the tree. Every few moments, she'd look over her shoulder or pause to listen for other footsteps; she couldn't risk being followed. Certain that she'd not been followed, Tera huddled beneath the oak, gathered her damp, sweeping skirts under her, and waited. Songs of crickets and sparrows broke the stillness. It was pitch black, and Tera had hoped that she wouldn't have much longer to wait for him. She wasn't afraid of the dark, morning was probably less than an hour away; but she wanted him to hurry to her, because she knew daylight must not find them together in that field. Tera looked toward the abandoned farmhouse in the distance. She savored the cool night wind, knowing that the coming day would bring stifling heat.

The crickets grew louder, and Tera's heart was heavy with disappointment. Morning was coming; would he even be able to make it? No sooner than she'd had that thought, it seemed, Tera heard a faint rustling of grass behind her. She sat stock-still, waiting for the signal. There it was: "crk, crk, kee". Was that him? Barely breathing, Tera listened closely. She heard it again, the near-perfect imitation of a speckle-bird. He was there! Tera turned to see him, her eyes straining into the darkness. Hearing her movement, he quickly stepped from behind the massive trunk of the old oak and swept her up from the wet grass into his waiting arms. "My love," she whispered. Her arms encircled him, warmed by the heat of his broad back. Her fingers stroked his sleek skin, marred in places by long-healed scars; Tera held on for dear life, knowing their precious moments together would be all too brief.

Forever, it seemed, they hung onto each other. When they finally released one another, Tera reached up and took his face between her hands, straining to see his eyes in the darkness; but she could not. She had tried to talk to him, had a thousand questions to ask, but knew that he would not answer; had never answered.

There was a sameness to their meetings, an indescribable mixture of comfort, anxiety, peace, joy, and anguish, which was replayed again and again each time they met in that dark, deserted field, under that secretive oak, in the hour just before dawn. They would lie together, huddled beneath the tree and cherish each moment; no words were ever spoken, and as the first faint rays of sunlight fringed the black skies, gradually brightening tree and field and sky, he would leave. Silently he would leave, running low through the tall grass, stopping once to turn and wave at her before cautiously moving on past the dilapidated farmhouse. For a few quiet moments Tera would watch him as he made his way further and further across the densely flowered field, growing smaller in the distance until he finally disappeared across a ridge...and then came the abrupt awakening that had spirited her away from that peacefulness time after time.

The first few times it had happened, Tera had awakened in tears; the sense of longing was almost more than she could bear. Now, she only laid in bed long enough to get her bearings, then got up, showered, and made coffee before getting ready for the long Metra ride into Chicago from the south suburbs. She'd once mulled over the idea of seeing a therapist to help her make some sense of it all; but couldn't quite get over her perception of a '*therapist*' being a '*shrink*'. And she most definitely didn't need a shrink. After all, everybody dreamed, didn't they?

Tera got up and walked through her small townhouse to the kitchen. She liked living out in Richton Park; she walked naked past glass patio doors facing the lagoon in the center of a wide field behind the loosely-spaced homes. No neighbors close enough to spy on her, she thought, unless they had high-powered binoculars or something. Standing at the spotless counter, Tera began a morning ritual that had become almost second nature: she measured enough coffee and water for half a pot, started the coffee maker, and headed back past the patio doors to the bathroom. Golden rays from the rising sun slowly crept across the quiet lagoon and flooded into Tera's living room, bathing it in a butterscotch glow, and she paused for a minute. Tera loved mornings like this; she sighed heavily, wishing she didn't have to make that long haul into the city, but it was the last day of classes and she had to be there for finals.

She stepped into the brightly-lit bathroom and pulled back the shower curtain. Setting the water temperature, she stepped in. The full force of the warm, cascading water was both relaxing and invigorating. She thought again of the recurring dream and had to admit to herself that, even though she didn't feel that a visit to a therapist was warranted, there was something strange and disturbing about that dream. She was having it far too regularly, and it left her with so many unanswered questions. Like *where was she? Where was that lonely field, so dark and deserted she'd never dream of visiting it, other than during her nightly journeys?* She didn't remember ever having been to a place like that. As a child, she'd never liked outdoor picnics or nature hikes or anything like that, and had only recently grown to appreciate the outdoors; she just couldn't stand all those bugs. *Why did she go to that place night after night, to meet God knows who?* On awakening, Tera could clearly recall the feeling of love and joy at seeing him...*but who was he?* The dream was always dark, so dark she could never quite make out the man's face. *But if it was that dark, how had she always managed to find their meeting place--that giant, twisted oak?* And her clothes! The stiff, sleeveless bodice and long, floor-length skirts of rough cotton, so long that she had to lift them in order to run across the grass without stumbling. The tattered shawl she sometimes wore tied around her waist in case the night air was too cool, that she might need to cover her bare arms. *Her bare feet!* It was mysterious, but only a dream, Tera concluded, letting the warm tide of water rush over her. She was no dream interpreter, and had no intention of trying to make sense of this one. She scrubbed vigorously, determined not to spend her precious morning time before work, *especially* a beautiful morning like this, trying to figure out something that obviously had no explanation. She turned the water off and stepped out of the shower. *Yep*, Tera thought, *just a dream.* Strangely vivid, but not really frightening. Now, if it had been some kind of nightmare that had left her tense and rest broken night after night, there might have been cause for alarm; but no such haps. Just a dream. *And the man?* Just a dream lover. Tall, thickly muscled, handsome (Tera had a feeling he was, though she'd never actually seen his face), and totally in love with her. *Not such a bad situation*, Tera thought, especially since there was no real, live, flesh-and-blood man totally in love with her. Or totally *in 'like'* with her. Or even especially fond of her. In fact, when Tera considered how long it had been since she'd actually been with a real, live, flesh-and-blood man, the memory of Dream Lover's strong arms wrapped around her had seemed almost *therapeutic*; hence, no need for a therapist, right? Laughing softly to herself, Tera dried off with a fluffy pink-and-black bath towel, and followed the aroma of strong coffee into the kitchen.

The sun's glare was blinding as she sat at the counter, still wrapped in the towel and sipping a mug of high octane Kenyan blend she'd gotten from a coffee shop in Chicago, down on Clark Street. The gourmet shops where you could buy practically anything from a coffee lover's dream, and the chocolate shops where you could buy plump, chocolate-dipped, juicy strawberries or creamy truffles were Tera's consolation for having to make the Metra ride, or--*heaven forbid!*--the drive into Chicago. Well, that wasn't exactly true; Tera worked in Chicago, and loved her job. She'd been an Associate Professor of Communications at Roosevelt University for the past two years, and felt that she'd found her niche. The intellectual stimulation and interaction with her students and colleagues was all she'd hoped it would be, ever since her appointment to that position. She'd spend countless hours during a semester working into the night preparing lessons, reviewing papers, grading exams, or reading current journal articles that her students might find interesting. Tera reflected on how satisfied she was with her life and career, and with that thought, glanced at the wall clock above the refrigerator. It was 7:30; in another hour, she'd be making the short drive to the Richton Park Metra station near the Windwood Condominiums. From there, she'd catch the 8:45 train into downtown Chicago and walk the few blocks from the Randolph Street Station over to Roosevelt. Tera sighed again, looking out on the shimmering lagoon and wishing she'd gotten a teaching assistant to proctor her final exams; she'd have traded almost any favor to still be sitting there in her kitchen and watching the ducks paddle lazily across the water. "Oh well," she said aloud, "duty calls." It was for the best, Tera thought. If she sat around much longer, she'd probably start thinking about that stupid dream again.

This was the last day of the semester, a beautiful late spring day, and after this she'd have the whole summer to kick back--that is, unless she opted to teach a class or two over the summer. Sitting there with another mug of coffee, she knew that summer classes would *not* be on the agenda. She'd worked hard that entire academic year, and wasn't entirely sure that all those late hours hadn't been the trigger that had started those crazy dreams in the first place. No, *this summer*, she promised herself, *Miss Tera Morton is gonna take it easy. Lay back in a chaise lounge in my back yard and watch the clouds. And ducks. Maybe even take a trip to some island and really max out. Yeah, I'll take a vacation! Then, see if Dream Lover will still be able to find his way into my dreams.*

Tera smiled, pleased with herself that she'd diagnosed her own problem and gotten to the root of what was causing her strange dreams. Why, that $75-an-hour shrink fee she *wasn't* gonna pay twice a week for the next however-long would go toward buying cute, wispy little things to wear on some sunny Caribbean beach. Tera dressed quickly and, exams in hand, stepped out into the warm spring morning.

###

The ride into Chicago, though long and interrupted by a number of passenger stops, was usually relaxing for Tera; that particular morning was no exception. The train was semi-packed with commuters making their way to work. Luckily, Tera had gotten a window seat and was able to focus her attention away from the influx of passengers filing back and forth through the narrow aisle. She watched the landscape, if one could call it that, whiz by. Sprawling strip malls. Office buildings displaying bronze-tinted windows and square, green lawns with built-in sprinkler systems. Densely wooded acres of land that might have been beautiful, had they been well-tended instead of used as a dumping ground. Construction sites with beautifully landscaped condo communities rising up on one side, and tractors, earth movers, and freshly-dug foundations on the other. Tera watched as a tractor's digging arm chunked deeply into the black soil, scooping up massive amounts of dirt and rocks. She wondered why in the world they'd never *finish* these complexes before letting people move into them. *I'd be pissed,* she thought, *if all I could see through the windows of my beautiful new home were dirty tractors and ugly gashes in the earth.*

She thought about her own comfortable little sanctuary with its rolling green lawn, tall slender willow trees, and shimmering lagoon...and again wished that she was laid back on a blanket in jeans and a t-shirt, whiling away the hours with a good book. "Soon enough," she whispered, and pulled a copy of her final from the worn leather attache her sister had given her as a graduation gift years before. She put on her sunglasses to cut the sun's glare on the white copy. For perhaps the tenth time she studied the exam item by item, looking for errors or ambiguous language. She'd been too absorbed in what she was doing to pay much attention to the person sitting next to her, until his deep voice broke her concentration.

"Tsk, tsk, tsk!," he said jokingly, "is *that* a way to pass an exam? And checking out the answer key, no less!"

Tera peeped over the edge of her sunglasses, caught off-guard by the stranger's boldness; not to mention distracting, coal-black eyes that held secrets in their depths.

"Excuse me?," she asked, giving him much attitude. She'd taken that train ride countless times, and could depend on at least three things: number one, the train would be punctual, number two, the ride would be *tedious*--and, therefore, a good time to catch up on reading--and last but not least, *no one* would dare make small talk with a perfect stranger. This man wasn't about to change the rules.

"Tsk, tsk," he repeated, " and got the *nerve* to cut your eyes at me 'cause I busted you!"

Tera took her sunglasses off and really gave him a cold once-over.

"Listen, brother--in the *first* place, you don't know me, okay? And in the second place, you dippin' up in something you don't know about. *Get you some business*, okay?"

Tera felt like two cents waiting for change when the

open, friendly smile faded.
"Whoa! I'm sorry miss," he apologized. "Just making small talk! Guess my friends in Atlanta were right when they told me Northerners weren't all that sociable. Excuse me for bothering you."
The man's perfect profile stared straight ahead. Tera could have kicked herself; he was only trying to be friendly, and she'd chopped him off at the kneecaps. She was ashamed of herself. One of the reasons why *she'd* moved out of the city was because everybody seemed so cold and aloof, and here she was, promoting that same image; she couldn't just leave things that way.
"Hey, excuse *me*," she said, "*I'm* sorry. I didn't mean to be so..."
"Cold?," he asked, finishing her sentence. Tera looked at him, mouth wide open. The warmth had returned to his eyes, and she had to laugh at her own foolish behavior.
"Yeah," she answered, "I didn't mean to be like that. It's just that I...I ride this train every day, and...well--"
"And you're not used to talking to strangers, right?"
"Something like that."
"Well, I was born and raised in Decatur, Georgia and lived most of my life in the South, and *I am* used to talking to strangers. I didn't mean anything by it...just making conversation."
"I know, and I'm sorry. Really. I was just sort of preoccupied, and you took me by surprise, that's all."
"Oh, I could tell," he laughed. "My name's Cameron."
"Nice to meet you, Cameron. I'm Tera," she smiled, extending her hand. Cameron clutched his chest, pretending to have a heart attack.
"Whoa!," he said, "do I believe *this*? This same evil Chicago girl who just chewed me up and spit me out is actually gonna *shake my hand*? I tell you, wonders

never cease."
Tera just looked at him.
"Hey, now! Don't be so serious. I'm sorry; I just like to joke around a lot, that's all. Cameron's big hand caught Tera's in a firm grip. "Nice to meet you too, Miss Tera."
His oval eyes crinkled into an easy smile, and Tera was glad she'd broken down the wall of ice she'd built. Small talk was awkward for her, but she tried anyway. "So, Cameron. You say you've lived most of your life in the South; what brings you here?"
Oops! What was she doing, asking this man his personal business? Hadn't she just put him in check moments earlier about getting in *hers*? Cameron smiled at her again; she could almost see him making a mental note of that contradiction, but answered anyway.
"Well...school, actually. Tying up loose ends, you might say."
"Oh," Tera answered. She was curious, but didn't dare pry information out of him.
They were both silent for a minute.
"So, Tera," Cameron began, "looks like *you've* got some kind of interest in school yourself." He pointed to the attache on her lap, exam sticking out of one of the side flaps. "Sorry if I was out of pocket about you having that exam, or answer key, or whatever; I was only joking, but hey, if that *is* the case, who am I to pass judgment, you know?"
"Well, you weren't out of pocket, not really...but you're wrong if you think I'm using it to cheat."
"Really wasn't my business, anyway."
"True. But you're still wrong if you think I'm skimming it to pass a test."
Cameron leaner over and looked closely at the papers; a slightly amused, slightly cynical look was on his face. "Well, Tera, *I* take your word for it, that you're not

using those papers to pass an exam but, uh, what would your Professor Morton have to say about you having that answer key?"
Tera smiled slyly. "I really don't think Professor Morton would have a problem with it," she said.
"No? You mean you got it like *that*?," Cameron asked.
"Yeah, I guess I do," she answered. "Let me properly introduce myself. I'm Tera Morton; Professor Tera Morton."
Cameron stared at her blankly for a moment before his eyes crinkled again in a look that was part surprise, part delight, part admiration. His smile widened.
"Well, this *is* a pleasure, Pro-*fessa* Tera Morton," Cameron said. I'm Cameron Wilson. Guess that's what I get for dipping. Sorry about the wrong first impression. Now, I feel like an idiot."
"No need," Tera replied, "I guess you could say we're even now; I felt like an idiot for raking you over the coals about getting in my business, then turning right around and jumping up in yours."
Cameron laughed.
"Yeah, come to think of it, I'd thought that was kinda out of character--for one of y'all Northerners, that is. My friends told me, '*don't talk to people, don't ask people questions...don't even* <u>*look*</u> *at people*'. That is, unless I was looking for trouble."
Tera smiled quietly, wondering if *she* was courting trouble, holding conversation with this strange man. She had no regrets about clearing the air between them--she knew she'd behaved badly--but she was at a loss as to where the conversation should go beyond that point. It was weird; a spark was struck, as they say, and Tera felt as comfortable with him as though they'd known each other for years. He seemed open and sincere, and Lord knows he was easy on the eyes; but he was still a stranger. And Tera Morton didn't talk

to strangers on the train.

They had lapsed into a comfortable silence, and Tera gazed out the window rather than grin at the man like a thunderstruck teenager. There was mutual attraction there, Tera admitted, but no way to check it out, and nowhere for it to go. She couldn't--*wouldn't*--give him her phone number; that would have been ill thought-out, *desperate*, and maybe even dangerous. He could be some kind of nut case, beautiful exterior or no. She could, of course, accept *his* number...but he hadn't offered it, and Tera wasn't about to ask. And even if he did give her his number before the train ride ended, Tera knew she'd have second thoughts about calling him; again, he might just be a psychopath or axe murderer or something. Cameron smiled at her, deep dimples creasing his handsome face. *There's no way*, Tera thought, *that this man could be dangerous...except maybe to a woman's heart*. Too bad he wasn't a cousin or uncle or brother of a friend of a friend, or *something*. That way, she'd have a chance to check him out, see what he was about...*what in the world are you thinking?!*, Tera asked herself. Even if she had known everything about Mr. Cameron Wilson's background, there was still no room in her life for getting to know *him*, or anyone else new, for that matter. She turned and started looking out the window again, watching scenery and morning traffic rush by. At that point in Tera's life, if someone wasn't one of her students, or colleagues, or old friends, or family, there was simply no time for them. Period. She was overworked, trying to hang on for a few more days until she could make simple, take-it-easy plans for the summer; and she was hopeful that the change from her hectic schedule would ease the tension she believed was causing her dreams. Her plate was full, and that didn't leave space for new relationships--even new friends.

The train descended into one of the tunnels beneath the downtown area, and would soon reach Randolph Station. In spite of herself, she'd enjoyed her brief encounter with Cameron but was still relieved that the ride was over, and she apparently wouldn't have to wonder what she'd do if he asked to see her again. As the train slowed to make its stop Tera turned to Cameron, ready to tell him she'd enjoyed talking to him, only to find him getting ready to stand, his hand extended a final time.

"Well Tera," he said, "this is my stop; it's been nice talking to you."

"Same here, Cameron. It's my stop, too. *And*, it was nice talking to you, too."

"Get outta here! Man, this is something; I wasn't really ready to say goodbye to you, and, well...now it looks like I won't have to."

"Well, Cameron..."

"Oh, hey--I won't make a nuisance of myself. I wouldn't want to mess up, after we finally got on the right track here. But if it's not a problem, maybe I can walk with you as far as you're going. Or *I'm* going. You know what I mean," he said.

"Okay," Tera answered.

They filed into the aisle as the stream of passengers emptied from the train, and they walked out onto the busy platform. They herded onto an escalator along with dozens of others and ascended to the brightly-lit station. Sunlight streaming through the skylight made Tera long to see the last, finished exam stacked on her desk. In a couple more days, Tera thought, one of the department secretaries would fax her the exam grades; she would calculate semester grades, fax them back to the registrar, and then--*Hallelujah!*--Barbados, Jamaica, Puerto Rico, or some other warm place had better clear an extra space on the beach.

Tera and Cameron left the station through the Wabash Street exit, walking south past Grant Park. Tera's pace slowed as she took in the surrounding greenery; she'd never understood how people could just scurry past the park without so much as acknowledging its beauty and tranquility.

Just across the street, tall brick buildings, restaurants, shops, and theaters stood shoulder to shoulder, a world apart from the endless stretch of massive trees, bushes, and velvet lawns where Cameron and Tera strolled. They paused for a moment, studying a huge bronze statue of a Native American warrior on horseback. The horse reared back on its hind legs, every muscle flexed, nostrils flaring, while the solemn-faced rider drew back the string of his heavy bow, aiming for the heavens. Age had tarnished parts of the gleaming bronze, darkening the sinews of both horse and rider.

"It's beautiful, isn't it?," Tera asked.

"Sure is," Cameron answered, his eyes sweeping across Tera's slender body.

Uh-oh, Tera thought. She was enjoying his attention, but had resigned herself to the fact that, for all the reasons she'd considered, *nothing* was going to happen between her and this man. Cameron hadn't offered her a number where he could be reached, Roosevelt University's gigantic stone archways were now directly across the street, and it was time for her to tell her new commuter friend goodbye. Maybe they'd run into each other again on the train; Tera hoped so.

When the traffic lights changed, they cautiously made their way across the wide street, which was choked with slow-moving cars jockeying for a position to move once the lights changed again. Standing in front of the university building, Tera turned to

Cameron and smiled.
"Well," she said, "looks like this is where we say goodbye. It *was* nice meeting you."
Cameron shook his head in disbelief.
"This is a *trip*," he said. "I was just getting ready to say something like that to *you*! This is where I'm going, too."
Tera eyed him suspiciously, thinking that he may have just been making it up; *kind of, sort of, not minding if he'd just been making it up.* Then, she remembered him saying that he was in Chicago because of school.
"Okay, okay...so *this* is where you've got the loose ends that need tying up," Tera said in amazement. "And this is where I teach. Small world! So, tell me about these loose ends; inquiring minds want to know."
Tera's reserve about dipping too deeply in the man's business flew out the window, once she saw that his business had brought him into *her* domain.
"Well, Tera--it's really kind of complicated. I don't talk about it much with people I don't know...or people I *do* know, for that matter, because they either don't understand, or think it's weird, or *both*."
"Try me," Tera said.
"I'm working on my doctoral dissertation," Cameron answered.
"Hmm! Impressive." She couldn't figure out what was so strange about working on a dissertation, though.
"So, what's your field of inquiry, your topic?," she asked.
Cameron took a quick look at his watch, then answered.
"Listen, I'm not only flattered that you're interested enough to ask about my work, I'm grateful I've finally met a woman who might be able to relate to it."
Tera blinked, feeling like she'd lost a chunk of the conversation somewhere.

"I...*don't understand*, Cameron."
"What I'm saying is, it's getting late. You've got to get to your class for finals, right? And I have an appointment with Dr. Mullins in a few minutes."
Tera knew Dr. Mullins; he was the head of the department of Religion and Philosophy, but she still wasn't following Cameron's train of thought.
"Okay...I'm still not getting you."
"Sorry, Tera. When I'm joking around, anything that comes to my mind just jumps out--usually quite bluntly, but when I'm being serious, I tend to beat around the bush too much."
"Like you're doing right now! What's the mystery? Are you gonna tell me about your dissertation, or what?"
"No...I mean, *yes*! I'd love to tell you all about it, but there's no time right now; what if we...talked about it over lunch?"
Cameron looked at her uncertainly. Tera's casual response barely concealed her delight that Cameron had made a move toward seeing her again. Before, she hadn't seen how it would be possible to get to know him better; they were just strangers who'd met on the train. Now, it seemed, Fate was providing not only an opportunity for them to get better acquainted, but one that fit into Tera's orderly, scheduled life perfectly. She'd decided that there was no time for anyone who wasn't her student, family, or colleague, right? Well, it looked like Cameron would fit neatly into the 'colleague' category; some parts of his research might even prove interesting and relevant for discussion in the future with her students.
"Well, Tera?," Cameron asked, 'now who's beating around the bush?"
"Oh, absolutely!," Tera answered, "I'll be finished around 12:30."
"Cool. How about if we meet at...1:00, at that cafe?,"

he asked, pointing to a restaurant
a few doors down with tables and umbrellas out on the sidewalk.
"I'll see you at one." They walked up the steps into the building, each heading for their destination.

###

At 1:00, Tera and Cameron were seated inside the cafe by a window, watching crowds scurry up and down the busy streets. Tera's finals were now in the hands of graders, and school was officially over until September. She casually sipped an iced cappuccino as she sat comfortably in the cushiony booth seat; relaxation settled into her body like a fast-acting drug. Cameron had politely asked how her finals had gone, but how much could be said about that? She was eager to hear about this mysterious dissertation. Cameron cleared his throat and spoke.
"Well, Tera, my study deals with a topic that's not very well-known or understood, at least not by the general public; it's about past life regression," Cameron said between sips of fresh-squeezed orange juice.
Tera leaned forward, intrigued.
"Past life regression? You mean, like, some of us used to have another life, and then...remember it?"
Cameron polished off his juice. "No, I mean, like, *all* of us used to have another life--possibly many of them--but most of us don't consciously remember anything; that's where the 'regression' part comes in. Volunteer subjects are hypnotized and walked backwards through time, if you will, to recall events of these past lives."
"That's fascinating. A little *unbelievable*, but fascinating just the same."
"It really *is* fascinating, you know. And if you'd been in on some of the sessions I've observed, you wouldn't think that it was so unbelievable."
"I don't know; anything's possible, I guess. And

obviously, *you* believe it's possible. You wouldn't have invested over two years of your life in something you didn't believe was founded in reality."
Cameron smiled. "True. I had my doubts at the beginning, but I can't say I was ever really a diehard skeptic. The field of religious study covers a lot of territory, you know."
"So, belief in past lives is a religious phenomenon?"
"Yes...but not *purely*, I'd say. The study of it involves a lot of different disciplines, or I should say, there's a lot ofoverlap; religion, philosophy, cultural studies, psychology.."
The word 'psychology' made Tera flinch. She thought of her dream.
"How do you find your subjects?," Tera asked.
"Actually, they find me. Ads are placed online and in various academic newsletters advertising for participants in the study, and then I wait to see who responds."
"I would think you'd end up getting a fair amount of crackpots responding; how do you deal with that?"
"Oh, there have been a *few*, mostly troubled folks looking for attention, but you'd be surprised; the people who volunteer go through and pass a very strict screening process. They're for real."
Tera leaned further forward, taking in Cameron's every word.
"And the troubled ones? What happens with them?," she asked.
"Well, they're referred to appropriate help, if they're interested. And they usually are."
"That's good. Now, your subjects that you do use, what is it that tips them off that they... how can I put this..."
"Might have had a past life experience? Almost to a person, they've reported having dreams, recurring dreams where they seemed to be in another place or

time."
A chill ran up Tera's spine. She sat back into the booth and gulped the last of the cappuccino. "Interesting," she whispered.
Another question about Cameron's research tried to form on Tera's lips, but he interrupted her.
"Tera," he said, "like I told you earlier, I'm really flattered that you're so interested in my study, but let's talk about something else, okay?"
"Oh...I'm sorry! I'm going on and on about it, like I've forgotten what it's like to be totally consumed by research; guess you're knee-deep in it *enough* without other people jumping in with both feet, too."
"No, that's not it," Cameron smiled. "I'd rather talk about *you*. You didn't think I'd rattle on about academics and waste an opportunity to talk to the finest woman I've met since I've been here, did you?"
Tera was totally charmed; and more than a little grateful for the diversion. Cameron's mention of dreams in past life experiences had been somewhat unsettling, but now his open flirtation was sweeping those disturbing thoughts into a far corner of her mind.

The server had finally arrived with their lunch of seafood salad and broasted potatoes, momentarily breaking the spell Cameron's intense eyes had cast. Tera watched him as they ate, fascinated by his lack of self-consciousness, humor, and overwhelming attractiveness. The man exuded sensuality, but Tera didn't feel uncomfortable. *What was it about him that was so unsettling and so soothing at the same time?* But with her determination to stick to the script she'd written for her life, what difference did his potent mixture of brains and masculinity make?
"None," she whispered.
"What did you say, Tera?," Cameron asked.
"Oh, nothing. Just thinking out loud. Say, it's getting

late, and I..."
"Of course. It's time for you to go. Sorry if I kept you longer than you'd intended."
"No! No, that's not it. I've just got a ton of things to do that have been waiting for me for the last few weeks until this semester wound down, and--"
"Say no more, I understand."
Cameron glanced at his watch, then outside into the street; it was an awkward moment. The server brought their check. Both Cameron and Tera seemed to move in slow motion, neither wanting the meal to end and neither knowing what to say to justify lingering a little longer. Tera gathered her things. *Ask for my number!*, her mind shouted. She slid out of the booth and stood up. With a sigh of resignation, she extended her hand to Cameron a final time to say 'goodbye, it was nice meeting you', but the words wouldn't come. Cameron placed some money on the check tray and began scribbling something on a napkin, ignoring Tera's outstretched hand. He finally grasped her hand, pressing the crumpled napkin firmly into her palm. His smile was that of a shy little boy.
"Here's my number," he said. "Now, I'm not trying to be pushy or anything, but I thought that I'd be more likely to hear from you again if I gave you *my* number instead of asking for yours. I hope you'll call; you will, won't you?"
Now it was Tera's turn to smile. On the outside she was gracious with just a hint of reservation as she accepted the number, but inside, she was shouting "*Yes, yes, yes!*"
"Yes, Cameron...I'll call you," she answered. Cameron stood up and he and Tera made their way to the door and out into the blinding afternoon sunlight. As they walked in the direction of the Randolph Station Tera promised to call Cameron soon, reminding herself all

the while that she'd just met a wonderful new colleague with a lot of interesting and exciting information to share; why shouldn't she be anxious to hear from him again? This was, of course, just a comfortable and respectable facade to hide behind; the truth of the matter was, she was just anxious to hear from him again, *interesting info or not*! Unexpectedly, Cameron walked Tera all the way back to the station; she'd thought that he was only going to walk her a block or so, since he still had some business to attend to at Roosevelt.

"Goodbye, Tera," he whispered, raising her hand to his lips. "Call me." She turned and hurriedly walked to the escalator so he wouldn't see the silly, dreamy smile on her face.

She barely remembered the hour-long ride back to Richton Park. Conflicting emotions simmered like a pot of gumbo: schoolgirl-swooning over a handsome stranger, elation over semester's end, anticipation of much-needed rest [maybe a vacation?], excitement and intellectual stimulation brought on by their lunchtime conversation, more swooning...and *anxiety* over the topic of that lunchtime conversation. *Past life regression*.

Tera didn't know much about it and decided that, other than by its inevitable mention in Cameron's work, she didn't want to know much more about it. Despite her firm (but getting softer by the minute) conviction that her itinerary for life should be followed to the letter, Tera *did* want to know much more about Mr. Cameron Wilson. *Who was he?* Oh, she'd already learned a few things over lunch--bachelor's degree from Morehouse, master's in counseling psychology from Clark Atlanta, parents still living in Atlanta, met Dr. Mullins at a conference in New Orleans and was persuaded by him to come to Roosevelt to pursue his doctorate work in clinical psychology. A sister in Virginia Beach. Brother, sister-in-law, and two nieces in Charlotte. *But what about him? Married? Divorced?* He was in his early thirties, like her; *any unfinished love chapters in his life?* The train slowed to an abrupt stop at the Richton Park station. Tera shook her head; for all her self-talk about 'research' and 'colleague' and 'intellectual conversation' as common ground for herself and Cameron, the questions that popped into her mind had precious little to do with any of that stuff. He was fascinating, and just *way* too fine for her to think about much else except when she might see him again. And she was thoroughly pee-oh'd with herself because of it.

"This is stupid," she said, gathering her things to get off the train.

Despite the air conditioning, her silk blouse was plastered to her back and her linen skirt was hopelessly creased; all she wanted to do was get to her car, drive home, jump into something comfortable, and get a grip on her galloping emotions. She was glad that there weren't many people riding back south; she felt disoriented. It wasn't until she hopped into her car and guided it into traffic that she began to feel in control again.

Before she knew it, she'd negotiated the short drive from the station, and was pulling off into her own driveway.

"Whew," she sighed, dragging herself and her belongings from the car. Once inside the house, she flopped down on the sofa and just sat there for a minute, collecting her thoughts.

"This is stupid," she whispered. Meeting Cameron had thrown her equilibrium off; he was a monkey wrench in the machinery of her orderly little world. Rather, it was the rush of emotions she felt. When she'd left for work that morning, her focus had been on finishing up the semester, and then taking out some time for Tera. Now, she sat thinking about whether 'time for Tera' would include time *with* someone: Cameron. Even thinking about him was too much of a departure from the way Tera usually operated.

Earlier that day when she'd thought about how long it had been since a man was in her life Tera had laughed, but it was the laughter of one who accepts things the way they are. There was no one special, no pressing urge to find someone special, and no time, no room in her life, no patience to accommodate someone special. *So be it!* She accepted it. All it really meant, Tera believed, was that she was free to plan and execute her life's events, free to cruise down life's road without worrying about potholes. But the pounding of her heart when she looked at the name and number scrawled on that napkin from the restaurant told her that something was changing, and she didn't like it. In the course of one day--*which wasn't even over yet*--Tera's thinking and behavior had begun to change drastically. She'd held a conversation with a complete stranger on her ride to work, she'd let him *walk her* to work, she'd had lunch with him, and she'd even taken his phone number, for God's sake, with a *promise* to call him, and soon! And the worst part of it was how much she'd enjoyed it all.

None of this stuff was fitting into her plans; it just wasn't like her. "*This is stupid*," she repeated, jumping up from the couch and heading for her bedroom to look for her jeans. The damp silk blouse and wrinkled skirt were soon in a heap at the foot of Tera's bed as she pulled on the comfortable denims and a Kool Jazz Festival t-shirt. She marched back to the living room, grabbed the stereo remote, and blasted Bob Marley's live version of "Natty Dread". *Just this morning,* she thought, *I was living for the moment I'd get done with classes, get home, and start planning a vacation.* "Nothing's gonna stop that now," she said aloud, looking around for the phone book.

She flipped through until she reached the "travel" section of the yellow pages. Closing her eyes, she waved her finger around a few times like she was doing a magical incantation, and planted it on one of the listings in the open book. "*Soleil Travel Agency*" was the name she saw when she opened her eyes. She dialed the number. Before the Marley CD had finished playing, Tera was booked on a flight out of O'Hare Airport for Montego Bay, Jamaica; she was to leave in ten days for a two-week vacation.

"Enjoy your trip!," the agent said.

"Thanks, I will," Tera replied.

This was more like it. Tera didn't like change, especially hated it when something made her change her plans; before she'd ever laid eyes on Cameron, she'd decided that she wanted—no *needed*—some time alone, and by God, she was going to have it. She wanted to kick herself for the way she'd let her feelings just take free rein before, but she felt better after the call.

When she gathered her things off the sofa and put them away in her room, a smile of satisfaction spread slowly across her face; order was restored. She'd created a situation where, even if she *did* go a little overboard about Cameron, it would only be a 'little'. She was going to Jamaica in ten days. Even if she saw him every day for those ten days [which she *really* had no intention of doing!], her travel plans were now set in stone. It was still very sunny, and unusually warm for spring, even late spring. Tera cranked up the volume on the stereo, opened the glass patio doors, and stepped out onto the thick carpet of grass.

###

The next morning began as mornings usually did for Tera; she awoke with a start, panting and sweating, after a long night of huddling in the darkness near trees and bushes. As usual, she'd seen Dream Lover the night before, in all his glory: tall and strong, muscular and sable-skinned, faceless. Tera had enjoyed the warmth of his arms, probably more than usual, for she'd already decided that her nights with the mysterious man of her dreams were numbered. She was now officially on vacation, looking forward to sun and sand and lazing around, and certain that the much-needed rest and relaxation would banish her anonymous lover from her dreams forever. She stretched lazily under the cool sheets; she'd miss him.

Tera got up and walked to the kitchen. Creature of habit that she was, she measured her usual half-pot of water, put a few scoops of coffee into the brew basket, hit the 'on' switch, and strolled to the shower. She wanted to shout! Even though she had absolutely nowhere else she needed to be, there she was, up at 7:30 and starting that damned coffee maker. She resisted the urge to turn on the morning news or lay something to wear across the bedroom chair; that would've been too much like a regular work day. Instead, she turned on the stereo and pumped Everton Blender's "Slick Me Slick".

The pulsing baseline made her yearn for that flight from O'Hare to Mo'Bay even more. She could just picture herself in a darkened corner near towering speakers, Guinness Stout in hand, bubbling to the rhythm of a *champion* sound system, feeling the motion and heat of countless other bodies jam-packed into a dim, smoky dancehall ...*escape!* Tera's love for the orchestrated chaos of dancehall was probably the greatest contradiction to her otherwise routine, predictable, orderly existence. Tera could hear the rhythmic thump of drum and bass over the roar of the cascading shower. She was tired of the predictability that had prompted her to get up, unaided by alarm clock, and begin the daily ritual of coffee-shower-dress-watch news that had become almost instinctive; she wanted something *different*--at least until September when classes started again.

She wrapped herself in a towel and walked back to her bedroom, acutely aware of the down side of her 'uncomplicated life'. No children. No special man. Everything on automatic pilot, more or less. Sure, she had freedom enough and money enough to do what she wanted, when she wanted; *but when in hell had she ever wanted to do anything*?! Her life revolved around work and family, and it was rare that she did anything that didn't involve one or the other. Her involvement with her family had become less and less frequent, since her sister was married and had a kid; her brother was away at college, and even her parents took long weekends or month-long driving vacations during the summer. Thinking about her trip to Jamaica was both exciting and frightening at once. It was a chance for her to do something out of the ordinary, but she was a little anxious just the same; she was afraid of change, even in the face of her realization that it was what she needed. Tera's life wasn't lonely, exactly; but her house echoed with the stillness of a lone existence, even over the blare of the stereo in the living room. She didn't feel that she needed more people in her life to make it less *lonely*, but to make it fuller, richer. Not just her family. Not just her colleagues from school. *Not just her students!* With more real people in her life, Tera reasoned, there would be less need for her mind to create dream folk to fill the empty spaces.

Sunlight had again flooded the house like the

morning before; Tera smiled. A feeling of freedom enveloped her, something she'd never allowed herself to feel before, at least not so completely. The changes she envisioned would come gradually, she knew. The vacation was only a start. Change wouldn't occur in a quantum leap. But for the first time in her life, she began to feel comfortable with the idea that, instead of being so obsessively focused on leading her life, she'd relax a little, and let life lead *her*. She glanced over at Cameron's crumpled napkin lying on the dresser, and reached for it.

Tera hurriedly dialed the number, before she lost her nerve. As the phone rang, it dawned on her that, just *maybe*, Cameron might still be sleeping. After all, it was early; just because *she* was awake, that didn't mean everyone else was. Flooded with embarrassment, Tera hung up the phone. A few minutes later, after her heart had stopped pounding, Tera decided she'd try the number again later--in the afternoon, maybe. Just as she'd gotten settled at the kitchen counter with her mug of coffee, the phone rang. *Someone else in the world besides me likes getting up early, too*, Tera thought as she answered, a little puzzled about who it might be.

"Hello."

"Good morning, Miss Tera."

Tera almost dropped her mug; *no*, she thought, *it couldn't be.*

"Who is this?," she asked, already recognizing the relaxed, masculine voice on the phone.

"It's me, Cameron! Boy, how soon they forget," he laughed.

"But...how? I didn't give you my number."

"Hey, slow down! No, you didn't give me your number, but--"

"Then how did you get it?," Tera demanded.

Cameron's throaty, sensuous laughter made her

conscious of her silly oversight...almost.
"Think about it for a moment, Tera. Now, didn't you call me this morning? A little while ago?'
"Yes," she answered, still not quite getting the connection.
"And you *still* don't know how I got your number?"
"No."
"Well, I'll let you in on a little secret; the phone company came up with this marvelous invention called 'star-69', and---"
The rest was a blur; Tera felt like such an idiot. Of course, that's how he'd gotten the number. There she was, borderline suspicious that she had a stalker on her hands. Like the other day when she'd snapped him up on the train, Tera felt ashamed.
"Don't make a lot of phone calls, do you?," Cameron asked.
Tera wanted to laugh; this man was having *too* easy a time reading her. She thought about who she usually talked to on the phone, and realized that she didn't 'usually' talk to *anyone*. The conversation she'd had the day before with the travel agent was the longest one she'd had on the phone in weeks. And she didn't have all the usual phone options, because she didn't have much use for them.
"Tera, you still there?"
"Yes...sorry, Cameron. You're right, I don't talk on the phone much. Otherwise, I'd have realized right away about the star-69. Sorry."
"Hey, it's no crime; matter of fact, it's kind of refreshing."
"What?"
"Someone who isn't a certified, card-carrying phone freak. I mean, most people nowadays are so addicted to their phones, they even carry 'em with them when they leave home. In their cars, in their purses or

pockets...even when they don't have one, they're carrying pagers to let them know who's trying to get them when they're not at home. It's kind of weird, if you ask me."

"Me, too. Listen, I was just rummaging around here, and came across that number you gave me, and..."

"And?"

"And I just thought I"d give you a call, like I said."

"Well, I'm glad to hear from you."

An uneasy silence followed, with Tera and Cameron listening to each other's breathing. Cameron finally spoke.

"So, just called to say '*hi*', did you? Or was there something else you wanted to talk about?"

Tera stood there holding the receiver, feeling as awkward and tongue-tied as she'd felt at age 16 when she'd wanted to ask Kenny Newsome to the Sadie Hawkins dance. She'd been crazy about Kenny and he *knew* it, and even though he liked her just as much he was determined that *she* would show some sign of her interest first. Kenny had wanted Tera to go out on a limb and let him know that she wanted *him* for her date, not just any available brother. And just as Kenny had stayed aloof and dragged every word out of her, Cameron was now doing the same thing. This little brush with *deja vu* was slightly pissing Tera off. She continued, trying to sound casual.

"Actually, yes I did want to talk about something else," she said, searching for a believable reason why she was calling, other than the most obvious and true reason--because she wanted to hear his voice.

"I was thinking about where we'd left off discussing your dissertation." *Yeah, that's a good one*, Tera thought.

"Do you have a fax at home?," Cameron asked, his voice sounding husky and languid.

"What?" Tera was confused; *what the hell did that have to do with what she'd just said?*
"Well," Cameron yawned, trying to sound disinterested, "if that's all you wanted to talk about, we could do that anytime, couldn't we? I could fax you some of the passages, if you want to review or help me edit them."
"Uh, well um..." Tera began stumbling over her words; *no, that was not all she wanted to talk about, and he knew it!* His arrogance galled her; *'review or help edit'-- I just know he didn't go there.* Why had she called him in the first place? She was about to breeze through some kind of *'catch you later'* dialogue when Cameron spoke up.
"Listen, Tera. I know you didn't call about research, or my dissertation, or anything else academic. You called because you thought about me, right?"
"You're pretty damned sure of yourself, aren't you?"
"No. Actually, I'm not. I don't know what's going on here, but...there's definitely *something* going on; can't you feel it, too?"
"Look, Cameron--"
"No, Tera *you* look. I don't know what's happening, but crazy sparks jumped off yesterday when we met-- don't tell me you don't know what I'm talking about."
Tera was silent.
"You felt those sparks too, Tera, or you probably wouldn't have called."
More silence.
"This is strange, I know; but it's like...we already know each other, or we *should* know each other. I'm not crazy, Tera. Nothing like this has ever happened to me before."
"Me neither," Tera finally said.
"So it's *not* just me who's picking up on this?"
"No."

"Well, what can we do about it?"
"I really don't know."
"Look now, I'm not suggesting we start shopping around for engraved wedding invitations or anything; I *am* suggesting that we--*very slowly*--start getting to know each other. Really know each other. Find out more about this vibe that's already got us feeling like we've known each other for years."
Tera laughed nervously.
"This is crazy; but you're right--I can't explain it, but I've never felt as close to anyone before in this short a time," she said.
"So let's be straight with each other then, okay?"
"Definitely."
"So...you called just because you wanted to talk to me; not about anything connected to work, right?"
"Oh, can you give it a rest?," Tera sighed. "What do you want me to say?"
"Just say why you called, and we can proceed from there."
"Okay!"
"Okay *what*, Ms. Morton?"
"Okay! I called because I wanted to talk, *alright*? Because I enjoyed having lunch with you yesterday, alright? *Because I was glad you gave me your number*, and I wanted to talk a little something-something--and not about your damned research, which frankly *creeps me out* more than interests me. Is that what you wanted to hear?"
"Whoa! I asked for honesty, but I guess I could've requested it in smaller, more specific doses," Cameron laughed. "Still, we're getting somewhere. I liked having lunch with you too, Tera. Matter of fact, I've enjoyed everything about you since the moment I saw you on that train, all preoccupied and everything... sassy, proud, into your own thing."

"Even the way I chewed you up and spit you out?"
"Well, yeah...even that. Once I figured out that it was just your game face. Guess you need it for the city."
"Hmmm."
"Anyway, I would like to see you again, Tera."
"I'd like to see you too, Cameron."
"Hey! We're on a roll. See how easy that was, just saying what's really on your mind?"
"I suppose that's never been a problem for you."
"Nope! One of the fringe benefits of my Southern upbringing."
"How nice for you," was Tera's dry response.
"Oh come on, woman. We were doing fine for a moment there; don't retreat on me now. Besides, I'm sure there are some fringe benefits to being born and raised north of the Mason-Dixon line, too."
"Of course; I just can't put my finger on what they might be."
"Well, we can find out together. Starting today. So, what would you like to do this afternoon?"
"This...afternoon?," Tera stammered. She was pleased, but totally unprepared for Cameron's quick response to her saying she'd like to see him again. She figured that they might see each other the next day, or the day after...not that same afternoon.
"Yes ma'am, this afternoon. Or, this morning if you'd prefer."
"This morning?! Cameron, you are a trip."
"Hey, just my 'south' coming out again. I meet a woman I like, I tell her. I think she's fine, I tell her. I want to see her again, I *tell* her. No problem. It's just now about quarter to nine. I know you probably got up with the chickens, probably already showered and dressed..."
"You're half right; I just got out of the shower a little while ago."

"Hmm...I won't tell you the image that just popped into my head of you coming out of that steamy shower."

"Cameron!"

"Just kidding, just kidding!," he laughed. "Anyway, I'll bet you could throw on something in no time flat, jump in your car, drive to the station, and meet me at the Lincoln stop in forty-five minutes."

"Forty-five...*minutes*? Cameron--"

"Come on, Tera! It's a beautiful morning, why waste it sitting around in the house? I want to see you, you want to see me...why wait, when we'd probably both just sit and watch the clock until it was time to see each other, anyway?"

Tera laughed. "Your honesty is a little scary, you know that?"

"Sorry. I'm just being real. We could meet at Lincoln, ride into the city, get some deli sandwiches and sodas, and stroll by the lake. How's that sound?"

"Sounds like I need my walking shoes."

"All-right! Really? Forty-five minutes?"

Tera heard the undisguised pleasure in Cameron's voice. She marveled at his spontaneity and enthusiasm; and she liked the way it was rubbing off on her.

"Forty-five minutes. And I'd better hustle if I want to make that train."

"I'll see you then. Bye-bye, Tera."

He hung up. Tera put the phone down and smiled to herself, a nervous but satisfied little smile. In the past twenty-four hours, she'd met and talked to a very nice man on the train; had lunch with him; gotten his number; actually *called* the brother, and made spur-of-the-moment plans to see him again ...and even planned a vacation for herself--to Jamaica!

Tera couldn't believe it. Not since childhood had she been so impulsive, and it felt *good.* She dashed into the living room, grabbed the stereo remote and clicked on 'cassette', and put in an old Freddie MacGregor reggae mix tape. *"Just like the rain that falls from the sky/my love for you will never...will never die, will never die,"* chanted above the thumping bass and smooth backing vocals as Tera dug furiously through her closet and dressers to find something cool and comfortable to wear. She chose a green and white nylon Nike jacket and sweats, a form-fitting white tank top, and white Nike joggers. A few strokes from a stiff brush quickly tamed her closely-cropped, wavy black hair. Her mother had practically went into cardiac arrest when Tera came back from the barber with the daringly short cut, but had to admit that it suited her, accenting her high cheekbones and oval face. Small gold hoop earrings completed Tera's outfit, and with a quick spritz of Moschino, she was ready. *"Just like the breeze that blows/I'll never let you go...never let you go,"* Freddie sang sweetly; Tera turned the stereo down, grabbed her purse, and zipped out the front door.

###

Standing at the Lincoln train stop, Tera felt doubt creeping up on her. *Was she crazy? What in the world had possessed her to go running off half-cocked to meet a stranger she'd only met the day before?* She looked around at the other people standing on the platform waiting for the train, searching for Cameron. *What if he didn't even show up, after getting her to rush down and meet him? Worse yet: she'd only seen him once-- what if she didn't even recognize him?* She put on her sunglasses, both to shield her eyes from the bright sunlight and to disguise her furtive gaze as she continued to look for him.

She found herself wishing Cameron had made it to Lincoln before her; every minute she stood waiting made her wish more and more that she'd never shown up. People moved closer to the platform's edge as an oncoming train slowed to a stop. Tera moved to the back of the crowd to allow others to board the northbound train, looking over their heads to see who was getting off; still no sign of him. She glanced at her watch, deciding to catch the next train south if Cameron wasn't there before it came. And if he *didn't* show, well, the day wouldn't be a big loss. There were a million things at home she could be doing; hey, she was on break! The doors of the train closed, and it rolled away heading for the city. Tera's uncertainty about being there momentarily left as she exulted over *not* being one of the passengers on that train, heading for work. She watched it pick up speed as it ran down the track, growing smaller and smaller in the distance.

"Good morning, beautiful."

Startled, Tera turned in the direction of the sexy bass voice. It was Cameron!

"Good morning," she smiled, looking him up and down behind her dark glasses. "I'm sorry, I didn't see you get off the train."

"I saw you as soon as I got off; you looked like you were in another world."

Tera laughed. "Hey, I probably was. Why didn't you say something?"

"I enjoyed watching you. You seemed so... beyond everything going on around you; like yesterday when I first saw you."

Tera just smiled. The doubts she'd had about meeting Cameron had disappeared when she saw him, like morning dew disappears from grass with the sun's first kiss. *God, he looks good*, she thought; *even more handsome than yesterday*. He was dressed casually in a loose cotton knit shirt and Levis. The loose-fitting shirt and jeans still didn't hide his powerful, muscular build, and Tera tried to catch a sly glimpse of thick biceps and massive shoulders behind her shades. Smiling broadly, he reached out and gently lifted the glasses from her long, straight nose.

"Mmm, mmm! Girl, you're looking good to me," he said, his eyes gliding appreciatively over her body.

Tera laughed to herself; there was that honesty again. *He* didn't try to hide that he was checking her out.

"Thank you."

"You're welcome, lady."

"Now, tell me again exactly *where* we're going?"

"Well, I thought we might ride into Chicago, get off downtown near Ziggy's--ever eat there before?--grab some food, and head over to the lake. Find a spot away from all the folks running to and fro, trying to get to their gigs, and just kick back. Parlez a little."

Another northbound train eased into the station, its doors sliding open.

"Let's do it," Tera said, and she and Cameron stepped aboard.

###

Tera and Cameron sat quietly for a moment, watching the boats skim across the choppy waters of Lake Michigan. Before either of them realized it, morning had stretched gloriously into a warm mid-afternoon.

They'd stopped downtown at Ziggy's and picked up flaky croissant sandwiches, a pint of potato & herb salad, bottles of sparkling apple cider, and Tera's favorite, chocolate-dipped strawberries. From there they'd walked forever--across Grant Park, past Buckingham Fountain, past the marina, and finally settled on a breaker near the lake where they could see the Field Museum of Natural History, the Shedd Aquarium, and miles of the Chicago shoreline. Again, Tera could hardly believe it was her sitting there, relaxed and full, with the humid afternoon air wafting across her body.

The rising temperature and bright sun had finally persuaded her to shed the warm nylon jacket and tie it around her hips. She was glad she'd worn the sleeveless tank top underneath; the wind felt good caressing her bare arms. Cameron sat with his back propped against a tree, looking out to the horizon. It amazed Tera how comfortable they were with each other, how each seemed to know what the other was thinking, what the other liked. It was as though Cameron was her brother, or childhood friend whom she'd known forever, or... lover. *Dream Lover.*

When she thought about that mysterious man from her dreams, Tera realized that she couldn't remember ever having felt as comfortable with *anyone* as she felt with Dream Lover...except maybe Cameron. But Cameron was *real*, not a figment of her imagination. It was eerie. Tera felt as though she would suddenly be snatched into wakefulness, just as she had countless time before when she'd laid down and dreamed about the nameless, faceless, tender lover who'd made her feel like a delicate and rare flower.

Cameron turned to her and smiled. Here was a man, a real, flesh-and-blood man whom Tera had only known for two days, making her feel that exact same way. They had spent over half the day together, laughing, talking, learning about each other's lives... while still feeling as though they'd always been part of each other's lives. Though Tera--the 'new' Tera--loved the experience of letting go, doing what she wanted, and making changes in her life, she was wary and cautious of the whirlpool of new, unexplored feelings that threatened to sweep her away; part of her did *not* like how right it felt to be with Cameron.

There was nothing about him that was

suspicious or insincere; and that's exactly what bothered Tera. If she'd been able to detect some shred of deceit or phoniness, at least she would have been able to identify what was happening as just a clever 'con game'. *But there was none.* And this left Tera trying to figure out what it all meant.

Cameron moved closer to her on the grassy slope and reached out to stroke the fine wisps of hair at the nape of her neck. Oddly, she didn't flinch or pull away; it felt as natural as though he'd done it thousands of times.

"Don't wrack your brain trying to figure this one out, Tera," he said, as though reading her confused thoughts. "I think it's beyond either of us."

Silently, Tera agreed. It certainly was beyond her.

Before she realized it, her eyes slowly began to close. The light, comforting touch of Cameron's cool fingers on her neck made her feel even more relaxed. Suddenly, her eyes snapped open and she looked at him with a mixture of embarrassment and caution. Sensing her uneasiness, Cameron stood and took her hands, pulling her up from the grass. "Let's walk," he said, gathering up empty bags and boxes from their impromptu picnic spot. Perhaps as much as Tera, Cameron had tried to ward off that feeling of familiarity which had *no* right to exist so soon; but unlike Tera, he wasn't afraid, and ready to allow the mystery to unfold.

His eyes drank in the sight of her; she was graceful, gentle, beautiful. Her full, moist lips curved into a dazzling smile, and the look in her velvet eyes evoked such depths of emotion...*emotions Cameron understood all too well.* He kept reminding himself, *no matter how good this feels, there's only so far it can go.* He tried to keep the mood light as they strolled along the shore, shoes in hand.

"Tera, there's something I've been wanting to ask about ever since this morning."
"Really? What's that?"
"That comment you made about my dissertation being more scary than interesting."
Tera smiled shyly. "Oh, *that*."
"Yes, that! I could tell that you were interested; what is there about it, past life regression, that scares you?"
"Well..." her voice trailed off.
As comfortable as she'd felt with Cameron up to that point, something wouldn't let her share her fears about that dream. Even though it was peaceful and she felt loved, something about it was confusing and unsettling, without even *considering* the possibility that the dream might be a...glimpse?...a connection to...? *No.* Not possible. Such a thought had never crossed her mind before meeting and talking with Cameron; there was *no way* she was going to go poking around it now, turning an ordinary dream into some 'doorway to the past', for heaven's sake. Cameron interrupted her thoughts.
"Tera? I'm listening."
"Oh! Guess I was in my own world again. Anyway, I don't know what it is that bothers me; I guess it's the idea that, well..."
"Go on. What bothers you?," he asked.
"What if someone finds that they've indeed had that experience? A past life, I mean."
"And?"
"And they *remember* what that life was like. And they *remember* people from that time and place; where do they do from there?"
Cameron looked thoughtful. Tera continued.
"I mean, what would it be like to recall those memories, those people, loved ones...and find yourself without a way to reclaim any of it, because it's all gone? What would a person *feel*, to discover through

past life regression that they haven't *lost* their mind, they've actually *found* another one?"
"Whew. That's definitely one for the philosophers, Tera; I guess that's why philosophy's such an important aspect of this field of study...for those of us who struggle with those kinds of questions."
"Well, that tells me exactly *nothing*! You've spent two years of your life with this, and all you can say is that, to actually recall a past life, to uncover past before past, leaves the one who recalls absolutely *nowhere*?!"
Tera's throat tightened, and she fought to hold tears of frustration at bay; her strong reaction surprised her. Cameron looked at her, feeling the sincerity of her question.
"No, Tera. That's not what I'm saying at all. The person who remembers is *not* suddenly thrown into chaos; they don't *lose* the life they've always had. If anything, they gain something."
"Oh really? What?"
"A new beginning. A greater sense of life's continuity. Just think about it, Tera. All our lives, we've been taught to believe that life begins on the day we're born. Now in purely scientific terms, we know that our lives begin *before* we're actually born, right? What if our lives begin over and over and over again? So often, so seamlessly, that life is like a circle, having no beginning and no end?"
They had stopped walking; Tera looked out across the lake, pondering Cameron's question. She slowly relaxed, and wondered why the topic had struck such an emotional chord with her in the first place. She had to admit, Cameron's perspective was much more positive than her own. Whereas she viewed the phenomenon as something to be feared, Cameron saw it as a welcome answer to a question humans have probably had since the beginning of time. She was

much more at ease, but she still had one more question. "Okay, Cameron. Say, for argument's sake, that it's true--life is circular and we pass this way again and again. And we recall our lives before. I *still* wonder about those who've been with us in our past lives. I still wonder how painful it must surely be, to remember loved ones...and realize that they're gone."

"Ah, but that's the beauty of it, Tera. They're *not* gone. Just as we return, *they* return. And whether it's in this 'life', or the next, or the one after that, *someday* our paths will cross again."

He took her hand, and they walked along the seemingly endless stretch of sand.

###

When Tera got back home, it was almost 9:00. She and Cameron had spent the entire day together; it had been more interesting and exciting than she could have imagined. *And to think she'd almost caught the train back home that morning.*

She sat down on the sofa, kicked off her Nikes, and put her feet up. She relaxed, her mind totally focused on the day's events. As much as she'd enjoyed herself, she couldn't give in completely to the heady feeling. She was happy that she'd thrown caution to the wind and followed her impulses for once; but she was caught off guard by the unexpected familiarity between herself and Cameron. The more she reflected on the day spent with him, the more she shook her head in disbelief.

Tera was actually embarrassed by the way she'd almost fallen asleep while Cameron massaged the back of her neck. And she smiled; it had felt so good, like the welcome, comforting touch of..."*Dream Lover,*" she whispered. Tera had no idea where things were going between her and Cameron--they'd already exceeded her expectations--but she felt confident about one thing:

with a real, daytime man taking up her time and attention, she was certain that her ethereal, nighttime lover would soon fade from existence. She curled up on the couch and was soon fast asleep.

###

Startled, Tera opened her eyes into inky darkness.

She sat huddled beneath the oak tree, nestled as far down into the tall grass as possible. Though humid, the air was slightly cooler than usual, and she pulled the tattered shawl from around her waist and tossed it over her shoulders. The grass where she sat was damp, but her legs were well insulated against the moisture by the sweeping length of her rough skirt and petticoat.

Tera sat very still as she waited, barely daring to breathe, though her heart pounded fiercely in her chest. Something was different this time; instead of the anticipation she always felt when waiting for her companion to appear, she was filled with terror. She mouthed a silent prayer that he would soon come to her, unharmed. Her strongest wish was that they could leave this place and never return.

She heard the grass rustling nearby, and her heart froze as she listened for the signal; if she didn't hear it, she would have to run...she'd never sit still for them to catch her! Barely audible, she heard it: "crk, crk, kee; crk, crk, kee."

The tightness in her chest eased, and she strained to see his powerful silhouette in the darkness. She wanted to call to him, but knew that she must let him find her, in case other ears listened. Her sharp ear, made more acute by the practice of listening for him when they'd meet in that field, picked up the sound of stealthy footsteps, and she knew it had to be him. No one, other than their friends, the Choctaws could move so silently. It was to the Choctaw land they intended to run, under cover of darkness; they would be safe there. Her heart still fluttered wildly, but Tera knew that everything would soon be fine. A firm hand gently stroked her head, and she could no longer sit quietly like a statue. She jumped to her feet, wrapping her arms around the broad, stout chest just inches away from her, and held on for dear life. He had made it! "Thank you, Lord Jesus," she whispered. His lips crushed hers in an urgent kiss that left her breathless; even more shocking was what happened next.

"Come on, Hannah, we got to go! Did you bring your things?," he asked.

He had spoken! After countless meetings under that tree, he had finally, actually said something!

The unexpected shock of hearing his voice reached deeply into Tera's sleeping consciousness, nearly pulling her out of the dream altogether...but somehow, she could not wake up.

"Hannah! Girl, we don't have time to stay here. This is the night, don't you remember? Where's your things?" Tera bent down and picked up a small bundle she'd hidden in the grass alongside her. Everything she possessed was inside it: another hopsack dress, similar to the one she wore; a short length of red cloth to wear wrapped around her head; a pair of worn knit stockings which she'd mended again and again; a sturdy pair of leather shoes; and a small, shiny mirror her mother had passed down to her when she'd turned sixteen. The long apron around her waist was pulled up and tucked to form a carrying bag for the food she'd managed to scrounge from the kitchen after everyone had gone to sleep. There was not much, but they wouldn't need much. They could survive on fruits and nuts, maybe trap a rabbit or two to cook over a small fire, if need be.

Tera strained her eyes into the blackness, trying to see his face; again, she could not. He pulled her to him and squeezed desperately, as though he might never let go. And through her fear, Tera felt the same incredible rush of love she'd always experienced when with him; and didn't want him to ever let go, even if the breath of life should leave her. She didn't understand the source of her fear, nor his need to leave in such haste, but she quickly gathered her things, tied the shawl around her shoulders, and took his hand. Gripping her hand tightly he led the way, moving across the open field as quietly as possible until they'd gotten past the farmhouse. Under the cover of a moonless, deep indigo night, they broke into a dead run until they reached the safety and cover of the dense forest.

After walking for what seemed like hours, he stopped to let her catch her breath for a minute; but they both knew they must move on. They must be as far away as possible before the sun's first light. He hugged her again, kissing and caressing her face as though for the first time; or perhaps, the last.

"Oh, Hannah," he murmured, "I love you so much, girl. Too much for us to keep on living this way. I couldn't just stand by and let them...let them...sell you. I don't care what happens to me, but I couldn't see that, and live. I'd die first! We're people, not animals, and they ain't got no right."

She laid her head on his chest and heard his heartbeat, vibrant and steady beneath the rough shirt and jacket he wore. He cupped her face in his palms.

"By morning, we'll be at the river--if we keep moving. In another day after that, we'll be at the base of those hills I told you about, with Tall Bear and his men. Those others won't dare follow us then! Oh, Hannah, my Hannah...then we'll be together forever, and we'll be free!"

Halfway between the dreaming and waking worlds, Tera didn't understand what was happening. She was frightened by his urgency, but knew that she must be with him, no matter what.

She reached up to feel the chiseled contours of his face. A light sheen of sweat dampened his brow, and his breath was warm on her questing fingertips. The absolute darkness hid his face, but her hands could feel what her eyes could not see.

Tight, soft curls covered his head. Thick, smooth brows curved over deep-set eyes, and Tera could feel a fringe of long lashes. Her finger lightly traced the long, straight bridge of his nose and the outline of his flaring nostrils. She felt the moist warmth of his even breathing on her fingertips as she touched his soft, full lips.

His mouth opened slightly, taking one of the probing fingers inside. Tera's fear and nervousness were slowly quieted by rising desire as his tongue swirled around and around the invading finger. His strong arms held her so tightly their heartbeats seemed to merge, and Tera's breath came in short gasps. Slowly, he drew her finger from his mouth, then quickly covered hers in a long, passionate kiss. His exploring tongue battled hers, and his sensuous mouth nibbled and sucked at her trembling lower lip.

Tera panted heavily now, as though she and her lover still raced for the shelter of the trees; his large hands, which had slowly, firmly stroked the length of her back now sought the lacings of her rough bodice and the smooth, warm flesh inside. Insistent, knowing hands found and caressed her body, and the two of them sank to the ground. Hungry lips touched and teased their way along her neck and the curve of her cheek, opening to capture an earlobe or to gently latch onto the firm mound of her chin. Tera was on fire as he lowered his full weight atop her and laced his fingers through hers. Moist, gentle lips next to her ear stoked the fire even hotter as he whispered, "I need you, Hannah Forrester;

love me now!"

###

"Oh, God," Tera groaned as she opened her eyes to brilliant sunlight flooding her living room. Her mind slowly dispelled the remnants of gnawing, leftover fear from her dream, but her body still tingled with desire as she recalled the hungering, exploring lips and hands of her mysterious nocturnal lover. *Shit*, she thought; *this wasn't like all the other dreams. What the hell happened?*

As Tera's breathing returned to normal, her body relaxed from its tight, fetal position and she sat up. What the hell had happened? Instead of the cozy, tranquil dream which had enveloped her in warmth and love night after night, Tera had just emerged from a twilight world of frightening, shifting figures, overpowering emotions.

Suddenly, the script had flipped, and very little of the original dream had remained. Yes, the man without a face was still there, and yes, they still shared a sweet, abiding love--the kind of love Tera had begun to fear she'd never experience in real life. But gone was the nightly scenario where he'd come to her silently across the darkened field, sweeping her up and tenderly holding and kissing her until the sun began its bold intrusion over the horizon. Gone was the knowing silence in which no words were ever spoken, but every emotion clearly felt and understood. Gone was the peace that had banished her fear of the night and open fields and creatures that scurried in the darkness. This dream had been too frightening, too real.

Tera got up and went to the kitchen to satisfy her morning addiction. As the coffee brewed, she showered, again mystified and disturbed by the dream. *Why had Dream Lover been so scared, so frantic to get away?* She recalled the painful pressure of his hand gripping hers as they fled into the forest. And he'd *said* something; for the very first time, the man had spoken to her. *And he'd called her Hannah.* Hannah Forrester. *Who was she?* It was all so confusing, so strange.

Even though her dream was dark, Tera knew that the woman was *herself*, yet the man had called her Hannah. She vividly recalled the clothes they wore, the rough burlap parcels they carried with them as they dashed across the clearing. She remembered generous hunks of cornbread and farmer's cheese stuffed in the fold of her apron, she could even smell them...and she thought of the meager contents of the bundle she'd placed in the grass. It was as though they were sharecroppers or something, farming people from olden days, or..."*slaves,*" Tera whispered. *They were slaves.* She remembered the man saying that he'd die before letting Hannah be sold; that was why they were running away!

Tera turned off the water and got out of the shower, realization lighting her eyes as she began to understand what had happened in her dream. For months, she'd buried her fear of the dreams, rationalizing that, at least they were harmless. All that happened was a rendezvous with a mysterious man. And a rendezvous with a man wasn't unusual at all, was it? Nothing to get upset about. No reason to seek so-called 'professional help', which was really Tera's greatest fear. But now, this latest dream had uncovered those old fears. This dream was *not* harmless. She was no longer just some farm girl running away each night to meet her lover; she was an escaping slave, running for her life. Determined *not* to consider the possibility that the dream's meaning might require the help of a psychologist to sort it out, Tera felt that if *she* could figure it out, no outside help would be necessary. She didn't want a shrink poking around in her head! She focused, trying to bring forth every detail, but nothing more came to mind. Hell, what she remembered was vivid enough.

"Forget this," she said, filling her favorite mug to the brim with steaming, black coffee. She picked up the stereo remote and in an instant the house rocked with the sounds of Steel Pulse.

She opened the refrigerator and pulled out a nearly-full pack of Marlboro Lights. She kept them there to prevent staleness, since she smoked so seldom. Right then, a cigarette or two was just what she needed to calm her rattled nerves. She lit one, went to the living room, and plopped down on the sofa. *That's more like it*, she thought.

As she willed herself to relax even more, Tera's panicked outlook changed. There was nothing significant about last night's dream, and she wasn't crazy, either. *It was just a plain old nightmare*; the reason why she and the mystery man were in the dream was because they'd been in that *recurring* dream. Her mind was simply used to seeing them, that was all. And with the heavy duty chilling Tera planned to do over the summer, pretty soon even *that* dream would be history. Though she had to admit, she would miss the loving attention of her dream man. She smiled. *Maybe*, she thought, *just maybe that attention will be replaced by a certain Mr. Wilson.*

All semester long--in fact, as long as she'd been an Associate Professor--Tera's plate had been full with lectures, exams, meetings, conferences, and such. She was now determined that these things would be replaced by music, dancing, outings, lounging out by the lagoon...and dating. She was almost all work, and that was going to change--along with a few other things. Tera decided that it was time to *make* time in her life for someone special. Maybe it would be

Cameron, and maybe not; but with all the circulating she envisioned, Tera felt that she'd have no trouble making friends and putting herself in a position to meet that special someone. Or at least, somebody with the *potential* to be that someone. In a very short while, she'd be going to Jamaica. She was sure to meet lots of interesting people there.

Music blasted from the speakers as she sipped her coffee and finished a second cigarette, and her mind was racing, thinking about all the exciting, different things her dull predictable life would soon include. She felt the dream was telling her that her waking life was too empty; *that's* why the dream had pulled her in so completely. It was time for her to open up her doors and windows, pull back the curtains, and let life's sweet breezes swirl around her; blow away the staleness of her world.

The terror and confusion of her nightmare faded, and Tera felt quite satisfied with herself, as though she'd solved world problems. In fact, she felt so good, she resolved to spend each day until her vacation doing something enjoyable and special. And she decided to start with a shopping trip!

Tera changed the CD to something more mellow, Roberta Flack's "First Time Ever I Saw Your Face", and went to the bedroom to dress. She looked at the clock. It was just after 9:00; the day was bright, warm, beautiful; she had *two* new credit cards she'd never used; and she was ready to plunge into the new life she'd envisioned.

CHAPTER TWO

Tera decided to drive into Chicago instead of taking the train. She'd need the trunk space for all the things she intended to buy. She laughed to herself, trying to remember the last time she'd bought anything for herself other than laser jet paper, pens and pencils, or 'sensible' shoes. Oh, there was the occasional gourmet treat; but clothes? Most of her wardrobe was either 'business professional', or 'sport'. She could count her sexy items on one hand. She was wearing her only sundress, a long, rayon knit number with cris-crossed white straps and white stripes running the length of each seam. Definitely not professional, but not exactly sexy, either; kind of casual-sporty-sexy. Cosmetics? She seldom wore any, so when there *was* an occasion for getting seriously dolled up, her lipstick and other makeup was either outdated or misplaced, and the only perfume she owned was the bottle of *Moschino* her mother had given her as a gift. *Pitiful*, she thought. But that would soon change.

All things considered, traffic wasn't too bad and Tera exited the Dan Ryan onto Congress, heading east through downtown. Another ten minutes or so of jockeying through stop-and-go traffic found her at the Grant Street parking garage, her destination; this was the same garage she always used on the few occasions when she drove to work instead of riding the train. Funny, but the drive into the city, and the traffic, and the parking, and the herds of people didn't seem so tedious. She plucked her ticket from the automated garage attendant and found a parking spot on the lower level. Tera was glad she'd worn comfortable, strappy white sandals; she knew she'd be doing a lot of walking. One had to range far and wide to hunt down the best bargains. She put on her sunglasses, which were like an American Express Card to Tera--she never left home without them. Catching the escalator up to the street, Tera was ready to get her 'shop' on.

###

Around noon, Tera found herself back over on Wabash, closer to the parking garage. She'd walked as far over as LaSalle and shopped her way back, excited about the bargains she'd found. It had been her intent to go on a spree, and indeed she had; but the sensible, practical side of Tera still needed to see a "sale" sign in the window before entering a shop. In any case, she was satisfied. And hungry. She saw the cafe where she and Cameron had eaten lunch a couple of days before, and headed in the direction of its yellow and green patio umbrellas; it was such a lovely day, it would've been a shame to sit inside. She seated herself at a table closer to the cafe than the street and tucked her packages under the table. She was starving, and looked over the menu. She didn't want the same thing she'd eaten when she came there with Cameron, though it *had* been delicious. In keeping with her promise to herself, she wanted to try something different. Everything on the menu sounded so good, she couldn't make up her mind.

"Try the blackened catfish, honey; it'll make you hurt yourself!"

Tera looked up over her shades. It was her mother, and her sister Mara!

"Look at her, Mara," Tera's mom laughed, "I don't know who's more surprised, her or us. Hey, baby." She leaned down and kissed Tera's forehead. It *was* a pleasant surprise; Mara lived in Minneapolis, and must have just popped into town for the weekend, as she often did. Tera was more surprised to see her mother, who lived only about ten minutes away from her; she and Daddy were gone out of town so often, it was like they used their condo for storage. Tera stood up and caught both her mother and sister in a group hug.

"Hey, Mommy! Hey, Mara girl, how you doing?"

"Hey, Tee. I'm doing alright."

"This is a surprise. What are you doing in town, just hanging out, what? Where's big Nate and little Nate?"

"Back at the house with Daddy. They let me out on furlough, girl. Nate said he'd keep Li'l Man so I could get out and kick it with Mommy for a minute. And you *know* your mother; she wanted to come down here and spend some money."

"When did you get in? *Why* didn't y'all call me?"

"We did, Tera Marchelle!"

Tera's mother had this habit of calling the kids by their first and middle names for emphasis; now that Tera was an adult she could handle it, but as a kid, it used to drive her crazy.

"That's right," Mara added, "but you were already gone, honey. What brings you downtown, anyway? I thought school was out till the fall."

"It is. I just came out to shop a little, you know, buy a few new things," Tera said casually, pointing to the bags under her table.

"*What??!,*" Mara and Mrs. Morton said in unison, shocked.

Tera smiled to herself; *they haven't seen anything yet.* They sat down at the table, ordering lemonade when the server came over. Mrs. Morton openly rummaged around in the bags while Tera placed her order for the blackened catfish and rice pilaf.

"*Unh, unh, unh!* I see it, but I'm not believing it. Summer dresses. Shorts! A *bathing suit*, two-piece at that!"

"Ma, you're kidding! I *know* Tera ain't bought nothing

like that, not for herself, anyway. Tee, you doing your Christmas shopping early?," Mara laughed.
"Very funny, Mara. No, I just felt like buying some things, that's all. Lord knows I needed to."
"Got *that* right," Mrs. Morton chimed in, "I don't know what's got into you, but child, I hope it *never* gets out! You even bought some *Design*, and...what's this? *Lipstick!!* Can you believe this? Mara Nicole, this child has even bought herself some lipstick. And a pretty color, too."
Mara rolled her eyes back when her mother doubled up on names with her as she had with Tera, and smiled, nudging Tera under the table. Mara took the bronze-colored tube her mother was examining, and looked at it closely.
"Ooh, Tee, girl this will look *good* on you! What color is it?"
"Something called 'Currant Wine'. I liked it, and another color I got too, called 'Desire'."
Mara looked at her sister and smiled. This was out of character for her staid, proper little sister, but Mara liked the change immensely. She looked at the shopping bags and felt that something really dramatic must have occurred; like a man.
"So, who is he, Tera?," she asked.
"Huh?"
"Girl, don't you dare play dumb on me, now. Look at you: makeup, summer clothes that you don't have to wear with stockings, a swimsuit...and look at this, even got new *Linga-ree!*," she laughed, deliberately mispronouncing 'lingerie'. "If there ain't a man up in this scenario *somewhere*, I'll pay for it."
"I didn't even wanna go there," said Mrs. Morton, "but I'm thinking like Mara. Who is he, Tera, is he somebody we know? Like Frank Williams?"
"No! No, Mother, you know me better than that."

"Jimmy Martin?"
"Ugh! No, Ma."
"River Bennett?"
"No, Ma! No!"
"Well, what was wrong with him? He was a nice fellow, I thought you two hit it off real well; whatever happened to him, anyway?"
Tera thought for a moment; *River*. She worked with him at Roosevelt. He was one of the first people she met after taking her position there, and she'd thought at first that they might hit it off well, too. He was nice, friendly--a bit introverted--intellectual, and very driven. In fact, he was probably too much like her for anything to have developed between them. They'd dated a couple of times, but things never seemed to go anywhere. They *did* get to be good friends and colleagues, and Tera was grateful for that. He was a real sweetie...even if a little strange.

Tera recalled an evening, maybe a year earlier, when she and River sat around his apartment discussing a journal article on cross-cultural communication; suddenly, River had switched gears on her, asking her what she wanted out of life.
"What?," she'd asked, puzzled. The question had been a complete turn-around from what they'd been discussing.
"What do you want out of life, Tera?" She thought about it for a moment.
"Well...I think I already have what I want, River."
"And what is that?"
"Come on! I'm young, I'm single, I have a job I really love..."
"Same here. So? Isn't there something more, haven't you ever felt that something was missing? Incomplete?"
"No. Not really. Oh, I suppose one of these good old days, I'll meet somebody, get married, have kids..."

"But?"
"But right now, my life is just like I want it to be. Besides, I'm too busy with my schedule to even think about all that. Hell, if 'Mr. Right' walked through my front door right now, I'd probably be too wrapped up in lesson plans to even recognize him."
"Knowing you, Tera, you probably would be."
"Hey, be nice! And what about *you*, Mr. Bennett? I suppose you'd know your Ms. Right if you met her, huh?"
"In a heartbeat...now, what were you saying about cultural differences in conflict resolution?"
Tera's thoughts came back to the present, the question her mother had asked.
"Well, Tera Marchelle? Did I guess right? Is it River?"
"No, Mama! No, no, *no*! Why does a man have to be involved? Can't I just do something different without everybody thinking that some man inspired it?"
"And what's wrong with a man 'inspiring' it?," Mara asked.
"Nothing, Mara. It's just that...you know how people take a look at life and say, 'hey, it's time for something to change'? Well, it's just my time, that's all."
Mara lifted her glass of lemonade in a toast. Mrs. Morton and Tera joined in.
"Here, here, baby sis; whatever the reason, it's *all* good, and it's about time."

###

Tera's mother and sister sat with her and shared an appetizer while Tera polished off the last of her fish and rice.
"So, Tee what you gonna do now? You done shopping?"
"Yep, Mara. I think I've done enough damage for one day; what about you all?"
"I'm ready to go," Mama Morton told them, "you girls

can do what you want."
"I thought you said y'all were down here shopping? I don't see any bags."
"We already put 'em in the trunk, Tera," Mara explained. "Oh, that reminds me; I kept one thing out, something I bought from that antique shop up on Clark. I was gonna give it to you when I came over to your place to see you--but I see you *now*, so here it is!," Mara said, pulling a small bag from her huge sack purse.
"Thanks, sis. Clark Street, huh? Man, you all have covered some territory *today*."
"That's why I'm ready to go," Mama repeated.
Tera was about to open the fancy-looking bag, but Mara shot her a knowing look that said *'girl, take that home! You know how Mama is when she's ready to step.'* Tera stuffed the bag into one of her shopping bags, preparing to go, and hugged her mom and sister.
"Bye, Mommy. Listen, Mara, I'll be over to see you later this afternoon, after I get back home and stretch-and-blow for a minute, okay?"
"Cool. Just give me a call, you know where I'll be."
"And what you'll be doing, too. You know how much Daddy likes to talk."
"Mara Nicole! Child, she just *said* she'd call you later; now come on!"

###

Tera walked into her living room and sank down onto the couch. She'd had a wonderful time visiting with Mama, Daddy, Mara and her family. The only one missing from their little gathering had been her younger brother, Xavier, who hadn't yet come home from college for the summer; knowing him as she did, Tera could see him opting to stay down at Hampton instead of coming home between semesters.

It was around 10:00. Tera had been gone all day, and was seriously tired. She did her usual--popped a CD into the stereo and relaxed as she listened to good music. *No matter what new things I might try*, Tera thought, *this is the one thing that'll never change.* She glanced over to her bedroom door, noticing that her shopping bags were still sitting there; she got up and pulled the bags back over to the couch to look again at the things she'd bought. A pretty, summery, orange sundress; a shorts set in chartreuse; two body suits, one white, the other pink; a white broomstick skirt, and a multicolored sarong skirt; and of course, a *bikini*, in the most vibrant shade of yellow, with a matching beach cover-up. She'd also bought a lot of little knick-knacks like bracelets, earrings, two more pairs of sunglasses, and an anklet. All of which would be *fabulous* for her vacation. She was still very excited about going, but just a little hesitant; going out of the country was *major*, as far as Tera was concerned.

She folded her things and gathered everything to take to her room. *I'm being silly*, she thought; *this vacation is just what I've been needing!* She was about to fold up the shopping bags when a thought hit her; snapping her fingers, she remembered the little bag Mara had given her. She hadn't looked at her sister's gift, it was still in the largest shopping bag.

She took the small bag out; it was from "The Unique Antique". She'd heard of that place before, but was never curious enough to go check it out. Since Mara had excellent taste, Tera knew it would be beautiful. She opened the bag and reached inside, drawing out something rectangular wrapped in delicate tissue.

When she peeled away the tissue, she sat transfixed.

No.

Her hands shook so violently, she almost dropped it, and set it down on the coffee table. *No, no, no! This can't be!*

Sitting in front of her, in her living room, on her table, was the *same* mirror from her dream the night before. The same mirror her mind's eye had seen wrapped in the burlap bundle she carried! It was the treasured heirloom given to her on her sixteenth birthday. Not *her*, this Hannah Forrester, whoever she was. Tera reached out slowly, picking it up. Its ornately designed frame was silver filigree, and the highly polished glass reflected her stunned expression. She still couldn't believe it. And she was frightened. First, a harmless dream of a silent, phantom lover. Then, a nightmare where she is someone else, someone who's being pursued by unknown people who mean her great harm; someone who is running for her *life*, carrying with her everything she owns. *And now this!* The most treasured possession of this runaway woman suddenly appears in Tera's waking world...turns up in *her* hands.

She felt her throat constrict with terror; what she feared most in life had come to pass--she was losing touch with reality. She was losing her mind! *What else could it be?* She fought for control as tears began to slide down her cheeks, but was soon sobbing hysterically. Tera cried until her fear spent itself, leaving her limp and broken like flowers after a windstorm.

Gradually, her breathing slowed as she began to calm down; she walked to the bathroom for a wet towel, pressing it against her burning eyes and nose. She felt a little better, and glanced at herself in the mirror. *A frightened little girl in a woman's body.* She smiled. Then laughed out loud.

"Fool!," she said. She was being ridiculous. *Ridiculous!* Yes, her dreams--*all of them*--had been vivid, but *no* dream is so vivid that it can make things materialize after you're awake. She wasn't losing touch with reality; she was just plain *tripping*, and the fact that

Mara's mirror *looked* like the one in her dream had spooked her. That was all.

She soaked the towel in more cold water and bathed her face. The gripping fear that she might be going crazy still lingered; maybe she *did* need to talk to a therapist, but...*no! I'm fine*, she told herself, *just fine.* The fact that she could *think* and *reason* that she might be going crazy...told her that she *wasn't* going crazy. "Whew," she said, looking at herself again; "get a grip, girl. This is just mind over matter."

She turned out the light and went into her bedroom. She'd been tired even before her crying episode, and was now truly weary. A slight feeling of anxiety throbbed in a dark corner of her mind, wondering if the nightmare would return. Finally concluding that there was only one way to find out. She settled down to sleep, reasoning that the worst was already over; it *had* to be.

###

"That wasn't so bad," Tera whispered, as she opened her eyes to the light of her third day of *not* having to get up and go to work. She'd had the dream again, but it had not terrified her as it had the night before. And like the night before, this dream had been the same, but slightly...different. Almost episodic, a mini-series or soap opera. There was the darkness, and the waiting for her lover to appear, and the desperate race to the forest carrying all her worldly belongings. There was the lovemaking on the grass beneath the thicket of trees. But there was more.

She and her lover had straightened their clothes, kissing sweetly, though they had little time to linger; and gathered their things so that they could continue their journey. Tera--or Hannah--was no longer afraid; her man knew the way to their destination.

For perhaps the first time in her life, she felt

secure. Whispering to her that they must still move as silently as possible, he headed deeper into the woods with Tera close at his side. They walked at a swift pace, trying not to tire themselves out too quickly so that they could keep moving. The night air was cool, but Tera's exertions made her slow down to remove the shawl and tie it around her waist. "Come on, Hannah," Dream Lover whispered, "don't slow down on me now, girl. We got to reach the river by daylight!"

He took her hand and pulled her along with him deeper into the night. They walked and walked, for hours it seemed, until Tera began to see the faint glimmer of rose and gold slowly lighting the skies. It was still dark, but they hurried their pace. Tera could smell the river; they were getting closer to it, closer to their freedom. Her man grasped her hand tighter, and they began a slow descent down an incline, through tall grass and bushes until he came to a stop.

"What is it?," Tera asked, "why are we stopping here?" He smiled, pulling on the thick underbrush until he exposed the mouth of a small cave.

"Here we are, Hannah. I found this place a little while back, and I cleared it out some. I didn't know then that I'd ever have a use for it except to just get away to myself, if I'd a mind to. This is where we're gonna stay 'till night time; then, it's on to meet Tall Bear at those hills."

Tera helped him move the brush away. Once inside the darkened cave, he pulled the brush back in front of the opening, making it look like the rest of the surrounding shrubbery. It would remain dark and cool inside, a refuge from the heat of the coming day--and their pursuers. The man unrolled one of his rough packs, and old blanket, which he spread out on the dirt floor. They lay down together on the blanket, snuggling close together.

When he wrapped his arms around Tera, there was that same feeling of security and love she'd remembered from the earlier dreams. This time, though, they whispered and shared with each other their excitement about the new life that lay just ahead.

"One more day, Hannah," he said. "Just one more day, darlin', and we'll be away from this place forever. We'll be free, do you hear me? Free! And we'll be together forever, Hannah girl; nothing will ever separate us again."

Tera wrapped her arms tightly around his broad shoulders.

"Oh, Mason," she murmured, squeezing with all her might. "I'm so happy! I could die right now, and just be happy that we had this time. If anything...happens..."

"Ain't nothing gonna happen, girl, 'cept we gonna get outta here! Hush, now; don't ever talk like that."

"But Mason, I...I'm just scared, I guess. Like something's gonna happen, something bad."

He pressed his lips to Tera's ear, speaking in soothing tones as though she were a frightened child.

"Hannah, ain't nothing bad can happen to us now! We left all the bad behind, ain't nothing but good from now on."

"Mason, honey...I just want you to know, if something should happen to me--"

"Nothing can happen to you! Nothing! I won't let it. You and me, we're meant to be together. I knew you was the one for me first time I saw you, first day you came to Master Walton's place; I been waiting for you all my life, girl, and wasn't no way I was gonna let them take you away from me!"

"Oh, Mason! I love you so much."

He cradled her in the crook of his arm, his large, rough hands caressing her with surprising tenderness.

"Let's get some rest, Hannah. We got a big day ahead,

and we're gonna need it."

"I know, Mason. But there's something I need right now more than I need rest," she said, drawing his lips to hers. "Please give it to me."

###

Tera lounged in bed a little longer, going over the dream again and again, noting the differences. *So, Dream Lover has a name: Mason.* In the past two nights, he had spoken to her and his name had been revealed. She still had never seen his face, but he'd become more and more real, and less an ethereal night visitor, this Mason. But who was he? And who was Hannah Forrester? These questions still haunted Tera.

She looked up at the ceiling, which the sun had tinted gold, and smiled to herself. *Damn. With my imagination, I should be a writer; not only are my dreams all too real, the people even have names, histories! But I'm not getting ready to sweat this--no!* "I have a real, live, *life*, and it feels like I just found it, and I'll be *damned* if I'm getting ready to let a dream make me lose it--just 'cause I have an overactive-ass imagination!," she said aloud, swinging her legs over the side of the bed.

She walked to the kitchen to make her coffee and looked in the refrigerator for her Marlboros. Sitting at the counter, she saw the notepad where she'd scribbled Cameron's number from that crumpled napkin.

It was around 8:30; not too bad considering she usually got up a couple of hours earlier. But she wondered if Cameron was up. She felt like talking to him. She called. Disappointed, she heard the phone ring and ring. "Oh well," she sighed. *His loss. Hers, too.*

She'd had such a wonderful time with him the other day; had envisioned spending a *lot* of time with him, at least until she left for Jamaica. *After* Jamaica, well...that could be negotiated when or if circumstances dictated. Her feelings told her that seeing *much more* of Cameron was a distinct possibility...but, hey! She was getting ahead of herself. Way ahead; first things first. And she'd promised herself to do something exciting and different every day.

She sipped her coffee, thinking, *what's on the agenda today?* More shopping? *No, save it for Jamaica.* Spa? *Hmmm...sounded good, but maybe a day or two before leaving.* Hook up with Mara and Ma? *Later in the afternoon.* Nothing seemed to scratch Tera's itch to do something right away. She thought about her mother and sister, and the wonderful time she always had with them. *Except* when Mama would start in on her about getting married or engaged or seriously involved, since her sister Mara had already done so, and given her a beautiful grandson to boot. But it didn't really bother Tera, especially now. She felt that her life was about to change, to become so full and fulfilling, she'd have an answer for Ma whenever she might ask "*Tera Marchelle, what are you doing with your life?*"

It was really kind of funny when Tera thought about it, how Ma was always asking, 'what about so-and-so?', this man or that, and whatever happened between him and her. Like yesterday, asking about yucky, thousand-hands Frank Williams. That man was the horniest, most frantic bastard Tera had ever seen. Even when he was so-called 'behaving' and trying to have a 'decent conversation', he kept his eyes glued to Tera's chest. *Like breasts could talk.* And Jimmy Martin. Ma thought that *he* was such a catch, but he was so pretentious, so devoid of substance that he was like...cotton candy. *Colorful, kind of sweet, but mostly puffed up with air.* If Tera had *really* been serious about not wanting an 'involved' relationship, Jimmy certainly would have been her man. And River; Mr. River Jordan

Bennett.

The son of a Baptist minister, he'd caught a lot of flack growing up with that name. Out of the three her mom had mentioned, only River's name had evoked positive memories. Nothing romantic had developed, but they'd gotten to be good friends. *Hmmm.* She hadn't heard from old Riv in a while; maybe she should give *him* a call. She dialed his number. No need to wonder if he was up at that hour. If he wasn't teaching summer classes, Tera was still sure he'd be up. And at home. On the third ring Tera almost hung up the phone, but heard River's voice just as she was about to put the phone down.

"Hello."

"Hi, River. Good morning!," she said cheerily.

"Tera? Hey, woman. Wow...this is a surprise."

"That's what it's supposed to be--a surprise. So, how you been?"

"Fine Tera, fine. Man, let me sit up and get my bearings. Wow! I mean, this really *is* a surprise; you're about the last person in the world I'd expect to hear from."

"Oh, River! Now, that's cold. You know I call you! I may not call *often*, but I do call."

"You're right--you do. Sometimes. So, what're you working on? What are you researching?"

"Nothing. Can't I just call to be calling?"

"Excuse me; is this Tera Marchelle Morton I'm talking to? Professor Morton?"

"Damn, Riv. I guess I must deserve that."

"I'm just kidding with you, Tee. But really, girl, this is just a social call? I'd be lying if I said I wasn't shocked, but I'm...pleased. And really glad to hear from you."

"I just thought about you and decided to call since we hadn't talked in a while."

"I'm glad you did; but you have to admit yourself, this is *way* different--for *you*. What's up?"

"Well, River, I've just been thinking--about a lot of different things--and I decided there really *is* more to life than what I've been doing with mine. You know, work, work, and more work."
"Hmmm...I wasn't sure before, but now there's no doubt--this is an imposter I'm speaking with, right? There's a candid camera planted somewhere in my apartment, isn't there?"
"River! See, I was trying to be serious."
"Well, at least *that* much sounds like the Tera I know."
"River..."
"Okay, okay, I'll stop. Wow, girl, something must have hit you like a ton of bricks. You're alright, nothing happened, did it? I mean--"
"No! No, I'm fine. Fine! Like I said, I'm just trying to attend to things in my life that I'd been letting slide...like talking, keeping in touch with my family and friends. Taking time out to 'smell the flowers' and stuff. And just doing things because I *feel* like doing them, instead of as part of some agenda I feel I have to follow."
"Well good for you, Tera, good for you! And it's about time, I might add."
"Not you, too. Mama and Mara already got on me about the same thing yesterday."
"Oh, Mara's in town? Tell her I said 'hi'. Your mom, too."
"Mama asked about you."
"Oh really?"
"Yeah; don't ask."
"Hey, I know Mama Morton! I won't. Anyway, they hit you up about 'doing something with your life'?"
"Something like that; it was more like, 'shock and surprise' because I *am* starting to do something unscripted."
"I'm happy for you, Tee. Go for it. We only pass this way once, as they say; make it count."
Tera was silent for a moment, wondering who was right

about how many times we 'pass this way'--River or Cameron.

"Well, River, like I said, I just wanted to call you and see how you were doing; I'm not gonna hold you."

"Hey, hey, what's the rush? I know you're not teaching this summer. Neither am I. Isn't *leisure* part of your plan for the new, improved Tera?"

"Most definitely."

"Well then, if you don't have any plans for this morning, why don't we meet at the nature trail, jog a couple of miles--"

"*Jog?!*"

"Okay, *walk* a couple of miles, then...I'll buy you a cup of coffee. How's that sound?"

"From the Bottomless Cup?"

"Of course."

" You ain't said nothing but a word, Bro Man! Meet you at the trail in fifteen minutes."

###

Tera and River strolled back down the nature trail toward the lot where they'd parked their cars. After nearly forty-five minutes of walking and--over Tera's protests--jogging, they had gotten two huge cups of coffee and a bag of chocolate croissants from The Bottomless Cup, a popular coffee bar located close to one of the nature trail exits.

They sat down on a grassy slope, looking out over a lagoon surrounded by acres of woods. Tera munched on one of the flaky pastries, at a loss to understand why she was so happy to see River. Oh, he was a dear friend, and they had both been caught up in the end-of-the-semester crunch and hadn't seen or talked to each other in a while; but she wasn't just happy to see him. She was almost...overjoyed. It was as though she hadn't seen him in years instead of weeks. And there was something different about him; or maybe, something she'd just never noticed before. Like the look of deep concentration in his eyes when he talked about anything. *His eyes*, for that matter. So dark and mysterious, they were almost black. Deep-set and piercing, with thick brows arching over, like wings. Eyelashes so long and curly, Tera was slightly envious.

River rattled on about some new area of research he'd gotten interested in, but Tera scarcely heard a word he said, studying his face intensely. *God*, Tera thought, *why haven't I ever noticed before? This man is gorgeous.* Not that it had mattered, though. Tera had always thought that River was a good-looking man. But they'd never really clicked, at least not romantically, and his looks had become so...secondary, she'd focused on other aspects of his personality, like his fine analytical mind and subtle sense of humor. What was it now that made her see the sensuality she'd overlooked all this time?

She looked up at his high, proud forehead, dampened with perspiration; the distinct, chiseled nose and full lips. The light sprinkling of premature gray curling through his shoulder-length dreadlocks. Something about him was so exciting, and yet so...familiar?

"Tera? Woman, you haven't been listening to a word I've said, have you?"

"Uh...sorry, River. My bad! It's just that I've been so tuned in to academics, and research, and all that stuff *all this time*, that--"

"Your mind needs a reprieve from it, right? Sorry. We can talk about something else; it's just that I'd never ventured into this area before, and that conversation I had with Cam Wilson was fascinating, and--"

"Wait a minute, River--conversation with *who*?"

"Cameron Wilson. Have you met him? This brother from Atlanta who's here working on his doctoral dissertation on--"

"Past life?"

"So you *have* met him! He talk about his research at all? Man, it's intense."

"Yeah, he did."

"So, what'd you think?"

"About him, or his research?"

"Well, *both*, I guess," River answered. He focused in on Tera, noticing a faraway look in her eyes, a look he'd seen before.

"Uh-oh," he said.

"Uh-oh, what?"

"Looks like you two must have found a lot of *other* things besides research to talk about."

"He's a nice man. Easy to talk to."

"Guess I gotta agree with you there; he seems to have that effect on people."

"I suppose."

"You *suppose*? Come on, Tera you look like you've been struck by *lightning*, don't be so... *oh, I get it.*"

"What?"

"This sudden change in you. I knew something--or *somebody*--must have happened; you like dude, don't you?"

"Huh? Aw, wait a *minute*, Riv. Unh-unh. You caught those dice *wrong*, okay? Yeah, I met Cameron, and we talked a little--we even had lunch, but...like him? It's too soon to say much more than *that*. I mean, I just met the man."

"So?"

"So, it's too soon to say anything more than that!"

"Remember a long time ago, Tee, when I told you I'd be able to spot my Ms. Right in a heartbeat? Well, maybe that's what's happened to you and you just don't know it. Maybe you've met your Mr. Right."

"Hmmm. That may work for you, River, but not me. I need time. Apparently, *you* must need time, too; I haven't heard you mentioning anybody's name."

"Your reasoning abilities are failing you, Tera."
"Meaning what?"
"Meaning just because you haven't heard me *talking* about anyone doesn't mean I'm not *thinking* about anyone."
"Oh, I guess you're right about that," Tera said, trying to suppress the sudden, inexplicable disappointment she felt just hearing River imply he was interested in someone.

She felt stupid. She and River had never been serious with each other; there was absolutely no reason in the world for her to feel the way she did. River was her friend. He'd always been very supportive of her, no matter what is was. Here he was, in his own aloof little way, trying to tell her about a woman he was interested in, and she was on a whole other wavelength. She wanted to show support, like he'd always done for her.
"So, Riv...who is she?"
He smiled at her, a mischievous twinkle in those marvelous eyes.
"Your reasoning's still faulty, woman. I didn't say I was *seeing* somebody."
"Well then, thinking about somebody!"
"Now, Tera, I didn't exactly say that, either--"
"River! Don't tease, just answer me. Have you met someone?"
Tera's heart sank just a little when he answered "yes".
"Well...Riv...that's nice. So, have you..."
"The answer to just about anything you'd want to ask, Tera, is 'no'. We haven't seriously dated or anything. Oh, we've seen each other, lots of times, and we talk...but that's about it."
Tera listened, hoping that she came across as neutral.
"So, it sounds like...like she doesn't know how you feel, River. How does she feel about you?"
"I think she likes me well enough. In fact, I know she cares about me."

"Mm-hmm." Tera felt her disappointment trying to flare up again and quickly squashed it.

"You like her. She likes you; what's the problem?"

"I guess I'm just, well..."

"Would 'stubborn' be the word you're looking for?," Tera teased.

"Alright, then. I'm stubborn; but as far as I'm concerned, it won't work between us unless Ms. Right realizes that she *is* Ms. Right, know what I mean? I don't want a woman I have to *persuade* that I'm the right man for her."

"Okay, I can see you not wanting to twist her arm...but how about a *hint* or something?! River, why don't you just tell her how you feel?," Tera asked, kind of hoping that he wouldn't take her advice.

"Nope. I've known her for a while, and it's been good; I'd rather keep her for a friend than mess things up by putting something on her that she's not ready to deal with."

"Riv, that's silly; if you *tell* her, maybe you'll find that she feels the same way you do."

"Maybe. But I already know about *me*; in order for me to know about her, *she* has to show me something. And I'm willing to wait to find out."

"If she feels the way you do, and *deals* with it the same as you, then you two have a stand-off; in the meantime, how many other good women are you gonna let pass you by?"

"Doesn't matter. I've waited this long. Hey, how 'bout that Cubs game last night; you check it out?"

That River, Tera thought. *The master of 'Presto, this conversation is over'*. She took his comment as a cue to talk about something else, anything else besides his personal business. The sun was high in the sky by then, almost noon. Tera thought about getting ready to leave. She would call Mama and Mara as soon as she got home.

She'd enjoyed her little outing with River, but--like most of the events of the last three days--it had left her with conflicted feelings.

On the one hand, Tera felt really positive about the difference her life had taken on in just those few days. On the other hand, though, she was angry with herself for the emotional whirlwind she found herself tumbling in. *Which was worse*, she wondered, *feeling almost nothing emotionally yet maintaining absolute control, or feeling everything, so much so that you lose control?* It was much more complex than Tera had imagined, or even allowed herself to consider; when one follows a blueprint for one's life--as Tera had been doing--there is no room for anything unexpected, or unpredictable, or imprecise. Like that crazy dream that had had her off kilter for weeks.

Or like love, for instance. Not that she was in love with anyone. Thinking about Cameron excited her, and the prospect of getting to know him better was like...the feeling she got while standing in line at the Chocolate Factory, waiting for a taste of those famous chocolate-dipped strawberries: she just knew it would be delicious, and satisfying, and an assault on her senses. But that wasn't *love*. And when she thought about River...that wasn't exactly 'love', either, but it was very nice. Like her first sip of morning coffee, jolting her into wakefulness and calming her at the same time; a constant companion, a lift that was always there when she wanted it.

Well, enough of these 'men as food' analogies, Tera thought.

One thing was painfully obvious--she didn't have the slightest idea what love was. She popped the last bit of croissant into her mouth, washed it down with coffee, and stood up.

"Riv, it's been nice, but I gotta go."

"Aww, Tee! Man...well, if you gotta, you gotta."
"I'm gonna hook up with Mama and Mara this afternoon."
"I hear you. Tell 'em both I said 'hey', and Tera?"
"Yeah?"
"This was cool, I had a good time; when we hang out, it doesn't always have to be about work or something work-related, you know?"
"Oh, I agree! But as I recall, it was *you* who started in talking about what research I was doing, and it was also *you* who brought up Cameron's dissertation."
"Oh yeah, that's right! That's really a thought-provoking topic, don't you think? Especially the part about--"
"River!"
"Just kidding, woman. I'll walk you to your car."

CHAPTER THREE

###

Boy, this is a twist, Tera thought, as she emerged from the shower. When River had walked her back to her car, it suddenly seemed so cut-and-dried that they should be saying goodbye after spending only a couple of hours together. She'd spent an entire day with Cameron, whom she hardly knew; River was her friend, and she wanted to spend more time with him, just kicking it and getting caught up on each other's lives. When she found that he was seriously thinking about a woman [and she'd had *no* idea], it let Tera know how lax she'd gotten in keeping up the few friendships she did have. No more of that; she invited River back to her place.

Instead of going over to Mama's, Tera decided to call her and Mara later to see what they were up to, and invite them over for a late lunch if they didn't have other plans. Who knows, River might even still be there when they came.

Tera put on a comfortable aqua tank top and matching drawstring pants.

"I'll be out in a minute, River; listen to some music if you want."

"Take your time, I'm fine," he answered, scanning the titles in the CD storage tree.

He selected a few CD's, put them in the carousel, and pushed 'random play'. From her room, Tera could hear the hauntingly beautiful tenor solo by Doug Richardson on the cut "Lonely Love".

The voice of the tenor was plaintive, longing...so bittersweet.

The melody wrapped itself around Tera's heart every time she heard it. *This man knows what love is*, Tera thought. And even if Tera herself didn't, the song could still touch that part of her that wanted to know what it was all about. She floated from her room, hairbrush in hand and swaying to the music. River just smiled at her.

"Your jam, huh?," he teased.

"I just love good music, Riv. But yeah, this *is* one of my favorites."

"It must be, to pull you out here half-done."

"What you mean? I'm dressed."

"Sit down, Tera; gimme that."

She obeyed, simultaneously sinking to the couch and handing River the stiff, boar-bristle brush.

"Mmm," she cooed, as River brushed her hair, gently raking through and taming her damp, tight curls. His hands were big but his touch had a childish gentleness.

Comfortable within the boundaries of their friendship, Tera allowed herself to enjoy the sensual feel of his hands stroking her close-cropped hair as he brushed, and to wonder what it might have been like if she and River had connected on a more intimate level. Of course, that was not a possibility now; River was a serious man, and apparently had his sights set on someone else. A part of Tera unselfishly wished him love and luck in winning over this mystery woman. Another part of her envied the prize this woman would be getting. *I just hope you deserve him*, Tera thought.

"All done, take a look," River announced, handing Tera the mirror she'd left sitting on the coffee table the night before. Mara's mirror. It no longer terrified her, but she still felt strange just holding it. Dismissing a slightly eerie feeling, Tera examined herself in the mirror. Her hair was brushed back neatly, and felt crisp beneath her fingers.

"Thanks, Riv. It looks nice."

"My pleasure, Tee." He looked her over, examining her as though he'd never seen her before.

"I don't know what it is, woman, but there's definitely

something different going on with you. Something good, and whatever it is, it's definitely working."

"Well, thank you sir," she answered lightly, enjoying the attention yet thinking about the unfairness of this so-called 'new' life of hers.

"Opening up" carried as many disadvantages as benefits. It might expose you to either acceptance or rejection, honesty or deceit, straightforwardness or vagueness. Tera wasn't afraid of rejection; she'd experienced as much of that as almost any other person. The possibility of acceptance was worth the risk of rejection. She felt she was a pretty good judge of character, too, and could usually spot and avoid a phony immediately. Vagueness was troublesome for her; she was not well-versed in subtleties, and wasn't always good at deciphering hidden meanings or motives. For example, if she didn't *know better*, she might have read something intimate, something flirtatious in the way River touched her. And the way he'd *looked* at her, but....no. He was her friend. End of story. That had been clear enough when he spoke of that woman. True, he'd said there was nothing going on between them--yet--but he'd also shown that *his* intent was definitely to get something going between them.

If there had ever been a chance for Tera and River to get close, surely it had been years ago. In any case, she valued his friendship and would have died before revealing her sudden, rekindled infatuation. She gently scolded herself; a couple of days ago all she could think about was Cameron Wilson, and now thoughts of River pushed him to the farthest corner of her mind. She felt like a fickle adolescent, and realized what her problem really was: she needed to meet and mingle with more menfolk. A *number* of intelligent, exciting, and--most of all--*available* men from whom she could choose. *Come on, Jamaica*, she thought.

"Earth calling Tera," River said, interrupting her thoughts. "Man, you were definitely somewhere else, woman."
"Hmmm...not yet, but I will be."
"Huh?"
"Never mind, I'll tell you all about it later. Do me a favor?"
"What do you need?"
"Fire up my grill, would you? I'm calling Ma and Mara."

###

Tera, Mara, Mrs. Morton, and River sat in lounge chairs out on Tera's patio, too full to move, and watched the sun slowly fade beyond the willows. As expected, Mama and Mara had been at home when Tera called, and she'd invited everyone over to eat. Daddy had sent his love--along with his request for a plate--but wouldn't come; his afternoon sports took precedence over almost anything else, especially the 'hen party' he'd envisioned between his wife and daughters. He'd even kept Li'l Man at the house with him, wanting to protect the child from the excessive mothering and clucking he would have had to endure outnumbered by his mother, grandmother, and aunt. Big Nate was left snoring in Papa Morton's recliner.

With none of Tera's male kin there to draw some of the fire, River was on his own. Tera occasionally helped him out by changing subjects or fielding her mother's and sister's pointed questions; but she was only too happy to have someone else occupying the 'hot seat' for a change.
"River, it's so nice to see you again, dear."
"Thanks, Mrs. Morton. Good to see you, too."
"And me? What about me?"
"Of course it's good to see you too, Mara," River laughed. "You really *are* Tera's sister, aren't you?"
"Now, exactly what's *that* supposed to mean, Bro Man?"
"It means you like giving folks a hard time, Mara Nicole," Mama said.

"Well, Mama, the apple don't fall too far from the tree, so I been told," Mara replied.
"Got *that* right!," Mama laughed, sipping her margarita. "So, River dear, when did you and Tera start dating again?"
"Mama!," Tera and Mara blurted in unison.
River smiled diplomatically but didn't answer.
"Oh, don't mind Tera, River; she's so closed-mouthed, this is the only way I can find anything out. You know, I was *just* asking Tera about you the other day, and--"
"And I told you *then*, Mama, that we hadn't seen each other in a little while. In fact, we'd both been so busy with school, we just got the chance to even hook up."
Mrs. Morton returned her focus to River.
"Hmm, you're a fast worker, huh River? That's good, my daughter needs a little push every now and then."
"*Mother...*"
"Uh-oh, must have struck a nerve or something. She's calling me 'Mother' now. Don't you get mad now, honey. I'm just happy that you two are seeing each other again, and I just wanted to let you know that, okay? Is that so bad?"
Mara wore a 'cat-who-swallowed-the-canary' smile; she'd tried to help Tera out, but wasn't about to sink any deeper in that mess. River's handsome face was a mixture of amusement, embarrassment, and discretion. He was too much a gentleman to contradict Mrs. Morton's assumptions. Meanwhile, Tera was doing a slow burn. She had to let them know--all of them--that she didn't need anyone to speak for her, didn't need anyone to fill in blanks or draw conclusions, and truly, *truly* didn't need anyone to patronize her.
"That wouldn't be bad at all, *Mother*, if that were the case," Tera answered evenly. "River and I have been friends for awhile, Ma, you know that. I just called him up, we talked, we got together for coffee, and then I

invited him over. *It's that simple!*"
Tera's mom smiled.
"So...that means you two have been together *all day*? Hmm. Guess I'm just behind the times, 'cause when I was *your* age, spending *that* much time with somebody meant something."
"It *still* means something, Ma," Mara interjected. "It means they're friends, okay? Tee just told you that. Don't embarrass folks; be nice."
"I'm sorry, Tera. Sorry, River. But y'all know me. If I wanna *know*, I ask. Or I drop hints. Anyway, I'd always thought that you two would make such a--"
"Nice couple? Ma, for the last time, you're barking up the wrong tree. River has his sights set on somebody..."
"Oh, that's too bad. I mean, that's nice for *you*, River. I suppose."
"Mama, you're a trip. *Of course*, that's nice; and I'm happy for him, too."
Mara's eyes followed Tera's every move as she spoke, looking for a chink in her sister's armor, something that would unmask her 'I'm happy for him' lie. Tera avoided looking in her direction.

River observed the exchange between Tera and her mother and sister with interest. It was always exciting to watch family dynamics at work, and he wanted to see how Tera operated under pressure. Not to mention, he was glad that he'd slipped from Mrs. Morton's scrutiny.
"Pay me no mind, River dear. I really *am* happy for you, if you've found a nice girl you want."
Tera looked at River, wondering when he was going to jump in and clarify things for her mother. The patient smile on his face told her that he planned to do no such thing. *Coward*, Tera thought.
"And as for you, Tera Marchelle--I'll be happy for *you*, too, when you finally meet someone you can put up with."

There was Tera's opening, and she stepped right into it.

"Well, Mommy, *maybe* I'll have that chance to meet someone--when I go to Jamaica."

It was a few moments later when Tera's words finally sank in.

"What?? *Jamaica?*"

"That's right. I leave in a week."

"But...but...," Tera's mom was sputtering, at a loss for words. Tera was the younger of her daughters, but had always been so responsible, so straightlaced...the idea that she was about to take a trip out of the country--probably alone--was so unlike her, it was...frightening.

"In a week? Who's going with you?"

"Just the three of us: me, myself, and I."

"Now, don't get flip at the mouth, Miss Tera. Goodness! Do you think that's wise, traveling alone?"

"Mama, thousands of people do it all the time, why not me? I'll be fine."

Well...you know, I *could* make reservations and go with you--that is, if you want me to."

"Mama, Tee ain't asked you about going with her," Mara interrupted. "Tera girl, you just go on, honey--have yourself a good time for *me* , okay?"

Mrs. Morton sat back in her chair, moodily sipping her drink. "Well, excuse *me*, I was just trying to help," she sulked.

"Mommy, it's not like that," Tera soothed. "Y'all are always getting on me about not doing anything; well, *now* I am. And I'm excited about it. That's why I went out and bought all those new things. Wish me a good trip."

"*Bon voyage*, Tera Marchelle," Mama said drily. "Look, honey, I really do want you to have a good time, and I do think it's good that you're making a few changes in your life. But don't try and make 'em all at once! And let people know when you're gonna do something like this, okay? Such a secretive child."

"Okay, Ma. You're right," Tera said, kissing her cheek. She glanced in River's direction.

"You're awfully silent about all this; what's up? No discouraging words to say?"

"No, no. Actually, I think it's a good idea. You'll enjoy it. Have fun." He stared at her strangely. Tera was puzzled.

"Well that's the most underwhelming response I ever heard," she said, returning his enigmatic stare. "Everybody but Mara sounds like I'm going to the electric chair instead of on vacation."

Maybe I am moving a little fast here, Tera thought. *But...no! No. I've been on the career track so hot and heavy, I scarcely know how to unwind and do anything else. That's probably the reason why I'm having those damned dreams. And that's why I'm taking this vacation, and doing a whole lot of other things I want to do--no matter who doesn't understand it or like it!*

Tera was feeling defensive and somewhat hurt by the lack of enthusiasm from her mother and River; thank God Mara was there, who always seemed to bolster her confidence, no matter what.

"It's getting late, Tera. I think Mara and I had better get going," Mrs. Morton said.

"Okay, Ma. Listen, I'm sorry if--"

"No dear, *I'm* sorry. I didn't mean to sound so negative, it's just that I worry about you. Going off alone, and all."

"Don't you sweat it, Tee," Mara said. "Mama, you act like you've forgotten how you used to do the exact same thing, and how Granny and Papa used to worry about *you*."

"That was entirely different, Mara Nicole."

"The only difference, Mama, is that it was you and not Tera!"

"Oh, I just can't win here! I apologized. I even said 'have

a good trip'; now, I think that's pretty damned good, seeing as how the whole idea concerns me."
Tera walked over to her mom and hugged her tightly.
"It *is* good, Ma. Now can we just squash this? I wouldn't have said anything at all if I'd thought it would cause this much commotion! It's just a trip."
Mrs. Morton smiled; she was used to Tera being her baby girl, and was simply having a hard time realizing that she was a full-grown woman. Lord knows she'd had enough time to get used to the idea; Tera was nearly thirty-two years old.
"If I can't go with you, can't I at least take you shopping for a few things? We can make a day of it: have lunch, the works. How about it?"
"Well...the 'old' me would have said 'no, I've already bought enough stuff myself', but the 'new' me says...it's still too much. But yeah, let's do it anyway!"
"All right! When, tomorrow?"
"I'll call you, Mommy. Mara, how long you gonna be in town?"
"Don't plan your shopping trip around *me*, girl. Mama already wore me out the other day, so y'all can go at it *without me*. Oh yeah, how'd you like that little mirror I got you? When I first saw it, something just said 'this belongs to Tera'. It just reminded me of you for some reason."
Tera shook off a momentary chill she felt at the mention of Mara's odd gift.
"It's beautiful, Mara; I love it," she lied.
"Good, sweetie," their mother interrupted. "Like I said, it's getting late. Talk to you tomorrow. You leaving, River?," she asked sweetly.
"Not just yet, Mrs. Morton," he answered, kissing her cheek.
"Well! Come on, Mara, let's leave these two...*alone*." Mama Morton winked slyly at Tera and River, waving

goodbye.

All Tera could do was laugh to herself at her mother's thinly-veiled innuendo about River staying on. Her mama's not-so-subtle matchmaking attempts were sometimes infuriating, but usually just plain funny.

Tera walked her mother and sister out to the car and said goodnight. She returned to the patio to find River comfortably laid back in his lounge chair, thoughtfully gazing out across the lagoon. When he glanced up at her, something inside her responded to the warmth and familiarity in those dark eyes. It was like a knowing look shared by lovers, and it angered and confused Tera. Her reaction to him earlier had had the same effect. *He's made himself clear enough*, Tera thought, *why am I getting these mixed messages?* She busied herself clearing away plates and glasses and taking them in to the kitchen.

"Need any help, Tera?," River called from the patio.

"Nope, I got it."

Why is he still here? She washed the dishes furiously, almost wishing that he'd left with Mama and Mara. Not that she hadn't enjoyed his company--just the opposite. But what was next?

I'm just tripping, she thought, ignoring the feeling of easy intimacy that still surrounded them even thought they weren't in the same room. She lingered in the kitchen as long as possible before going back out.

River had moved to the grassy slope where Tera had spent many lazy hours reading or watching the willows sway. She joined him, sitting down next to him on the lawn, their eyes staring out into the darkness; no one spoke. That was one of the things Tera had always liked about being with River. When words ran out, silence was never a problem. She felt herself relaxing, whereas moments before she'd felt tense and uncertain about the strange vibes between them. The uncomfortable feeling slowly dissipated into the indigo night, and Tera allowed herself to enjoy the inexplicable closeness she felt with River.

She wasn't the only woman in the world to have a close male friend; surely others had found themselves in a similar dilemma, not knowing exactly where the lines were drawn between friendship and something deeper. It was somewhat mysterious, but she felt no immediate need to figure it out. It had been a long day, and she was getting tired.

"Come on, Tera, let's go inside. You look like you're ready to hit the sheets, and I'm gonna hit the road."

Tera yawned and stretched, getting up from her comfy spot.

"Whew! Sorry, River. It came on all of a sudden, but yeah, I guess I better call it a night."

As they walked back to the house, Tera thought about how good it had been, seeing River--and how good it would be to see him go! They'd barely spoken since her mother and sister left; and though the silence hadn't been uncomfortable, it had *still* been...silence. It had reminded her of her parents--how they could go for hours without saying a word, yet still be in tune with each other.

Such a connection was common—even expected--between people who'd been together for years and years like her folks; but that wasn't the case with her and River. Tera couldn't figure it out, and decided again not to even try. There was enough unexplained stuff in her world without adding to the pile.

They were almost at the patio door when River grabbed her hand, shaking her out of her scattered thoughts. She turned, expecting him to say something and was caught totally off guard when his lips met hers in an urgent kiss. For a split second, Tera wanted to pull away. She and River had kissed before, but those chaste, brother-sister kisses were nothing like this. His lips on hers were warm and inviting, and kindled a heat that surprised as well as consumed her.

River drew her closer, wrapping his arms around her waist. *This is crazy*, she thought, even as she responded to his kiss. Her mind swirled madly as her hands gently crept up to River's solid, thick shoulders and neck. *What am I doing?* Her fingers now toyed with his shaggy, curly locks and worked their way to his scalp. Their warm breath mingled as River's arms tightened around her, and Tera knew that if their kiss lasted *even a moment longer*, she would make love to him...passionately and without restraint. But she couldn't do that! She had just firmly convinced herself that River was her friend, her running buddy, her home boy, her *colleague*, for God's sake...and there she was, reaching under his shirt to caress the short, crisp hairs on his chest.

His big hands tenderly framed her face as he nibbled on her lips and tongue. Tera hooked her thumbs into the belt loops of his pants and began walking slowly backward, pulling him along with her. She didn't understand what had brought all this on, but clearly understood the fiery passion building between them. *Oh my God*, she thought, as his hands stroked and massaged her back. Even her wildest fantasies of romancing River hadn't prepared her for the sensuous reality; his touch sent desire rippling over her like the wake of a pebble dropped into peaceful waters. Tera felt her legs weakening as she steered him to the bedroom. His eyes remained closed as he allowed himself to be led. Tera paused at the bedroom door, trying to get her bearings and calm the furious pounding of her heart. River opened his eyes enough for Tera to see the desire smoldering behind his sooty lashes. He drew back for a moment, staring into Tera's upturned face.

"Ever been to Heaven?," he murmured.

"I'm already there."
"Uh-uh, woman. Not yet. We're only at the outskirts."
"Well, since you seem to know the way, why don't you take me there?"
"It would be my pleasure."
River lifted her easily in his strong arms and carried her to the bed. Just as he'd eased her top up to expose her smooth, taut midriff, the phone rang. She sighed, releasing some of the tension threatening to explode inside her. River sat up, and Tera rolled to the other side of the bed to grab the phone. As she took the phone, she couldn't decide whether she was more annoyed or relieved that the caller had interrupted them. What happened between her and River had been almost magical; *but magic is an illusion, one that may have disappeared with the first glow of morning.*
"Hello," Tera whispered.
"Well, hey, Miss Tera; what's up?"
"Oh...hi, Cameron." Tera looked at River, who was calmly studying her face. The fire of passion still burned between them, but slowly subsided to glowing embers with the phone's intrusion. Tera was disappointed to see River's guard slipping firmly back into place; though he didn't seem upset, he'd drawn himself over to a neutral corner of the bed at the mention of Cameron's name.
"Wow...you were sleeping, I'm sorry; I just thought about calling you when I got back in, and I really should have waited until tomorrow, but...I just wanted to hear your voice," Cameron said.
River quietly rose from the bed; a tiny, little-boy smile tugged at the corner of his mouth as he waved goodbye and mouthed *'I'll call you tomorrow'*. Tera felt caught between a rock and hard place. She remembered the electric magnetism between her and Cameron, had thought of their next meeting almost constantly...until River. Had Cameron not called, she would surely have

spent the night with River.

It was strange, being emotionally caught between the two of them. Neither of them was her man, her options were open... but Tera wasn't well-versed in this so-called 'mating game', and wasn't comfortable with the constantly shifting variables. She didn't *really* understand what was 'fair' versus 'not cool' in that situation, though she was clear on what *she* personally considered 'stank'. She wasn't comfortable flitting from one to the other...*but wasn't that what she planned to do in Jamaica? Mix and mingle with a number of fine, available men? Maybe relax her mind enough to chase away the imaginary lover who'd become a fixture in her life?*

She heard the door close softly behind River; *so why the inner conflict about being attracted to both Cameron and River--maybe dating them both?* She'd just be getting a head start on her Jamaican adventure, that's all.

"No, it's alright, Cameron," she said. "It's not that late."

"Still, I'm sorry I disturbed you. So how've you been?"

"Fine, thanks. I spent the day with my mom and sister, threw a few steaks on the grill...that kind of stuff."

The memory of River's kiss was still on her lips as she recounted the events of her day to Cameron, studiously avoiding any mention of River.

"Sounds like your day was good," Cameron said.

"Wasn't yours?"

"Yeah, I suppose...just in a different way. I spent most of my day with one of my research participants, gathering data on her experiences."

"Oh really? Anything interesting?"

"Of course; one thing I can say about this study, there's almost never a dull moment."

"Wanna talk about it?"

"Thanks for asking, but confidentiality prevents me from getting into too much detail, you know? Besides, I didn't call to talk about that. What you doing tomorrow? I thought we might hook up, you know, do something. Whatever you want. How about it?"

"Well, I'm going shopping with my mother tomorrow, probably early, but...yeah, later sounds good. I'll call, okay?"

"Good enough, Tera. Talk to you tomorrow."

"Good night." Tera hung up.

She rolled over onto her back, staring up at the ceiling; she sighed. She was beginning to understand why she'd always felt so secure in the orderly, well-planned confines of her life. It was predictable. It was stable, no curve balls or wild cards. It may have gotten boring from time to time, but at least she always knew what to expect. The moment she'd made a decision to explore the *less* predictable, emotional side, it seemed she'd been inundated with all these surprising feelings and turns of events. But it was good, Tera told herself; *I already know the other side--this is the side of life I need to know more about.* While the thought of possibly making some mistakes offended her meticulous nature, Tera realized that she'd probably end up making quite a few as her sheltered, closed life began to open up. And she almost welcomed the bumps and bruises that a life well-lived would bring, because they were often the precursors of joy. She felt her eyes closing in sleep.

###

Tera woke up in the same position, still wearing her clothes, which smelled faintly of barbecue smoke and River. She lay there for a second, wondering what was different. Then it hit her; the dream. For the first night in months, there hadn't been one! For the first morning in months, she'd awakened slowly and naturally, without being wrenched from sleep by the events of the strange dream. Tera was both relieved and bewildered; her undisturbed night's sleep had relaxed and refreshed her, but the dream had become such a constant, she almost *missed* it, and wondered what had happened. She sat up and swung her legs over the edge of the bed.

She'd almost forgotten what it felt like to wake up rejuvenated and rested; maybe the lightning pace she'd maintained all during the school year really *had* been the problem, and now that she was taking a break from it, well...she could think of no other reason for the sudden absence of the dream. She couldn't have cared less why she hadn't had it--she was just grateful. And once again, pleased with herself for having diagnosed her own problem.

Tera glanced at the clock on the dresser; it was almost 9:00--far later than she was used to getting up, and it felt good to actually *sleep in*. *Now, that's what I'm talking about*, she thought. *Life is good!* As she got up and started her coffee and turned on the shower, Tera thought about the few remaining days until her trip; and decided that, if the days to come were anywhere near as exciting as the days that had just passed...ah, what a life!

###

This wasn't exactly how Tera had planned to spend this particular morning, but it was certainly for the best that she'd finished calculating semester grades. With a feeling of relief, she faxed her completed grades back to the registrar's office at Roosevelt.

Finding the exam scores in her fax that morning had thrown a kink in her plans, but now she was free of any work obligations until the fall. But that freedom from obligation had come with a price tag; she'd had to postpone her shopping trip with her mother and settle on meeting Cameron that afternoon. He'd been a little disappointed that they couldn't get together earlier and spend more time, but neither of their schedules had allowed for it. Still, Tera was excited about seeing him. They planned to meet at this new seafood restaurant in

Richton Park, *The Fillet of Soul.* The restaurant wasn't far away, thank goodness; that gave her a little more time to carefully groom herself.

When she started rummaging through her closet, she was dismayed that she couldn't find a thing to wear that she was satisfied with. The crisp tailored suits and blouses were for *work*, and she had absolutely no intention of putting anything like that on until September. She liked her nylon joggers, but...no. No sweats and sneakers. *Her casual-sporty-sexy dress?* Uh-uh; fine for shopping expeditions and such, but not special enough for a date. *Damn*, she thought, as she continued to dig through the closet. She hadn't wanted to wear any of her new stuff until her trip to Jamaica, but it was looking like she might have to break down and choose something from among those things.

"My kingdom for a sexy dress," she mumbled. As if in response to her request, Tera suddenly saw a flash of aqua blue near the back of the closet; puzzled, she reached for it. A pleased smile creased her face. It was the dress she'd bought last summer, then felt foolish for having chosen something so...frivolous. The price tag was still on it, because she'd intended to return it but just never got around to it. The dress was a lovely, summery shade of blue with a low cut back and halter neckline, and it was so totally unlike something she would wear, she wondered what had possessed her to buy the dress in the first place.

She clearly remembered the day she'd stopped in her tracks when she saw it in the window at *Eccentricity*, went in, tried it on, bought it--full retail price, no less--then took it home and shoved it to the back of the closet. The old Tera had chided herself for buying something that wasn't acceptably professional; the new Tera found herself deeply appreciating old Tera's effort to break out of the mold. She laid the dress across the bed as she searched for sandals to wear with it, glancing at the clock. It was about a quarter to one, and if she was going to meet Cameron at 1:30, she'd have to hustle.

###

"Can I call you later?," Cameron asked, as he and Tera prepared to leave the restaurant.

"That would be nice," Tera answered.

"Sorry my schedule's so crazy."

"Cameron, I understand what it's like when you have heavy-duty research staring you in the face. No need to apologize."

"Thanks, but...I'd like to make up for this... this abbreviated excuse for a date."

"Hey, don't trip; when time's looking a little better, we can get together."

"You're a sweetheart, Tera," Cameron said, giving her an appreciative peck on the cheek.

"Gotta run. I'll call you."

"'Bye," Tera whispered, watching Cameron as he hurriedly walked to the front door of the restaurant.

He paused for a moment, smiled, and waved before disappearing out the door. Tera sighed, thinking that her sweats or even a burlap sack would have gotten as much attention from Cameron as the beautiful dress she'd worn especially to impress him. *It was deja vu.*

Like when she'd first met River, and the initial sparks of attraction had shot off fast and furious before cooling off to slow steady embers of a comfy friendship, Tera could see the exact same thing happening with her and Cameron. Truthfully, she'd had no set-in-stone expectations about what would happen the next time she and Cameron saw each other. She knew that there had been a strong mutual attraction, and wanted to see what might develop. With that thought in mind, she'd dressed attractively--*not* seductively--and met up with him as they'd planned. The restaurant was nice, the food and conversation were even better...but somehow, Tera had slid into the 'friend zone' with Cameron. Which wasn't exactly a *bad* place to be; but it was a little like unwrapping a sandwich and finding peanut butter instead of steak. "Oh, well...I like peanut butter," she whispered.

CHAPTER FOUR

Tera was tingling with excitement; at long last, the day of departure for Montego Bay had arrived! The last few days had alternately dragged or flown by, but she was finally on her way. The reggae music pumping softly in the background was replaced by the voice of one of the flight attendants instructing the passengers to fasten their seatbelts in preparation for takeoff. She felt the pressure of lift off, a little like the feel of going up in an elevator, and her spirits soared as well.

She recounted the events of the previous days. After her somewhat disappointing date with Cameron, Tera had decided to just stop projecting about what might happen between them; from all indications, it probably wouldn't be much--like with River. Oh, they'd talked a few times since that day when he'd had to rush off to a hypnosis session, but their conversations had mostly centered around the progress of his dissertation. And much as she'd have preferred a different slant on things, Tera understood; she clearly remembered eating, breathing, *sleeping* research, and such a life left absolutely no time for cultivating relationships that weren't already established. So it was no surprise that Cameron didn't have much time for her.

River, however, was an entirely different story. Tera didn't have a clue about what was happening with him. Just thinking about the night she'd almost spent with River gave Tera an incredible rush--followed by maddening frustration. As he'd promised, River had called Tera the next day; but he'd been his old self, cool and reserved. If he'd even shown some type of jealousy or frustration, Tera could have handled that. It would have at least given an indication that *something* had happened between them. It would have confirmed that it hadn't just been her imagination that he was interested in her. As it was, they seemed to be right where they'd started. Tera shrugged; *so be it!* She shoved all the confusing or conflicting thoughts from her mind and ordered a rum punch from the flight attendant. In an hour or so, the plane would touch down in Jamaica, and it would be *on*.

"Let the games begin," she smiled, savoring her fruity drink.

###

If Tera had thought that *anticipating* going to Jamaica was exciting, actually being there was so much more intense. The dreamlike quality of the island was apparent even before the plane landed; as the aircraft made its descent, Tera saw eruptions in the crystal waters that she soon recognized as dolphins, leaping to break the clear turquoise surface of the bay. Massive palm trees and indescribable, colorful blooms created a profusion of color that was almost otherworldly in comparison to the predominant grayness of Chicago. The feeling of entering another world continued as she exited the plane, greeted with tropical warmth and the scent of hyacinth and gardenia.

Going through customs was painstakingly long as Tera and the other passengers stood in a long line with their belongings, waiting to be checked through. Air conditioning in the terminal was sufficient to battle the humid weather, but only if one kept movement to a minimum, which wasn't difficult in the slow-moving line. This was perhaps the only lag in Tera's vacation, but she finally got checked through and was free to board the hotel minivan which would whisk her and some of her flight companions to *Lavish*, one of the newer beachfront resorts.

After a short ride through narrow streets filled with people, other vehicles, and goats, the van reached a less congested road and began to pick up speed; more speed than Tera had ever experienced in Chicago, where drivers are notorious for flagrantly breaking the limits. Their driver flew down the road, narrowly missing cars and motorbikes, it seemed, as he darted around sharp bends, and the fact that they rode on the left side rather than the right only increased the illusion that they were careening out of control. It was impossible for Tera to relax and enjoy the lush scenery of the countryside. *That would be all I need,* Tera thought, *for this damn van to go plunging over the side of the road down into the sea!*

Soon enough, the van reached a level stretch near a beach, and Tera found herself enjoying the exhilarating ride. Minutes later, the van pulled up to *Lavish*, a cluster of modern suites and villas located close to the beach, with its sparkling water and glistening white sand. A four-story hotel rose from the center of a great complex, encircled by villas with rooftop decks and flanked by specialty shops, clubs, restaurants, and the largest pool Tera had ever seen. She could hardly wait to get settled in and changed so that she could do a little exploring.

Tera's single bedroom villa may not have offered the same spectacular ocean view as the hotel balconies, but it was beautiful, cozy, and private; she was more than satisfied. Sliding glass doors provided an impressive ground level view of the beach, and she envisioned wonderful, early-morning breakfasts up on the deck. She hurriedly unpacked and hung up her things to let any wrinkles fall out. Rather than being tired from her flight and the drive to the hotel, Tera was energized and ready to get out into the center of the complex. It was late afternoon, and Tera was antsy...but reminded herself that she'd just arrived. She had *two whole weeks* to be there! On that note, she opted to read through the visitor's guide on the wicker coffee table in the living room; it would give her an idea of the featured activities of the complex and allow her to make more choices of what to do.

In the same way that Tera wanted to find out what activities and events were going on, she also wanted to be prepared to check them out, so she took a quick shower and dressed in comfortable white pants and halter top before skimming the guide. *Hmmm,* she thought... *what'll it be?* Snorkeling? *Nah; well, maybe later or next week if things*
get boring. Parasailing? *When pigs fly, I'll fly.* Shopping? *Tomorrow.* Casino? *Just say 'no'.* Nightclub? *Most definitely! But not right now.* Excursion around the bay? It sounded perfect; the whole trip would take about two hours, she'd get a chance to see many of the surrounding attractions, the salt sea air would do her a world of good, *plus* she'd be back in time to dress and go out to the local nightclub, *Kickit.* Tera threw on a wide-brimmed straw hat, sandals, and shades, and closed her door softly behind her.

###

From the bow of the *Arawak*, Tera scanned from shore to horizon. At the ship's closest point to the shore she could see the beach, peppered with folks in colorful swimwear. An occasional jet ski or powerboat would pass by, and Tera got quite a sampling of the island's offering of handsome men. From her vantage point, she could scope them all out--somewhat anonymously--from behind her dark glasses. Appreciative smiles and open flirtation from some of them let her know that this vacation hadn't been a mistake.

Back at her villa, Tera was delighted to find that a tray of chilled fruits had been placed out on the deck for her to enjoy, and she relaxed and savored a sliced starfruit as she watched a picture-perfect sunset. The sun was a burnished golden ball, sinking into a calm sea of orange and gold and framed by delicate green palm fronds. As far as she was concerned, it just didn't get any better than that. Her first day in Montego Bay was almost surreal...and it wasn't even half over. Back home, it would still be light outside; Tera's internal clock was still tuned in to Chicago time, and the fact that it was now dark in Jamaica didn't bring on any drowsiness. She loved it! It made her feel like she had an advantage, even more time to enjoy herself. Sleep was the last thing on her mind. Still, she thought it might be a good idea to lie down for a short while before going back out. If the night life in Jamaica was as exciting as the daytime hours she'd just spent, she could very easily see herself getting worn to a frazzle in the next twenty-four hours; no way would she enjoy the whole two weeks unless she paced herself. Tera went inside.

She settled down on the comfortable, overstuffed chaise, almost too pumped up to think about relaxation. Eventually, flesh conquered spirit and she found her taut muscles loosening involuntarily. Wide awake but totally relaxed, she allowed her thoughts to wander...to her chance meeting with Cameron on the Metra...her 'date' with him...her surprising romantic interlude with River...*to the dream*. Suddenly, it was there in her mind.

The experience of recalling it while fully awake was slightly...uncomfortable, but not nearly as troubling as it had been while Tera slept. In any case, there it was, scrolling through her mind practically without her permission.

Tera saw herself running to meet her lover, felt the mist dampening her bare arms and feet. The memory of their escape to a hidden cave at sunrise, and the secure feeling of being nestled in her lover's protecting arms brought Tera a sense of peace; but at the edge of that peace, she could feel disaster looming. Her eyes stared off into space. She wasn't asleep, yet she wasn't quite part of the waking world, either. She was perfectly aware of her surroundings, didn't feel overwhelmed or terrorized by these waking visions; it was more like being forced to sit through a movie you didn't *really* want to see. She was ready to snap out of it...but found that she couldn't.

And then Tera saw herself and Dream Lover emerge from the cave at dusk. This was slightly different from what she'd remembered. In fact, after not having the dream for a few days, Tera had begun to believe that it was a thing of the past--up until that moment. "Go away," Tera whispered. "Just leave me alone." But it continued.

Barely visible in the gathering darkness, Mason, her dream man, and Tera--that is, Hannah--made their way stealthily down to the water's edge, trying to keep their packs of belongings from brushing up against bushes or low branches, or anything that might make noise. They were so close; the last thing they needed was to attract the attention of those who stalked them.

A feeling of desperation overtook the lovers as they continued to search for the small canoe that Tall Bear had promised would be waiting for them, hidden close to the shore. Where was it? Had something prevented Tall Bear's warriors from placing it there? Worse, had the patrollers found it first? Barely, Hannah heard Mason sigh in relief. He guided her hand to a curved expanse of wood jutting out from beneath willow branches skimming the river's surface; it was the canoe!

Placing a finger over Hannah's lips, Mason cautioned her to keep quiet. They waded noiselessly into the waist-deep water, holding their packs high. Only crickets, bullfrogs, and other night creatures could be heard as they slid themselves and their belongings into the canoe. Blackness covered them completely; no moon lit the sky. Still, they could not afford even a momentary lapse in their caution, for they knew beyond a doubt that the patrollers wouldn't rest until the two of them were *either recaptured, dead...or <u>free</u>. Freedom was their only option. Hannah knew that Mason would die before letting either of them be caught. And she knew that she would rather be dead than to live without Mason.*

Once they'd safely reached the middle point of their river crossing, Mason sat up and began to slice through the silent waters with his oar, rowing for the opposite shore which was barely visible. "It's alright, Hannah; you can sit up now. Here, take this oar, girl! Sooner we get across, is the sooner we get away from here forever," Mason whispered. "Don't cry, honey, just keep rowin'. We almost there."

Well, Tera thought, *at least this obtrusive, repetitive-ass dream/daydream has a happy ending; doesn't it?* Though she could feel herself slowly coming out of it, there was more unfolding....

once ashore on the other side they huddled silently, listening for any sign that they may have been heard. It was a certainty that they were being followed, but Mason and Hannah knew if they continued as quietly and cautiously as they'd been up to that point, they could make it. Their pursuers were slow, and stupid, and hateful, and overconfident of their ability to catch runaways because they were, after all, just niggers. Their dogs would be useless by now, so unless they'd paid an Indian to track them, there was little chance that the patrollers would catch them. Their hatred of Indians was as intense as that of the slaves they were trying to find; Mason and Hannah comforted themselves that the patrollers would never catch up. They managed to slide their canoe close to shore, using overhanging willow branches for cover just as Tall Bear's men had done on the other side; it might still come in handy in an emergency. With God's help, *Hannah prayed silently,* we won't be needing this canoe again!

The vision dissipated like fog after the sun rises.

"Oh, so it's like *that?*," Tera said aloud. "I have to make up my *own* ending?"

She got up from the chaise, annoyed. She hadn't wanted the daydream in the first place, hadn't wanted to sit through its familiar story line. She'd finally stopped battling the impulse to 'turn it off', and allowed the waking vision to unfold. And what had it gotten her? *A classic 'soap opera' treatment, where she'd been given just enough of a glimpse to keep her hooked--just short of revealing the most exciting part.*

Tera shook her head, again thinking that she should have been a writer; then again, if she *were*, she'd have brought that story to an end long ago and moved on to something else!

"Bump this," she said, glancing at her watch. It was almost 10:00. She knew that *real* dance hall didn't start jumping until the wee hours; by then, she would have met plenty of folks at the nightclub, maybe a local or some fellow tourists who'd want to venture out past the confines of the self-contained little world that was *Lavish* and check out some real sounds. In the meantime, she would dress up and sashay down to *Kickit.*

###

To Tera's great surprise, *Kickit* was, well...*kickin'*. Massive speakers of fabulous sound quality and power dropped an exciting mix: reggae, r&b, soca, rap, house—even a little contemporary jazz.

When she stepped into the club, she saw that the dance floor was packed. She paused for a moment, checking things out...and smiled. Her light touch of makeup was flawless, her short hair lay in glossy, crisp waves, and she could tell from the admiring glances that her body-hugging, aqua dress would not get the same reaction it had from Cameron. She was ready.

Her slight nervousness disappeared when a handsome young serving attendant walked up to her, asking if she'd rather be escorted to a table or the bar.

"The bar, please," she answered. She didn't want to sit alone at a table. That might be interpreted as an invitation to someone she *didn't* want to get to know.

She slid onto one of the tall barstools, marveling at the bar itself. Its design emphasized art as much as utility. It was long and unusually curved, with a clear surface which was softly illuminated from below. The muted glow was as complimentary as candlelight--without the wax drips. The bartender took Tera's order, and she checked out her surroundings while waiting for her drink.

It was a fantasy world of flashing colored lights, music, laughter, writhing dancers. She was momentarily saddened by the whole scene, which was almost *too* intense--as though the people felt obliged to dance, and laugh, and flirt...or their trip to the island would have been in vain. And she was not exempt from that observation, either. *She'd* come to party like her life depended on it, too. That glimpse of frantic energy turned Tera's own level down a few notches; after all, her original intent with this vacation had been to *relax*.

The bartender returned with her drink, a Malibu and fresh pineapple juice. When she tried to pay, he shook his head.

"It's from the gentleman down there," he said, pointing to the far end of the bar. Tera turned slowly to see who'd sent the drink, and sputtered, nearly spilling it on herself when she recognized the sender. *There at the end of the bar, smiling and raising his own glass in acknowledgment, was River!*

Tera's mouth gaped; she'd never been good at dealing with surprising situations, and sat there opening and closing her mouth like a fish tossed up on the sand. *What the hell was he doing there?* He'd sat at her house and heard her say that she was going to Jamaica--*why* hadn't he said that he was planning to go, too?

Tera gulped the icy drink. Was he

following her? *Why??!* These questions raced through her mind like sprinters, but after the initial shock of seeing him in this most *unexpected* place...she was... happy to see him. Confused about seeing him. *Furious* at seeing him! He looked wonderful, which made Tera even angrier. *Of all the nerve*, she thought, slamming her drink when she should've been sipping. She hadn't forgotten about the night they'd almost spent together; nor about his crisp, "business-as-usual" attitude ever since. His being there made absolutely no sense.

She waited at her end of the bar for River; he had some explaining to do. Her eyes followed his image in the mirror as he walked down the length of the bar toward her. The image stopped right next to her and she faced him.

"Hey, woman," he boomed over the loud music, "having a good time?"

"So-so."

The pineapple in her drink suddenly seemed tart, and her mouth went dry.

"Fancy meeting you here, Mr. Bennett."

"Guess you're not the only one who needed to break away from the grind, Tera."

"Mm-hmm. Looks like I'm the only one who had *no problem* letting *other folks* know I was breaking away from the grind."

Tera grew more annoyed. River's casual air could be irksome even on a *good* day, and his standing there and acting like their running into each other was *coincidental*--the most natural thing in the world--well...it was insufferable. Why didn't he say something before?

"So River, why didn't you let me know you were coming here?"

"It was pretty 'spur-of-the-moment', you know? Sort of like *your* decision to go."

"Right. Still, it would have been nice to know that one of my best friends was going to Jamaica at the *same time* that I planned to go, and--lo and behold!--even staying at the same hotel."
Tera struggled to keep her emotions in check, but wasn't doing a very good job; she was confused and somewhat hurt. She'd thought about their almost-night together a thousand times, and accepted that things hadn't gone any further. She'd even told herself that the whole thing had been an impulsive mistake; that was why River had gone back to his same old aloof self. *They'd known each other too long to be embarrassed by what didn't happen.* She figured that River had caught himself before things went too far. The woman he admitted being sprung over had a definite hold on him, and probably didn't even know it. But none of that mattered, it was water under the bridge. No matter how she tried to look at it differently, Tera couldn't help thinking that River had followed her to Jamaica--his aloof act just wasn't working! *Well*, she thought, *maybe he didn't follow me, maybe it's a so-called 'coincidence' and we're just pawns in some cosmic chess game or something...*no! Even if that were the case, how would that explain his distant behavior? With everything in her, Tera believed that River had come to Jamaica to be with her...if not to be with her, why had he come to this specific hotel? If he wasn't thinking along those lines...why had he even bothered to let her know he was there? Tera didn't know what to think.

River leaned back against the bar, gazing out onto the dance floor, then suddenly turned to Tera. *Was it her imagination, or did she momentarily see a flash of anger in his eyes?*
"I agree, Tera--it *would* have been nice to know that 'one of my best friends' was going to Jamaica. Who

knows? Maybe me and my 'friend' might have made plans to go together, or hook up there later...or at least spend more time together beforehand."

Tera's hurt feelings shifted to anger. *Go together? Spend more time beforehand?* He was acting like she was his lady or something, and had neglected to tell him that she'd secretly planned a getaway without him! She was even more confused; if he'd had a change of heart about the woman he loved at a distance and was thinking of Tera instead, *why* the arm's-length treatment? She was seething. Her words were calm but cutting.

"Don't blame your 'friend', River, that *you* walk around all the time with a broomstick stuck up your--"

"Stuck up my what?"

"Your...well, you know what I mean! If you weren't always so busy keeping your 'game face' intact, maybe your friend would have known that you wanted to spend some time together."

"My friend *knew* that. I thought my friend understood my feelings the last time I visited her. Oh, but that's right--my friend is so popular and busy these days. Phone just jumping off the hook, all hours of the day and night."

So, Tera thought, *Cameron's call had upset him. Idiot! Why didn't he say anything? Why hadn't he just stayed?* She sighed; *why was any of this even an issue, since he'd already said he cared about someone else?*

"River...are we or are we not friends?"

It was clear that her question had caught him by surprise. River turned and stood directly in front of her, and they stared at each other for a long moment. River's handsome face was solemn as he rolled the question over in his mind.

"Of course we are, Tee."

"Then let's not talk about each other in the third

person, or keep throwing out stupid hints instead of saying the things we need to say to each other, okay? Why aren't we talking about what's really wrong?"

"Huh? Well, I...did I tell you how *fire* you look in that dress? Blue is definitely your color."

"*What?* Dammit, River--be serious, would you?"

"I *am* serious! You look good, girl. Square biz."

"River..."

"When you walked in, Tee, all heads turned. I mean, for a minute there I thought the music was gonna stop. You--"

"You're full of shit, River," Tera said, turning from him.

"What? Wow, can't a brother give you a compliment? And you think *I'm* the one walking around with something stuck up my behind."

Tera grabbed her purse from the bar and turned to leave, stinging River with one of her most withering looks. He stood there looking confident and poised, and totally innocent of the mind games she knew he was playing. She was tempted to toss the rest of her drink on him, but the sight of his well-defined chest in a soaking wet knit shirt might have made her forget how truly angry she was. She could still hit below the belt, though.

"What's the problem, River, were you playing it too close back home? Scared your lady friend might have found out you were trying to dip up in this? Is that why you *followed me here*, so we could finish what we started--without her being anywhere around?"

A look of surprise spread across River's face. *Bingo*, Tera thought; *score one for me.* She turned on her heel and was about to strut triumphantly away when River called her.

"Touche, Tera. Touche! Whatever I may have thought doesn't matter, does it? Looks like you've got Mr. Dissertation on call to take care of any situation, night

or day, right? And as for picking up where we left off, well...it'll never happen, because she *is* here."
Tera stopped mid-stride. She felt like the wind had been knocked out of her. The music swelled in her ears until she felt her head would pop; *River's lady was here with him in Montego Bay?* She spun around. Now it was her turn to look shocked. River just stood there looking at her, cool as the hour before sunrise. She felt her insides turn to jello.

It was suddenly clear why they'd never talked about that last time he'd come to her house and what had almost happened; *the sonofabitch had been playing games with her, just as he was now.* Minutes ago, he'd *just said*--in so many words--that she should have let him know of her plans to come to Jamaica so that maybe they could have come together, or at least spent more time together before she went. Now he was throwing it in her face that someone else was there with him! *Bastard!*

Hot tears formed in her eyes, blurring her vision, but she would *not* let them fall. Not with River standing there. *How could she have deluded herself into thinking that he might be interested in her...how could she have ever thought this man was her friend?*
"Maybe you ought to go where she is, then," Tera said calmly. "Have a good time. I certainly intend to."
This time she walked away, hips swinging and head held high amid inviting glances. She looked straight ahead, not daring to look back. It would have been too much for her if River saw her crying. How she managed to keep striding without breaking into a frantic run, she didn't know. Once outside of the club, she walked faster and faster as tears fell and she ran the rest of the way back to her villa.

###

After crying herself to sleep, Tera got up early

and watched the sun rise as she sat up on the deck. Apparently, others at the resort enjoyed watching the sunrise too; fresh water, steaming coffee, and a breakfast tray were already on the table when Tera went up to the deck. The hotel staff anticipated the guests' every need.

As swatches of fuschia and cayenne red and gold tinted the horizon, Tera sipped the strong coffee and smoked one of the Marlboros she'd stashed in her purse before leaving Chicago. Each puff eased away a little more of her misery, and the beauty of sunrise lifted her spirits as well. When she'd gotten in the night before, she'd thought she should probably just pack up and go back home. That scene with River had ruined everything and the prospect of a laid-back, peaceful vacation seemed impossible. But with sunlight bursting out over the Caribbean Sea bathing everything in its gentle glow, Tera had a change of heart. If nothing else, she was analytical and determined, and she mulled over the reasons why she'd wanted to go away on vacation in the first place. She thought about the vow to herself to let life lead her for a change, and to open herself up to the less predictable side of life--whether it brought joy or pain. And she wasn't going to let River or anyone else change that!

She was determined to view her episode with River as just one of the many bumps she would experience along the road of life. *There was no reason to stop driving, just because the asphalt wasn't always smooth.* No, she would *not* go back to Chicago, not until she was ready. She would not leave that hotel either, just because River happened to be there. She would get up every day--early--and hit the streets, or tour the rest of the island, or water ski, or whatever... and hope like hell she didn't run into River and his lady. And, probably toughest of all, she wouldn't allow herself to hold a grudge against River for what had happened the night before in the club. It was childish, uncalled-for, and even a little mean, but she would not trade wrong for wrong. She *would*, however, protect her feelings in the same way River had always done. That way, the boundary lines would always be clear concerning what was fair in their relationship, and what was not. They should never have blurred that line with anything even faintly resembling romance, and Tera realized the part she had played in their mutual mistake.

Hurt feelings would cool off, she knew--and she resolved to just keep dealing with River as she always had, accepting his friendship "as is". No matter that he was elusive and distant at times; after all, everyone had their quirks and flaws...was River any different? Was she?

Having made peace with herself about that, she felt no need to either avoid him or seek him in order to straighten out the previous night's mess. *It'll happen when it happens*, she thought.

The sun was high, and birds darted across the endless, cloudless expanse of sky. The beach and streets were still deserted, except for the workers whose job it was to keep the sand and walkways clean. Maybe the other hotel guests had partied a little too hearty the night before; whatever the case, Tera saw it as a perfect opportunity for her to roam undisturbed. She went inside to throw on a swimsuit and shorts, then headed down to the beach, shoes and sunglasses in hand.

###

The sun was a soothing balm to Tera's tense, over stressed body and its warming rays seemed to penetrate to the center of her being. She understood why the ancient Egyptians had worshiped the sun as the Giver of Life. She could hear a car or two passing on the road behind her but had seen only a few other people on the beach, farther down. *Good.*

She was enjoying her solitude immensely, and wanted to stay exactly where she was for at least another half-hour. The new day held promise; the events of the night before were a million miles away as Tera lay on the sand, eyes closed behind her sunglasses. She felt much better but found that she couldn't stop her thoughts from flashing back to the things she and River had said to each other. Her stomach turned over with shame when she thought of what she'd said about him trying to pick up where they'd left off. *She didn't really think that; why had she said it?* And the way he'd relished telling her that he wasn't in Jamaica alone; *why had they both tried to hurt each other with cruel and foolish words?* Suddenly, something above her blotted out the sun. She opened her eyes to find River standing over her, and she bolted up from where she lay. He knelt down, then sat next to her on the sand; it was an awkward moment that felt like an hour.

"Hi, Tera."

"Hello, River."

They sat in silence for a short while; River seemed at a loss for words and Tera looked around, expecting to see a woman approach.

"Listen, Tee about last night...I'm sorry. That's not the way we are, it should never have happened."

"It's alright, Riv. Hey, I'm sorry too."

"For what? I was the one acting like a jackass."

"I said some things I shouldn't have...I--"

"You reacted to the shitty way I came off."

"Yeah, maybe so...but I didn't have to trade shit for shit."

"Hmm. Interesting way of putting it."

"No, really. You know, at first I had wanted to talk about...that time you came over; the time you almost spent the night."

"Tera..."

"Hear me out, Riv. I wanted us to talk about it 'cause I didn't want to be caught out there thinking the wrong thing about what it meant--if anything. I didn't want to fool myself like we might be heading in a...a certain direction, but you know what? *That's what happened anyway.*"

"Tee, I wish like hell I'd never said the things I said."

"Well, in a way, I'm glad you did. It put me back in the right frame of mind."

"What do you mean?"

"I mean, Riv...I was thinking about you in a way I shouldn't have in the first place. You already told me what time it was. You made it clear that your mind was on someone else."

"Tera...about that...I think you misunderstood."

"Unh-uh. I heard you loud and clear, *regardless* of what almost happened between us. I shouldn't have let it happen."

"I was the one who started it."

"But it takes two. And I knew I wasn't the right one."

"Tera, I'm telling you--you didn't understand what I was saying."

"Didn't I ? I think I did. I mean, you *did* tell me you were in love with someone else, right? Someone who didn't know how you feel, right?"

"I didn't exactly say 'love', Tera."

"Dammit, River! Man, don't drop semantics on me. Be for real! You *love* the woman, am I right?"

"Yeah...yeah, I guess I really do."

"And she's *here with you*, right?"

"Tee, you don't have the whole picture--"

"Shit!" Tera wanted to explode; she closed her eyes and took a few deep breaths to calm down the pounding in her chest. She'd told herself that she wouldn't let River's caginess upset her, but it wasn't

working. The stinging behind her eyes told her that she'd cry if he didn't stop playing games and avoiding this important issue between them. Without their clearing the air, how could
they continue to be friends?
"Okay River, okay. I don't have the whole picture. Fine! Why don't you clarify things for me, okay? Is she or is she not here, like you said?"
"Yes, she is, but--"
"No buts!" Tera's hand flew up, motioning River to be quiet.
"If she's *here*, and you *care* about her...they why are *we* at each other's throats? You should be happy, and I want to be happy *for* you, but--"
"But you think you might be falling in love with me."
"That's not...what I was gonna say."
"But it's what you feel, isn't it?"
"River, that's got *nothing* to do with anything! Look...*all* I wanted to do was clear the air between us so there wouldn't be any drama *when* or *if* the three of us were ever around each other. I mean, I'll probably be meeting her one of these days...right?"
"I don't know."
"Whatever, Riv. *Whatever.* You know, this whole conversation was a mistake. I figured we'd have to talk sooner or later, and I really thought it would turn out better than this," Tera said, getting up and brushing sand off her shorts.
"Why is it so important that you meet her? Why are you so angry?"
"Just forget it, River. I guess it shouldn't be important to me if it's not to you. And I'm not angry, either. I'm just seeing the boundaries of our friendship, and...well, things are just different than I thought, that's all."
"Unh-uh. That's not it."
"Well then Mr. Bennett, *you* tell me what's up, since

you seem to know everything."
River got up, standing dangerously close to Tera. His eyes lovingly consumed her from head to toe, and she felt herself melt down under such close scrutiny. She began to tremble; *what the hell was wrong with her? What was wrong with him?* In an instant, River drew her close, crushing her soft lips with his kiss.
"River, don't!," she whispered, but her plea was useless; her passionate response had made her protests null and void. Tera was again caught up in the heat generated between her and River. She molded herself to his embrace, a perfect fit that felt so right...but it was all wrong!
"No!," she shouted, pulling away from him. She felt cold and alone, like a child snatched from its mother's warmth. And she felt betrayed; *why was he doing this?*
"You asshole! What the hell are you thinking, huh? What are you trying to prove?"
"I just proved it. Know all that shit you just said about 'seeing the boundaries of our friendship', and all that jazz? There *aren't* any, we crossed 'em, Tera. You love me."
"*Love* you?? *You make me sick*, you arrogant bastard!"
"Maybe I do, baby girl, but you know I'm speaking truth! The only reason why you're mad, why it's *so important* for you to meet the woman in my life, is so you can *prove* to yourself that you don't love me--that all we are is 'friends'."
"No, you're wrong! You're crazy...why would you *want* that to be true?? So you can brag about having two women strung out on you?"
"You know me better than that, Tera."
"Right now, I'm not sure I know you at all!"
"Oh, you *know* me. And you know what I say is true; just admit it to yourself."
"*For what?!* If I did love you--and I do *not*!--that would

be some sticky shit, now wouldn't it? I can just see it: you, me, and Miss Perfect make three! What the *hell* would I need that for?"

"I keep telling you, but you're not trying to hear me; you *don't* have the whole picture, Tee."

"And I keep telling *you, you said you love her, and you said she's here.* What else do I need to understand?"

Tera stepped away from River, who'd once again gotten just inside her comfort zone. Her angry face relaxed in shock for a moment as a sickening thought occurred to her.

"Oh, you *sick* ass--River! Please, please, please don't tell me...I *know* you don't mean that you wanna screw *both of us!* Is that it? Is *that* the whole fucking picture you want me to see??!"

She took his shocked silence for assent; before she knew it, she'd slapped him with all her might. Anger blazed in his eyes as he stepped to her and Tera shrank back, afraid for a moment that he might actually slap her back. Catching herself, she stood her ground defiantly. He pulled her roughly to him and covered her mouth with his. She struggled vainly, only to feel the resistance draining from her body into the warm sand beneath her feet. His firm grip eased when he felt her body loosen and press against his chest. When his moist lips finally released hers, he began to nibble and kiss along the curve of her neck.

An angry sob caught in her throat; his touch was intoxicating, but this was not right. He was playing her. The low moan of pleasure rumbling in his chest inflamed her even more and her body rocked from the intense emotions warring inside her. *He was playing her, like a violin.* And not just a plain old violin, either--*a Stradivarius.* No matter how good it felt, she wasn't going out like that. No! She was *not* going to make love to River, right there on the beach. And she was definitely, definitely *not* going to be his piece on the side! And she was *not* going to compete with his woman for his affection; and she hated him for the passionate kisses and caresses that made her *feel* like competing with the nameless, faceless woman. It took everything she had to pry herself away from his arms.

"Leave me alone, River. This is the craziest, *stupidest* shit I ever...man, this is *not* cool, okay?...and I'm having *nothing* to do with it!"

"You love me, Tera. You want me right now, as much as I want you."

"I hate you! *Love you?* I hate your damn guts for this, River. So--you pushed my buttons, okay? You pushed 'em just right, I admit that. So what?! That's not love, that's just plain *horny*--it's been a long time! And you know what? It'll be even longer if you're my only option!"

"Cameron Wilson can't make you feel like I can."

"Oh, what is the damn *deal* about Cameron?! There is *nothing* going on between us! And if there was, you're right--it *wouldn't* feel like this, 'cause right now I'm sick to my stomach!"

Tera's words hurt River deeply; he pulled her to him a final time, kissing her until she was breathless before letting her go.

"Sick to your stomach, huh? When you wanna get well, Tera, come see *me* for the cure," her said, rubbing his hard body against her.

"Fuck you, River!," she screamed, running away from him down the beach.

###

Once safely back at her villa, Tera's rapid breathing gradually slowed. She could not believe what had just happened, nor decide whether she was more hurt, shocked, angry...or excited. She flopped into a chair and put her legs up, immediately lighting a cigarette to calm her jangled nerves. *Well, that's that*, she thought; *I have to leave that man alone.* No more being patient with his strange ways. No more 'accepting his aloofness'. *No more friendship*, not anymore. As open as she was to exploring other areas of her life, she was *not* open to being played for a fool. "Fuck you, River Jordan Bennett," she hissed.

Losing his friendship hurt, but from that moment on, he would definitely be a closed chapter in Tera's life. She'd miss his off-beat sense of humor, and his brilliant insight into things. She'd miss his confidence, his enthusiasm...even his reserved, stand-offish air. She shuddered, remembering the thrill of his touch; she was grateful to have never found out exactly how much she might have missed...*other* things about him.

She knew just from the way he kissed, his loving would have been an addiction she couldn't easily shake. It didn't matter, though, whatever she may have lost with his friendship; the price was more than her heart could pay.

She made herself focus on how much of her vacation she had left to enjoy. Even though the past twenty-four hours had felt like days, she intended to spend the rest of the two weeks of vacation in a leisurely way. She showered, put on a green tank top and matching wrap skirt, and joined the tour group headed for Negril.

###

The rest of Tera's day progressed beautifully. After her bumpy start with River, she and eleven others from *Lavish* had taken an even bumpier ride south into the Jamaican countryside to Negril. It was beautiful, and Tera almost wished she'd made reservations there instead of Montego Bay.

The sand on the beaches was fine and white, and the waters crystal clear and laced with colorful coral beds. Rough thatched huts sat a short distance from the shore, where you could change into swimsuits or lounge in woven hammocks. Sun-burnished young children were eager to run and get fresh coconut water, or sky juice, or patties from the vendors up near the gravel road for a small fee. Tera had been spoiled enough at *Lavish*; she walked to the vending carts herself and divided her change among the kids. She strolled along the beach drinking a syrupy lime, mango, and orange sky juice. It was like sno-cones back home, only with a different variety of flavors to choose from.

It was completely 'touristy', she knew, but Tera spent the next couple of hours collecting seashells. She discovered large intact conch, abalone, spiraling nautilus, and clam shells lodged or buried in the sand, and collected them in the fold of her skirt until she could get something larger to put them in. She'd done it unconsciously, but the way she'd draped her skirt reminded her of the woman in her dreams--Hannah--and the way she'd folded away stolen items of food in her skirts. She shook off the thought and continued down the beach.

The air was humid and warm, and the strenuous walk had Tera's cotton top and skirt clinging to her body. She was on a deserted stretch of beach, thinking how nice it would be to take a quick dip; but she'd forgotten her suit. She approached the lone thatched hut she saw a few yards away, and was relieved to find it empty. She immediately stripped off her sweaty clothes. She peeked outside; it was as though this was her own private beach. Finding the coast clear--as one *would* on her own private beach--Tera sprinted down to the water, naked as the day she was born. She plunged into the surf, giggling from the shock of cool water against her skin and the outrageousness of her daylight streak.

She laughed even harder, hoping the beach would stay deserted long enough for her to go back for her clothes! Swimming nude was a new and...liberating experience. She was an excellent swimmer, but the only time she'd ever been naked in the water was during a bath or shower.

She floated and dived, relishing the feel of the waves pounding against her bare flesh. *Uh-oh... wouldn't you just know it?* She could see someone in the distance approaching at a pace too fast to allow her to get out of the water and back to the hut before being seen in her birthday suit. *Damn!* Tera hoped they'd just keep on walking past. She continued to tread water; maybe the passerby wouldn't look too closely. She could see that it was a man. *Damn!* He was sure to notice a lone woman swimming. Maybe her short hair would fool him. She stayed neck-deep in the water, her eyes glued to the man. She dived under for a few moments, thinking he might not even notice her. When she couldn't hold her breath any longer Tera surfaced and saw that the man had taken a seat on the sand, watching her and smiling. *Surely*, she thought, *the gods must be laughing.* It was River. His smiling face had her seething with anger, but she was still somewhat relieved that it wasn't a stranger watching her swim naked.

"What do you want, River?," she shouted, "Why are you following me?"

"I've been looking for you all day," he yelled back. "I found out at the front desk that you went to Negril, so I drove down; I came to apologize."

"What?," she hollered.

The distance between them and the ocean's roar made it almost impossible to hear him.

"I said I'm *sorry*, Tera."

"Sorry's not good enough, River!"

"What? Tera, I can't hear you! Why don't you come out so we can talk?"
"No! I think enough was said last time we talked!"
"Huh? Tera, this is ridiculous. You wanted to talk seriously before, and I put some other stuff in the game...and I'm *sorry*. Please come on out and sit down with me, let's talk."
"What?"
"I said come on out! I can't hear you, you can't hear me--"
"No, River, just leave me alone! Go back to your lady, why don't you? I'll be fine, don't worry about me. We can talk another time."
"Tera, I'm not going anywhere until you come out and talk to me. I have a lot to say to you...*we* have a lot to say to each other, things that needed saying a long time ago."
"No, I said! Look...I'm just having a nice swim here, trying to relax...go away! You already said enough."
"Why won't you come out, Tee?"
Tera's paddling act was getting old. She was tired of treading water but if she back floated, River would see that she was naked. If she came in closer to shore, he would see that she was naked. *The salt sea was like glass; his smug ass could probably already see that she was naked!* So, he wanted to get an eyeful, did he? She decided to show him exactly what he *wasn't* going to get.
"Don't ignore me, Tera--stop being foolish! Come out of the water! Please?"
"Okay," she whispered.
She swam closer until her feet touched sand and began wading in. Her shapely body glistened like diamonds as she emerged slowly from the waves. River sat glued to his spot on the beach, mouth and eyes wide open.
Bingo! Score two for me.

"You wanted to talk?," she asked innocently. River finally found his tongue.
"Where are your clothes, Tera?"
"I thought you said you came all this way because you had something to say to me; say it."
"Tera, <u>where</u> are your clothes?"
The annoyance in River's voice was controlled but unmistakable; he looked up and down the beach to see if anyone else was nearby. *Good*, she thought. Tera hoped Miss Wonderful *would* suddenly appear. She assumed that was why River looked around so frantically, and relished the idea of giving him a lot of explaining to do.
"What's wrong, Riv, isn't this what you wanted to see?," she teased, running her hands lightly up down the length of her body. "Scared Lover Girl might see, hmm?"
River jumped up, his face clouded with anger.
"Tera...get-your-damn-clothes-on-*right*---<u>now</u>! I mean it!"
The look in his eyes said game time was over.
"They're in that hut...over there," she whispered meekly.
"What? Aw, man...well go on! Now!"
She walked quickly over to the hut with River close on her heels, still furtively scanning the beach. He stood outside while she dressed, his brows knit into one angry line across his forehead.

Tera was ashamed. They'd both done some inexplicably stupid things lately, stupid enough to have killed their friendship a dozen times. Indeed, Tera had thought it was already dead and buried; but he'd tried to make amends...and she'd shut him down.

Tera tried to rationalize by telling herself that this was his fault; that he shouldn't have come looking for her in the first place, knowing that he'd already hurt her. But he'd tried to meet her halfway, and in her heart Tera believed her latest stunt had likely driven the final coffin nail into an already failing relationship. She was grateful that River's girlfriend *hadn't* been there to see anything!

When she came out of the hut she was too embarrassed to even meet River's gaze. She could feel his eyes on her and finally looked up at him. Even though a frown pinched his beautiful face, his eyes still held the same adoring look. Tera was confused. Right at that moment, she longed for the familiarity of classrooms, and lectures, and research discussions. She felt that she no longer knew the man standing before her...that she never had. She began to cry. River gently placed his hands on her shoulders. His touch made her cry even harder, but when he tried to hold her close she pushed him away.

"River...what are we doing?"

"I don't know, Tee."

"What happened to us?," she sniffled. "We used to be friends; *strange* friends, maybe, but we were tight, River...we were cool with each other! What's happening?"

"I can't explain, Tera...all I know is that I was wrong to try and make you admit to something you're obviously not ready to deal with. And I'm truly sorry for that."

"I don't get it...I don't get *you*! I don't understand *why*--if I was in love with you--*why* you would want that, why you would want me to care about you in that way... knowing that you have somebody else already. That's out of pocket, River, and you know it!"

"If it helps any, I *really* feel like a fool, Tee. I didn't intend for things to get out of hand like this, but believe me, my intentions are good. I...have my reasons for not saying too much...but you gotta trust that I'm not trying to hurt you."

"Oh, *well*! 'You-have-your-reasons'! Of course, how stupid of me...I guess *that's* supposed to make everything alright."
"I know it doesn't, Tee. I messed up...I see that. That's why I'm backing off."
"Fine!! You play all kinds of head games with me, and *now* you want to 'back off'! I suppose that means I won't be hearing anything about why you're here in the first place, and we won't be getting to the bottom of *how in hell* we got into this crazy vibe, and--"
"Tera..."
"Don't you *dare* use that calm tone of voice with me, like *I'm* the only one who's been tripping!"
She stopped talking for a minute, trying to give herself time to cool down.
"Okay, you're right, Tera...can we have a truce, please?" River ran a hand through his hair, pausing to collect his thoughts. "Tera, there's a million things I could say right now, but none of it would untangle this mess. The one thing I *can* say...that I hope you'll believe is that I'm sorry."
They stood there on the beach, looking around at everything except each other. Tera felt helpless. She could feel the sincerity of River's apology, but couldn't just forget everything that had been said and done before. But there was really nothing else to do, except drop it...maybe give things time to cool off. Tera could feel River's eyes on her as she walked back into the hut to retrieve her seashells.
"Walk me back, River. It's almost time for the van to go back to *Lavish*."

###

Their walk back along the beach road might have been enjoyable and serene, had it not been for the tension of unanswered questions built up between them. Dozens of them crowded Tera's thoughts. *Why*

had River ever kissed her that night at her place? Why had he come to Jamaica--with some woman, no less? If this woman was the one he wanted to be with, the one he claimed to love...then why was he pursuing her, why did he kiss her again? What kind of games was he playing, what was he trying to prove? Tera bit her lip; *why does it hurt so much?*
"Tera?"
"Yeah?"
"Um...I know you probably don't want to hear what I've got to say, but...we can't just leave things like this."
Everything was still very raw, as far as Tera was concerned...but at least he seemed ready to talk about the situation rather than evade it; at least, she hoped so.
"I'm listening," she said.
"Tera, right from the start, you've misunderstood my intentions."
Tera could feel tears welling in her eyes again; she couldn't *believe* that, once he'd finally decided to 'open up' and talk about things, he'd *still* be trying to evade the truth by convincing her that *she'd* 'misunderstood' him! It was too much.
"Really? Well, what *exactly* did I misunderstand, River? Is this about me *'misunderstanding'* that you love somebody else--but you were trying to lay *me* down?"
"Tera, wait--"
"Or is this about me *'misunderstanding'* that she's here...but every time I turn around, you're in *my* space?"
"See, you still aren't giving me a chance--"
"Oh, that's right, that's right--this is about me misunderstanding why you're even *here*! Why *are* you here, River?"
Tera had expected a different kind of response from River than the one she got.
"Look at what's *obvious* for once, Tera," he answered

calmly. "Everything you just asked me, you already know, without me saying *anything*...the answers you're looking for just aren't that deep."
Even though Tera believed it when River had said he wasn't trying to hurt her, that's exactly what was happening. When she did as he suggested--'*look at the obvious*'--she could come to only one conclusion, and felt totally ashamed that she'd not been perceptive enough to figure it out before. There was no big mystery to why River had kissed her, or pursued her...or even why he'd come to Jamaica. *He was attracted to Tera, just as she was to him.* But attraction was *not* love; and he was in love with this other woman...that's why he'd brought her with him to Jamaica. He'd probably already had plans to go, but never mentioned it beforehand. Tera could see how River might be hesitant to say anything, especially after she'd told him that she planned to vacation there. It was hard for her to be angry with him for being caught between his feelings for his woman and for her...after all, hadn't *she* had conflicting emotions about him and Cameron?

She couldn't honestly say she knew what River was thinking, because each time anger had heated up between them, she'd never let him explain anything. She'd thought he was just being evasive, and indeed he was...but who *wouldn't* be, when faced with the task of telling a friend--a good one--that they don't share that friend's romantic feelings? And that was another bust--she wasn't even in love with River! But how could she convince him, though? It galled Tera that he *believed* she was...and fancied himself *too much of a gentleman* to keep throwing it in her face that he was interested in someone else.

Tera's analysis of the situation *almost* made sense and she was even prepared to shoulder the blame for what had gone wrong between her and River...but there were just *too* many things she couldn't dismiss. The incident that very morning on the beach, for one; she remembered how he'd taunted her, stirring her emotions to fever pitch and then saying "*when you want to get well, Tera, come to me for the cure.*" Were *these* the words of a man trying to explain that there could be nothing but friendship between the two of them because of his commitment to someone else? *Hell no!* Those were the words of a man who wanted her to understand, in no uncertain terms, that he was game for some loving on the 'down low' if she was...no strings attached.

Tera's head was spinning; *how naive and gullible had she been to not see how 'obvious' that was??!*

"Say something, Tera...why do you always have to over study *everything*? I'm sure by now you can see what's going on with me, can't you?"

Sadly, she could. Much as Tera *hadn't* wanted to think that River was just like some other hormone-driven hound dogs she'd known in the past, the conclusion she'd reached was simple and straightforward: he wanted to have sex with her, whether they were supposed to be friends or not. He was the one who had insisted that she look at the surface of things--the obvious--instead of digging deeper, and once she had, nothing felt the same anymore.

She looked up at him, wondering what was going on behind those dark eyes. He didn't *look* any different. He didn't *look* like he was suggesting they creep in private while maintaining a 'buddy-buddy' facade in public...but he was. *Obviously.* Well...it just wasn't gonna work with her. Tera still couldn't believe she'd somehow given him the impression she would go for an arrangement like that. She couldn't despise him, though, even after realizing his intent. He was being a world-class jackass, but she wasn't yet willing to throw away their years of friendship; she would make him see how crazy this whole situation was. If the years they'd known each other meant anything to him, he'd have to forget trying to walk the line between friend and lover with her! *He'd be the same old River...or get out of her life forever.*

"Well, Tera? Tell me what you think."

"I think I *do* understand what's happening here, River."

His eyes widened expectantly. "You...you do?"

"Yeah; I can hardly believe it, but...yeah."

"Oh, Tee," he said, scooping her up into his arms and sending her seashells clattering onto the gravel, "I've been waiting for this, hoping you'd finally open your eyes."

"Let me go, River!," she said, struggling to get away from him.

They were just a short distance from the *Lavish* van, and some of the other passengers smiled at them in amusement.

"Tera...what's wrong now? I thought...well, you already *know* how I feel; I guess I thought you'd be happy."

"*Happy*?," she snapped. She had meant to keep a cool head. She'd *meant* to let him know she still cared about him and wanted his friendship, but was not going to be 'monkey-in-the-middle' between him and his lady. She had meant to be rational and reasonable and tell him there were no hard feelings, just a big-time misunderstanding... but the resolve to say all that flew right out the window.

"Did you say *happy*? About *what*?! I finally understand what I'd already guessed before--*that you want to screw me on the sidelines*--and I'm supposed to be 'happy' about that shit?"

"Tera--"
"Oh, hell no! No, I'm not happy worth a damn! How could you think I would even consider—"
"Tera, you still don't understand! I--"
"You're right about that, River--I don't! And you know what? *I don't want to understand!* Ooh, I could just *strangle* you for this, you know that?"
Hot tears boiled over and rolled down her cheeks, which made her even angrier. *How did he manage to upset her so easily lately? Why was she crying? This was crazy; why didn't she just tell him to go to hell?*
"Go to hell, River...I know I'm not going to stay as mad as I am right now, but until I feel like I can talk to you, you stay the hell away from me, do you hear?"
"Tera, don't--"
"I mean it!," she hissed. "Just leave me alone."
She turned and ran over to the van, not daring to turn around. The other passengers had already gotten in the van, and pretended not to notice Tera's tear-swollen eyes as she got in and sat alone next to a window. As the van began moving, Tera finally glanced in River's direction. He was gone.

CHAPTER FIVE

For a couple of days after their argument on the beach Tera's nerves remained on edge, expecting yet another face-off with River. Surprisingly, though, he had kept his distance just as she'd asked. She had seen him a couple of times, once on the beach and once coming out of a jewelry shop in the hotel complex. Both times she'd watched him anxiously, hoping he wouldn't even approach her; both times, her heart sank with disappointment when he did not. It soon became clear that he intended to leave her alone, and Tera half-heartedly accepted that *this* is what she had asked for. She focused on trying to enjoy what was left of her vacation.

As the days flew by, she felt less and less like cramming every hour with excitement. That wasn't a hard thing to admit to herself; that was probably true of most other visitors who'd come to Jamaica with big plans and a non-stop itinerary. Tera had gone with another tour group, this time to Ocho Rios, but she'd spent most of the remaining days of her vacation taking long walks on the shore, or swimming, or relaxing up on her deck, deep in thought. And during these periods of contemplation, Tera had made peace with herself about a few things.

First of all, she'd come to a decision she'd tried to avoid for months. Much as the idea of seeing a therapist repulsed and frightened her, Tera realized it was probably the only way to finally get to the bottom of her mysterious dream and why it continued to hang on. Her self-diagnosis that she'd only needed a break from the stressful demands of her job had been wrong;

the dream had not only persisted, it had intensified--even spilled over into her waking consciousness.

She had finally convinced herself that she must see a psychologist in order to root out the dream, hopefully banish it forever. She had told herself that if the dream ever got to be more than just a semi-harmless distraction, she would forget about her aversion for shrinks and find one *asap*. Tera shuddered, remembering the latest dream and how serious it had become. Something new and terrifying had happened...Tera had seen her own death.

Mason and Hannah had continued on through the pitch-black forest, having left the canoe hidden by the shore. There was nowhere for them to go but onward; they could not turn back, and prayed they would soon reach the clearing Tall Bear had described. At the clearing, Tall Bear's men would meet them with horses and escort them to the foothills where Tall Bear himself would lead them away, deeper into the land...where the others would not dare follow, where they would be free! They had moved on silently but swiftly, carrying their packs.

Suddenly, Mason stopped, straining to listen; he placed a finger to Hannah's lips. Her heart beat wildly as she waited alongside Mason, not knowing why they'd stopped. Had he heard something, maybe someone following them? A barely audible rustling in the grass made Hannah freeze, afraid to even breathe too loudly. Someone was near! Mason gripped her hand reassuringly. He gave the signal he'd used to let Hannah know when he was near, the call he'd learned from his Choctaw allies.

"Crk, crk-kee...crk, crk-kee."

Moments later, his call was answered from a few yards away. Mason called again, this time adding his own signature warble to identify himself; the answering call let him know that it was Tall Bear's men in their midst, and not the patrollers.

Waiting on their cautious approach wore on Hannah's nerves. She was almost overcome with fear, and fought an overwhelming urge to run. She could feel the subtle motion of bodies all around her, and just as she thought she might cry out, a hand clamped over her mouth and a muffled voice in her ear whispered "come." She and Mason followed the warriors the rest of the way to a clearing, and her heart leapt with excitement at the sound of horses tethered nearby. When Mason lifted her onto one of the gentle beasts, she began to believe that freedom would actually be theirs; that they would finish this last leg of their journey and meet Tall Bear at the foothills.

They rode on through the night, putting as much distance between themselves and the patrollers as possible. The first faint glow of sunrise found them crossing a plain, and to Hannah's great joy, she could see the foothills in the distance. Mason and the others rode just ahead of her, keeping their horses at a steady pace. The gradual brightening of the sky illuminated the hills and distant treetops, and Hannah could barely contain her anxiety. They had gotten away; they had crossed a treacherous, swiftly-flowing river, then rode on horseback all night; at last, she and the man she loved were within reaching distance of freedom, and all should have been right with the world...but Hannah couldn't shake the feeling that something terrible would happen. She watched Mason's back, loving the confident way he sat his horse...and hoping some of that confidence would rub off on her, too. Suddenly, the morning calm was shattered by the sound of gunfire. Hannah's horse reared in fright, throwing her to the ground before breaking into a dead run; dazed, Hannah turned to see where the shots had come from. The worst had happened...the hated patrollers had picked up their trail!

Mason whirled around, reaching for Hannah to pull her up behind him on his horse. Just as their hands touched, another shot rang out. Hannah felt herself thrown forward by a powerful blow as an indescribable pain tore through her; then everything became a blur. She heard Mason shout "Oh, God, no!", saw Black Sky return the patrollers' gunfire to give Mason cover as he tried to lift her onto his horse. Hannah wrapped her arms around Mason, aware that her blood soaked the back of his jacket where she held him; she could feel herself slipping away, but struggled to hang on. Mason's horse lurched forward, racing for the foothills.

The horse bolted, and Hannah moaned as a sharp pain ripped through her; she was too weak to even cry out, and Mason feared the worst. Through a fog, it seemed, Hannah heard gunshots coming from ahead of them, instead of behind; as they got closer to the hills, she could see them...the one Mason called Tall Bear and his men, pouring from the wooded foothills like a swarm of angry bees. By the time the patrollers saw the men, it was too late; their fate was sealed as Tall Bear picked them from their horses one by one. Not one escaped with his life. By the time Mason reached the safety of the trees with Hannah, all their pursuers had been killed...but there was nothing he could do to save Hannah. Black Sky helped Mason lift Hannah from the horse and lay her gently on the grass. As Black Sky walked away, Hannah thought to herself, 'he knows I'm going to die'... For the last time, Hannah looked up into the eyes of her beloved; for the last time, she felt his salt tears warm her own cheeks as he cradled her head. And as she breathed her last, telling him how much she loved him...Hannah heard Mason promise that someday they would be together again...that he would love her forever.

And then...there was peace. She felt herself rise up from the ground, up above the tops of the pines, up...until there was.....nothing.

That dream had left Tera shaken, and convinced she could no longer ignore the fact that she needed help. Even if she wasn't ready to accept that she *needed* therapy, she couldn't deny that she wasn't at her best; and she needed to be at her best when the school semester resumed in September. If therapy offered even a *small* chance that she could get back to her old self, well...it was a chance she was willing to take.

Another thing Tera had realized while on vacation was how much "home" really meant to her. Sure, it was fun going abroad and seeing how other folks lived; but the biggest eye-opener had been to realize that the people who lived there led everyday, routine, *normal* lives--just as she did. Only the *tourists*--herself included--chased the ideal of endless excitement. She had gone to Jamaica with the intent of exploring the island from shore to shore, skiing, wandering, shopping, and hitting every dance hall from Negril to Morant Bay...and had found instead that the simple pleasures--the same things she enjoyed doing back home--were the things she'd enjoyed most.

Finally, and with as much reluctance as she'd acknowledged her need to see a therapist, Tera admitted the hardest truth of all: she *was* in love with River. After their last disagreement, she'd believed it would take only a short while to cool off her fury and get her emotions under control. She thought that staying away from River would help speed up the process. While physical distance had taken the edge off her irrational anger, nothing seemed to ease the strange pangs she felt whenever she thought of him. Tera didn't understand *how* it could have happened, but ever since the day she'd seen him coming from that jewelry shop her heart had burned with curiosity and yes, *jealousy*, wondering if he'd been shopping for a gift for his lady love. And she finally had to sit down and ask herself why it mattered to her.

Tera couldn't avoid examining her deepest feelings for River...and wondered if it was *really* love, since she had nothing to compare it with. She knew he was by far the sexiest, most handsome man she'd ever gotten to know, and her heart did *crazy* things whenever he was close to her; but that wasn't love--it was just powerful physical attraction. Even though she thought him a *strange* man, she marveled at the way his mind worked, and how easily he tuned in to her thoughts and feelings... but that wasn't love, either--they just had an undeniable connection, a "meeting of minds". Tera fought against a lump in her throat each time she thought of the mysterious woman River had managed to keep under wraps the entire time he'd been there. *What was she like? Was she beautiful? Were they happy together?* Tera reminded herself that this feeling wasn't love either; it was plain old jealousy. Being attracted to him, physically and mentally, and feeling heartsick about River's attraction to someone else did not convince Tera that what she felt was love; there was something more. When she could accept that *she* was not the one for River, yet wished him and his lady only the best...she knew. When she saw that she couldn't stop thinking of him any more than she could stop breathing...she knew. When she realized that she wanted *his happiness* even more than she wanted *him*...she knew that she *loved* River Jordan Bennett.

Having made that realization, Tera wondered what was next. *Should she tell him?* He had recognized it long before she had, even urged her to come clean about it; *but if she did, how would that change their relationship? Would it create an awkwardness between them that might eventually end their friendship?*

If Tera couldn't have him as her lover, she still wanted him as her friend, and realized that it wouldn't be fair to lie and cover up her feelings. But it wouldn't be right to push her feelings off on him, either. After more thought and deliberation she decided that yes, she *should* tell him how she felt--letting him know that these were *her* feelings, and there was nothing she expected from him *except* to continue being her friend. If they both knew where they stood, it shouldn't be a problem... should it? She vowed to never let her feelings cause problems for River and his lady, but realized she could only speak for herself; whether or not River could accept things and resume their friendship--*the way it used to be*--was up to him.

Her mind was at peace, though; she'd faced some difficult issues and called on strengths she didn't even know she possessed in order to deal with them. Tera went up onto her deck to watch the Jamaican sunset for the last time. The next evening would find her on the return flight to O'Hare Airport; it would be *good* to be back home.

Watching the huge orange ball gradually fade in brilliance as it sank below the horizon, River crossed Tera's mind for the hundredth time and she wondered what he was doing at that moment. *Did he watch the same sunset from his suite balcony? Did she enjoy it with him...or had they left the island already?*

"Stop it, girl," she whispered to herself. If she was going to be honest about not letting her feelings cause problems for River...she had to start with not letting them continue to cause problems for *her*. There was nothing she could do about the dull ache in her heart--time would have to take care of that--but she didn't have to torment herself, wondering what might have been under different circumstances. And she didn't have to plan on a special time to tell River all she'd been thinking. Sooner or later their paths would cross, and that would be the right time.

Tera sat quietly in the gathering darkness as orange became maroon...then purple...and then, deepest indigo; and she indulged in a fantasy of her and River lying there together, enveloped in each other and the magical night.

It didn't matter to Tera that her fantasy was something that could never be. The next day would be soon enough to deal with the realities of her situation. And she laughed to herself at the irony that, in both her dreaming and waking worlds, *the man she wanted was somehow always just beyond her reach.*

###

Early next morning Tera strolled along the beach, reflecting on Murphy's Law and its uncanny ability to kick in when least expected. She thought about running into River on her first night in Jamaica at the nightclub; about going skinny-dipping for the *first* time in her life, only to be seen by--guess who?--River. Definitely two incidences of Murphy's Law--that whole idea that "*whatever can go wrong usually does go wrong*". And the stupid 'law' was still in effect. Almost the entire time she'd been in Jamaica, she'd anticipated being bombarded with attention from single, attractive men also vacationing on the island...and it hadn't really happened. Now that she was about to *leave*, it seemed that men were crawling out of the woodwork wanting to take her out, or call her, or buy dinner; there were messages for her at the front desk when she'd gone there to mail off some postcards. *It figured, with less than twenty-four hours left before her flight home.* And it wasn't just a simple case of Murphy's Law--Tera was sure that River had something to do with it. A number of people had witnessed their confrontation at the nightclub. In fact, the bartender she'd gone water skiing with had thought River was her boyfriend. If any of Tera's travel mates had been paying attention when she'd stormed away from River in Negril, certainly they'd have gotten that same impression. And naturally, if people thought he was her man, Tera could see why the brothers had kept their distance.

A wry smile touched her lips; it was ironic, but she had long since adjusted her expectations of fun, fun, and more fun on this vacation. She continued on down the beach, appreciating the peace she'd found, and ready to return to the familiarity and security of home.

The day was slightly overcast but very warm and humid. Almost no breeze could be felt, and Tera was glad she'd remembered her bathing suit this time. She reached a lonely stretch of beach that wasn't fenced off like most of the private beach close to the *Lavish* complex; the waters were more choppy, and larger waves pounded the shore, but it was secluded and serene. Gulls soared above, silhouetted against the blue-gray sky and sand crabs darted in and out of tiny holes near the shore. A coconut palm jutted out from the sand, arching almost to the ground, and Tera plopped down under its long, sheltering fronds. If the sun came out strongly, her spot would provide ample shade.

She sat for a long while, just looking out to sea. Further up the beach she saw a pair of lovers walking and holding hands; from time to time they'd stop and kiss, holding onto each other as though no one else in the world existed. Seeing their forms entwined against the slate sky, hearing the roar of the surf, Tera was filled with longing for what those lovers shared. Love was missing in her life, and she fought against the feeling that River should be the one to fill the emptiness. He was not, nor would he ever be hers. Still, she remained optimistic that one day, she would find the kind of love that people dreamed of, and wrote of, and sang of; the kind of love that could free her from this spell poor River had no idea he'd cast.

She stripped down to her suit and waded out into the warm water. She paddled around for a while, enjoying her swim but keeping conscious of the time. She still had a few things left to pack before leaving for the airport later that evening. Before long the sun came out and the crystal blue waters shimmered like liquid sapphires. Tera floated on her back, feeling the sun's warmth caress her face and arms. It was heavenly...she couldn't think of a nicer way to spend her remaining hours in this tropical paradise. Reluctantly, she swam in to shore. She walked in slowly, her body feeling heavy as she left the buoyancy of the salt water. She looked up and caught her breath. Her heart plunged to her feet as she realized Murphy's Law had caught her yet again; River sat on the sand beneath the arching palm.

She paused for a minute, blood pounding in her temples. Seeing him was shocking, not only because of his powerful impact on her emotions, but also because she'd convinced herself that he was probably already gone back home to Chicago. She'd envisioned her day of reckoning with him *in the future*, not right that moment...but there it was. Tera froze and stared at him like a deer caught in a car's headlights. Her mind reached frantically for something to say or do. *Wave at him, you idiot! Smile.*

"Don't trip, Tera," she whispered to herself, "just act natural."

Her nerves were going haywire, and she hoped her slow approach would give her time to get herself together, as well as give the impression she wasn't fazed at seeing him--although she most certainly was. Her mind squirmed with runaway emotions. *Why was he there? Oh, Lord he looked good in those trunks! How did he find her, had he been looking? Lord, please don't let him touch me! Where was his woman, and why did she always seem to be absent at the damnedest times??! Please, Lord--help me to keep my hands to myself.*

Tera was aware of him watching her every move, and the way his eyes traveled up and down her body weakened her like she'd suffered heat stroke. They finally made eye contact, and for the longest moment on record they just stared at each other in silence. River spoke.

"Hello, Tera."

"Hi, River." She continued to stand over him until he patted the sand next to him, beckoning her to sit down. She hesitated.

"Please sit down, Tee. Let's talk."

"What do you want?"

"I just want us to talk; can we do that?"

Tera sat down; she'd hoped River might think her trembling was caused by a slight chill in the air but it was even warmer than before, now that the sun was out. Whether she was ready or not, it seemed the time had come for her to come clean about her feelings and just hope for the best.

"Tera...*aw, man* I'm so sorry for all that's happened."

"Me too, Riv." Tera swallowed hard. "River...I've got something to say to you--"

"Same here," he responded, taking a deep breath. "This is so hard...you know, at first I thought I could just keep my peace and let things happen however they're supposed to happen, but... I can't. I have to say what's on my mind."

Tera's heart sank. Fear tasted sharp on her tongue as she prepared herself to hear him say *he couldn't deal with the drama; that the swirl of emotions had been too much, ever since he'd first told her he was romantically interested in someone else.* She waited for him to say that... their friendship couldn't bear up under the strain and...perhaps they shouldn't...see each other any more. Just thinking that these would be River's words was like a knife in Tera's heart. She would still tell him what she had to say...right or wrong, he would know she'd been honest with him.

"River...remember when you told me I was in love with you, and that was the problem between us?"

"Yeah, and I was wrong for saying it. I shouldn't have—"

"But you weren't wrong," Tera said softly.

River turned slowly to face her, an incredulous look in his eyes. It was as though he was seeing her for the first time. Tera thought her heart might shatter into a thousand pieces; River was speechless, and Tera was so afraid that her admission had just cost her a friend. Had she just ruined any chance for their relationship to heal?

"River," she continued, "you saw something I couldn't, and I was angry with you for saying it. I couldn't see that...I was in love with you, I didn't *want* to see it...that's why things went so crazy."

River's eyes softened, and Tera wanted to cry; *she didn't want his pity!* Having already said so much, she was forced to continue and get it all out.

"Look, I'm not saying this for you to do anything about it--I knew from jump that you cared for someone else, it's not like you didn't tell me. I just wanted you to know I'll always be your friend if you want me to; my feelings are just that--*mine*. And I'll never put them off on you."

He just stared at her, and she couldn't bear to look him in the eye. She'd misinterpreted his intentions before,

and couldn't stand to sit there feeling such love beaming out from his black eyes, when she knew it was probably only embarrassment at her outpouring of words. *There's no kind way to tell me he doesn't want me*, Tera thought; *but if he doesn't say anything,...oh!* If she lived another hundred years, she could *never* feel as ashamed and rejected as she did at that moment.
"River, please say *something*. I mean it when I say that I won't let my feelings cause problems for you and your lady; and I'm sorry if they already have."
River's mysterious woman was nowhere around, and Tera got a terrible, sinking feeling at the thought that *she* might have been responsible for the woman's absence. River moved closer to her under the tree and gently placed his hand on her shoulder; Tera shivered and his arms drew her closer as if to protect her from a sudden chill. *It was unbearable!* Tera knew that if they could just get over this hump, past this terrible awkwardness...they would be alright. She'd *never* allow herself to be this vulnerable with him ever again.
"Tera...you don't know how long I've waited to hear you say those words."
"I...I didn't mean to mess things up between us, Riv. You said I needed to admit it to myself, and now I have...and...you don't have to worry that it'll keep on being a problem. I promise."
River just shook his head, laughing softly to himself. "Tee...woman, you *still* don't get it, do you?," he asked.
She didn't.
"All this time, I've been wanting you to say you love me, Tera...so I could tell you how much I love *you*. How *long* I've loved you, girl."
"What??!"
Tera heard, but didn't believe. Her body stiffened. A part of her wanted it to be true, but...*it couldn't be*. River could see how she was suffering; why was he

doing this? What was he trying to prove?
"It's true, Tera," he said, turning her around to face him. *I love you, woman. I always have.*"
"No, River! No! You don't expect me to...to believe that, not after all that's happened! Not after... after...*coming here with your woman!* Why are you doing this?," she cried. She snatched away from him as though his touch burned.
"Remember when I told you to open your eyes--to see what was obvious, Tera? Look around!," he sputtered. "Do you *see* a woman? Have you seen me with a woman since you've been here?"
"Well no, but--"
"I kept trying to tell you that you'd misunderstood me from the start!"
"Fine, fine--maybe I did, but...what about that night at the club, when I said that stupid stuff about you wanting to finish what we'd started without your woman around, and you said 'no it'll never happen because she's here'--why did you tell me somebody else was here with you?"
"I didn't exactly say that anybody was here with *me*--"
"You're doing it again, River!! You know damn well you said--and I quote--you *love* her, and she's *here*."
"Yeah, I did say that the woman I love is here; and you are, Tera Marchelle Morton."
"But...River, this is *not* making any sense. I mean...okay, okay--that day we hung out? And went jogging, and you talked about all that 'Mr. and Ms. Right' stuff?"
"Mm-hmm, and I told you that your reasoning powers were failing you something fierce?"
"Right. Hmmm...I don't know about all that '*failing me something fierce*', but...oh, you know what I mean! You said then that you'd met your Ms. Right, that you could recognize the right woman for you in a heartbeat,

remember?"
"Yep, I remember; and I *had* met my Ms. Right, Tera--
you. And I've known you were the one ever since that first day you walked through the door of Dr. Mullins' office more than three years ago."
The sincerity in River's voice and on his face melted Tera's heart, but she still couldn't dare to believe he spoke the truth.
"Riv, this is me you're talking to. *This is Tee*! We've been partners since day one, a few years now, and I think I would've known *something* if you had really felt that way, for that long! You know I was attracted to you right from the start, I'll be first to admit that. And for a minute, I thought things might jump off between us...but they *didn't*. I just thought, 'hey, me and this man just aren't meant to go there'. End of story. And I *accepted* that. If you really felt that way, *why* didn't you say so?"
"It's like I told you when we talked about this before: *it does no good if I know you're the one for me, but you don't know I'm for you*. What good would that be?"
"I just swallowed every bit of pride I had left telling you how I feel, River. I *do* love you. I know that now. But I still don't understand why you never said a word."
"Probably for the same reason *you* never said anything to *me*--afraid of losing our friendship. I couldn't risk that, Tee. I'm sorry about lying, but...I couldn't think of any other way to deal with it at the time. Besides, I didn't *lie*, exactly..."
"No, you just abused the hell out of the truth," Tera smiled.
"Maybe just a little bit. But don't leave yourself out of the mix, woman."
What?! Me? I didn't lie about anything."

"No, but just like I didn't *say* anything, you didn't *see* anything. Some things about me were so obvious, Tee, I still can't believe you didn't pick up on 'em. I mean, didn't you think it *strange* that I just happened to show up in Jamaica at the same time as you? At the same hotel?"

Tera thought for a moment. "Of course, I did. As a matter of fact, I wanted to ask about that the first time I saw you."

"And didn't you wonder, *at all*, why you never saw my 'woman'?"

The puzzle pieces began to fit together slowly, one by one, and Tera felt like a complete fool; *why had none of that occurred to her before?* River pushed her back onto the sand, looking down into her upturned face.

"That day you came out of the water totally naked; didn't you wonder why I was so upset with you?," River asked.

"Oops! Yeah...I just...thought you were afraid your lady friend might have seen us and got the wrong impression. God, it's hard to believe that I actually did something *that* shitty."

"There *is* no lady friend, Tera. My being mad had nothing to do with another woman! I had wanted to tell you what I'm telling you now, and...when I saw you like that...I wanted you so bad, Tee...I couldn't even think straight. That messed me up *big time*," he smiled.

He kissed her forehead lightly, caressing her short, soft hair.

"And I was pissed, just *thinking* that somebody else might see you like that." River's eyes grew serious.

"You hurt me, Tera, that day you accused me of wanting to--and I *quote*--'screw' both you and my woman."

Tera felt even more foolish.

"I'm sorry, River. I was just...hurt, and confused too, 'cause I didn't understand why you kept coming at me like that, if you already had somebody."
"That's my fault for letting you think I had someone else. But you're still not off the hook for thinking I'd 'screw' you."
"Well, what about you? Saying that if you made me '*sick*' I should come to you for '*the cure*'? What's up with that?"
"I *meant* that, Tera. But that's got nothing to do with screwing. No, baby. When the time is right, I'm going to make *love* to you."
River moved closer, positioning himself next to Tera. He covered her mouth with his, stroking her lightly and kissing her until she gasped and squirmed against his hard body.
It was all so crazy, just like the first time when River had kissed her; and like that first time, Tera instantly responded with a boldness that surprised her.
"Still want to go to Heaven?," she breathed. River just smiled at her.
"Oh, yes. Definitely. And I still know the way; but let's wait until we get back home, okay?"
"Oh, River...why?" Tera was on fire. She wanted River badly... just as she had the other times. *Why was he hesitating?* He pulled away gently, cupping her face in his hands.
"Heaven is waiting for us, Tee," he said softly, "but we don't have a lot of time right now. And I want everything to be *just right*. You don't know it, but for more than three years I've wanted you, and now...there's no way I'm going to rush."
This time when he kissed her, it was soft, and sweet, and electrifying...and Tera couldn't stop shaking. His voice was a subtle, sweet whisper in her ear.
"*When we make love, Tera, you're going to remember*

it...you're going to know everything you've forgotten...baby, you're gonna remember me."

###

River rescheduled his return flight, and was able to ride back with Tera. Fortunately, the passenger next to Tera was willing to trade seats with River and he and Tera sat together, her head snuggled against his chest. The gentle pressure of her body at his side and the feel of her warm, even breathing on his neck made River's heart turn over with love; *after all that time, they began moving in the right direction. His patience had at last been rewarded.*

He shifted so that she could slip more easily into the crook of his arm, and tenderly stroked her close-cropped hair. *They'd come so far in such a short time!* He had loved her for so long, loved her forever...and now he knew that she loved him, too. It had taken all his energy, and concentration, and patience, and most of all, *love* to help get them to this point. The time had seemed as nothing; he would have waited even longer for this moment. He reminded himself that they still had a long way to go. *There was still so much Tera didn't understand, still so much she had to remember... and when she did, then their lives could truly begin.*

###

Tera tried in vain the sleep during the flight as she lay resting her head against River. Though his broad chest and strong arms felt like her home, she was too distracted by his overwhelming sexual aura to even think of sleep. Like the night they'd almost spent together, Tera couldn't believe this magical thing that was happening between them.

She smiled, sliding her fingers slowly upward to trace the masculine curve of his chest, the column of his neck and its pulsing artery, his chiseled jaw. She played among his thick locks; she wanted to know every inch of him--every line, or mole, or childhood scar. It was as though he'd become brand new for her and she wanted to know him in ways she never had before. River caught her hand as it crept just inside his shirt collar to fondle the fine hairs at the base of his throat.

"Baby, don't," he moaned. "What are you trying to do, kill me?"

Tera found it hard to keep her hands to herself, but reluctantly draped her arm across his taut stomach. Their closeness was so intoxicating and new...but at the same time, as familiar as though they'd been in love all their lives. It was a little unsettling, just as River's last words on the beach had been..."*you're going to know everything you've forgotten...you're gonna remember me...*"; what did he mean?

Something about what he'd said struck her, and Tera tried to put her finger on what it was. The first, most *obvious* thing that had crossed her mind was 'verbal foreplay', but she quickly dismissed that thought. She knew River well enough to know that *hinting at sensual delights he had in store for her* was *not* his style; Lord knows, she didn't need any prompting to get ready for him. No, his words definitely meant something, and at the furthest edge of her memory... she almost knew what it was. River's fingers playfully rumpled her hair, pulling her thoughts back from that shrouded place.

"You okay, woman?"

"Mmm. I can't remember when I've been better."

"Good. You know we'll be touching down pretty soon."

"I know," she smiled.

"And soon after that, we'll be home."

"Mm-hmm. And then?"

"And then, baby girl...it's you and me. And heaven."

###

Tera and River went straight from O'Hare to River's place. Tera had thought she should check in at home first and drop off her things, but River had urged her to forget about all that and just come home with him.

"But Riv, it'll only take a few minutes."

"I know, Tee, but I want to spend even those few minutes with you."

"Oh, you sweet thing...well, why don't you come with me while I drop my stuff and grab a toothbrush and nightgown and--"

"Nightgown? I hope I'm not being too presumptuous in saying you won't be *needing* anything like that; trust me. And I always keep extra toothbrushes. Guess it's a habit I picked up from my old man. You never know when company's coming, he'd say, so always keep extra towels, blankets, and toothbrushes."

"Sounds like your daddy had it *together*; but I still want to check in. What if I have messages or faxes or anything?"

"They won't spoil, Tee. Besides, you know your Moms kept an eye on all that stuff while you were away."

"Ooh, that's right! I need to call and let her know I won't be home tonight like I'd first thought. I wouldn't want her to call and find me not there; she would worry."

"I hear you; but can't you call from my place?"

"Hmm...I guess I could at that. Okay, looks like it's on to your place."

###

It was late evening when they reached River's apartment. They struggled up the walk with luggage and boxes, which they plopped onto the sidewalk while River fished for his keys. When he swung the door open, Tera's eyes widened in surprise. She stepped inside into a fragrant lover's paradise of tropical

blossoms like the ones they'd enjoyed in Jamaica. The living and dining rooms were alive with colorful hyacinth, jasmine, roses, and bird of paradise blooms. On the kitchen counter were trays of sliced fruits, Tera's favorite chocolate-dipped strawberries, and other delicacies. The dining room table was set for two with covered dinner plates at each setting, and delicate wine goblets on the side. Tera was stunned.
"Oh, my God...River! How...<u>when</u> did you...?"
He slipped his arms around her waist from behind, nuzzling her neck. "Surprise, baby."
"Oh, River, this is so beautiful! Oh...but how?"
"With a little help from my friend and your sister, Mara."
"Huh? You mean *Mara* did all this?"
"No, honey--I couldn't let her know *everything* I was planning," he chuckled, "she let the florist and caterer in for me."
"She had the keys..."
"Mm-hmm. I told her where I keep my extra set."
"And so...Mama already knows I'm coming here?"
"Yep, Mara told her. I talked to them this afternoon before we left *Lavish*."
"Well, I'll be---Mara knows."
"Honey, she knows just about everything; how do you think I knew *exactly* where you were staying in Jamaica?"
Tera turned to him, linking her arms around his neck; she molded herself to him.
"My River...ready for any situation," she said in amazement.
"No, just ready for *you*."
He plucked one of the chocolate strawberries from the tray and steered Tera over to the couch to sit; standing over her, he held the berry by its stem and guided it to her parted lips. Tera's moist mouth closed around it

leaving nothing exposed but the stem, and she closed her eyes blissfully as she devoured it.
"Ooh...even the way you *eat* is sexy as hell," he purred, "look, you stay right here--I'll be right back."
River dashed out the front door and hurriedly collected as much of their luggage as he could and brought it inside to the hall closet as Tera watched from the sofa. When she offered to help, he insisted she stay put.
"Thanks baby, but I got this. Stay there--or better yet--look around, put on some music, okay?"
Tera kicked off her shoes and got up to investigate River's apartment. It had been quite a while since the last time she'd visited it, and was impressed by the many changes River had made. It had always been a neat, tidy place but definitely a man's apartment--furnished in a Spartan style that was more about simplicity and utility than aesthetic beauty. That is, that's how it used to be. Now, tasteful art prints hung from the walls and there were West African wood sculptures, plants, a new stereo--even a huge oak bookshelf against one wall, replacing the neatly stacked milk crates that once held River's staggering collection of books. There were already five CD's in the stereo carousel; Tera didn't bother to change them, knowing she'd enjoy them since she and River had similar musical tastes.

The sweet, haunting melody of Yanni's "One Man's Dream" filled the room when Tera touched the stereo 'play' button. It was a beautiful song, one of her favorites from the New Age musician's live performance at the Acropolis. River had turned her on to Yanni's music when they'd first met. She began examining the varied titles on River's bookshelf. There was the expected collection of communication texts and she skipped past them, not wanting to look at anything that even remotely reminded her of a classroom.

Hmm, she thought, *interesting*. A few of the volumes on the far left side of one shelf immediately caught her attention with titles like "Life After Life", "The Way Back Home: Memoirs From a Past Life", "Mysticism and Reincarnation", and "Emerging From Darkness: Patient Accounts of Past Life Experiences Gathered Under Hypnosis". Tera was fascinated. She pulled the heavy book from the shelf and thumbed through it, seeing pictures of people slumped in chairs or lying on couches, their eyes shut and jawlines slack under the effect of hypnosis. She read a caption under one of the photos: *"For many patients, hypnosis is the most reliable means of breaking through barriers which prevent total recall of past life events."*

The hairs on Tera's neck felt charged with electricity; again, she felt on the verge of remembering something very important, very traumatic--and again the memory escaped her. River crept up behind her, catching her earlobe between his lips.

"Find something interesting?," he asked.

"Yeah...Riv, I remember you saying how much you'd enjoyed talking to Cameron about this stuff, but I had no idea you got into it like this; where'd you get these books?"

"Actually, I got that one you're holding from him, and the others from the Occult & Esoteric Bookseller in downtown Chicago, near Roosevelt. And I got that one," he said, pointing to the "Life After Life" book, "from Unique Antique."

Tera remembered that shop; it was where Mara had gotten that mysterious gift, the filigreed mirror.

"Mara bought me something from there...small world."

"Mm-hmm," River murmured. "And I feel it closing in on me right now."

He took the book from Tera and laid it on a nearby table. He folded her into his arms and brushed her lips with the most tender, feathery kiss. All thoughts of the books were forgotten as River walked her to his bedroom.

"It's our time now, Tee. I need you, woman...let's make the world go away."

Tera crossed the threshold into his bedroom and into another world. The room was filled with the soft glow of a dozen candles. A bottle of fine champagne and two wine flutes rested in a chilled bucket near the bed, which was draped with a beautifully woven aqua comforter and matching sheets. Tera trembled in anticipation as River closed the door softly behind them. She watched him move carefully and deliberately, in almost dreamlike slowness; as though he didn't want a sudden move to startle her. He moved toward her with catlike grace, eyes locked to hers. Moments stretched unbearably until they stood close to each other, barely touching and still looking into each other's faces. River stepped back and began unfastening the buttons on Tera's blouse. She reached up to help him, but he gently took her hands and placed them at his neck.

"No, baby...let me, let me do it all. I've waited for this moment longer than you know."

Tera's eyelids fluttered, then closed as she gave in to the luscious sensation of River's large, gentle hands undressing her. The removal of each garment was accompanied by soft kisses, sensual caresses, and teasing fingertips probing her pliant body. She quivered, a powerful chill running the length of her spine. River had said he was going to take his time with her, but Tera didn't know how much longer she could take this tender onslaught. She opened her eyes, standing before him naked. Her clothes billowed around her ankles like the foamy, white waves of the Caribbean, and River stood transfixed, unable to take his eyes off her.

He unbuttoned his own shirt, letting it slide from his shoulders.

Tera caught her breath at the sight of his tight, athletic body, and she couldn't stop her eyes from traveling downward as River's pants slid to the floor. He stepped out of his clothes and into Tera's arms. He reached for her hands, lacing his fingers with hers; it felt as though energy pulsed from his hands into her own. Suddenly he bent and scooped her up into his arms, covering her open mouth with his. River's eyes were bright with desire in the warm glow of candlelight, and he carried Tera and laid her softly on the cool sheets. He stroked, massaged, and teased her body until she tingled with pleasure. His warm lips blazed a trail from the hollow of her neck and down across her shoulders, pausing for a moment to slide on protection before moving to her breasts.

"River...River," she moaned over and over. Her hands roved his body frantically. Her hands gripped his shoulders as she strained
against him. It was still a wonder and a delight, just thinking of how they'd come together; she wanted him more than she'd ever wanted anyone...and she ached with the need to feel their bodies merge. It was a feeling of forever, and she wanted forever to begin right then and there.

"River...oh, my baby...love me."

Tera cried out as he entered her, sending shock waves throughout her. River's body was satin-steel under Tera's eager, exploring hands as he moved and flexed, exploring her body and soul. Never in her life had Tera felt such total sensuality; she called River's name again and again as tears slid freely down her cheeks. *She was melting down under the heat of their lovemaking*, and there was nothing she could do about it; nothing she *wanted* to do, except beg him to never stop. She moaned as tension increased to its breaking point, arching to meet River at the threshold, and Tera felt herself sliding over...falling...her body rippling with ecstatic release. Their tempo increased as River reached for that same pinnacle, and he held her tight, moving more urgently until his rhythm pushed Tera toward fulfilment once more. All Tera's senses were startlingly alive; this was beyond anything she had ever felt...what she had yearned for...waited for all her life.

She lay beneath him, still molded to the contours of his powerful body, still feeling the pressure of him inside her...and felt herself bathed in warmth and light. Enveloped in the peace of afterglow, Tera felt herself slowly drifting...drifting. Neither asleep nor awake, she drifted away free, it seemed,...to another place... the hidden place...the concealed cave where Mason had just made love to his darling Hannah.

They lay together in the blackened cave, Mason and Hannah, their bodies spent from the intensity of their loving...just as Tera and River lay.

Tera moaned softly in alarm; this was not the time for the vision to insinuate itself into her thoughts. River stirred, again craving the comfort and pleasure of Tera's body, and Tera felt a wave of renewed desire coursing through her, seeking to dispel the vision. She marveled at how River's slightest touch could ignite such a fire inside her, and her body came alive once again as she strained and rocked with him...*but the fantasy of Mason and Hannah alone in the dark, humid cave slowly, subtly fused with the reality of her and River alone in the candlelit bedroom.*

Scattered thoughts and lost, fragmented memories flooded her brain, and Tera's cry was mingled with both passion and fear as she felt herself...fly away. "Tera...talk to me," River whispered huskily; "tell me how you feel...what you see." He worked relentlessly,

loving her until passion erased all her fears; it was crazy...*but it was as though they were suddenly one in mind and body, and he could see and feel everything she experienced.*
"Tell me, baby...what do you see ?," he urged.
"I...I see...us, River," she moaned, fighting to push the image from her mind.
"Let it happen, Tee...tell me...I'm with you, I'm *right here with you.*"
As their lovemaking took them higher, Tera felt her body trembling, bridging the world between her and River and Hannah and Mason; it was as though she and River were no more...*only the impassioned lovers clinging to hope and to each other in that cave existed,* caught up in desire and the rushing sound of the river filling their ears.
"I see you, River...I see...Oh, God, I see us..."
"Do you remember, baby? It's been so long, Tera...tell me you remember me, darling."
Oh, baby yes! Yes!," she whispered between clenched teeth, her body rocking in unison with his. "I remember everything...*I remember you!*"
Her words were enough to drive River over that delicious brink along with her as he realized they'd truly been reunited at last; his body clenched forcefully, claiming her as his forever.
"Mason! Oh, my baby...Mason...I love you," Tera cried. River's whisper was barely audible as he buried his face against Tera's neck.
"Hannah...my sweet, sweet girl...I told you I'd love you forever...Oh Hannah, *this* is forever...nothing can separate us ever again."

###

Tera awakened hours later, nestled in River's arms. *What happened?*, she wondered. Her mind was in a whirl, as though she'd emerged from a dream too wonderful to be true...but the candles, and the beautiful man lying next to her, and the peaceful, satiated glow of her body told her that it *had* been real. River lay propped up on one elbow, looking into her face; he had watched her as she slept, and kissed her eyelids as they opened.

Tera wanted to cry; she was so happy...happier and more alive than she'd ever felt in her life...but she was also afraid. *What had just happened to her?* A couple of past lovers had been very good...but no one had ever reached down inside, to the heart of her and touched her very soul as River had. *Is this what it means to be 'whipped'?*, she wondered. If so, then she had to confess that she was. That in itself was frightening enough, but it was more than that; she could feel River in her blood--*the salt taste of his skin, his scent, the warmth of his breath against her fingertips, the steady, even tempo of his heart beating against her own*--they had left a permanent imprint. She was his, and no one else would ever do. Each time she looked into his gorgeous, soft eyes, her heart ached with love for him.

But instead of being filled with joy, fear gripped her as she realized she was even more troubled by the dream that she'd ever imagined. It was with her night and day now, invading even her most private moments; the dream had again broken in to her waking consciousness.

Painfully, Tera recalled that she had even shouted *Mason's* name during her most intimate moment with River, and she bit her lip to keep from crying out in frustration and fear. *Why* had she done that? It was as though she'd had no control over what she said or felt. And what must River be thinking? *In the same instant she'd found whom she knew to be the love of her life, Tera agonized over having to give him up;* she didn't see any other answer. She and River had revealed their love for each other, had just made wonderful, passionate love that affirmed their intent to be together. But Tera was *not* ready, and it broke her heart to know she wasn't. Not with the specter of her unexplained, unrelenting dream hanging over her. It wouldn't be fair to lay all her troubles at River's feet, right at the beginning of their relationship. She was even more reluctant to tell him about her problems than she'd been about admitting them to herself; she was afraid that the magic they'd just shared would disappear in a puff of smoke. *No...she couldn't let that happen!* She wanted him, wanted *whatever* life they'd have together to begin right then and there. But she couldn't spoil the joy they'd found with this scar that had dug so deeply into her psyche, it might take years to heal it. No, she had to root out the unknown origin of the dream *without* River's help...it was enough of a burden without having to consider how it might affect him.

With deep sadness, Tera regretted that she and River hadn't clicked before. *Why couldn't they have met years and years ago? Why couldn't they have known each other all their lives?* It killed her to think they had to stop before they'd even had a decent start; but she wouldn't let go of the hope that someday, when all of this was behind her...they might still have another chance. River noticed the thoughtful crease between Tera's brows and playfully kissed the tip of her nose.

"How you feeling, beautiful?," he asked in a husky tone that spoke to Tera of the passion still burning inside. She smiled lazily, stretching in his arms.

"Mmm," she purred. "I feel just fine."

"I don't know...where'd that frown come from? I kinda *thought* I was making you smile."

"Oh River," she sighed, her arms encircling his neck; she buried her face in his hair, wishing she'd seen a therapist months ago...*that she'd never had the dream in the first place.*

"Whoa, whoa...Tera, baby--what is it?"

"River, it's...well, you see, I..." Everything in her told her she should allow herself to trust; but she couldn't find the words to tell River what was troubling her. *How could she?* He would think she was crazy, indeed, *she* wondered about that herself. *If she told him, what would it help? What could he do?* All she could envision coming out of her confession to River was a trip to Tinley Park; she could see herself locked away in a padded room wearing a straitjacket.

When he gently drew her arms from around his neck and laid her back so he could see her face, the concerned look in his eyes was more than Tera could stand. She knew from his face that her own was a mask of pain; she fought a losing battle against the anguish inside and broke down, crying uncontrollably.

"Tera! Oh, Tera honey, what is it? What's wrong?"

"I...I'm scared, River...I'm so scared!"

He pulled her close and held on tight, stroking her back. "Of what, Tee?"

"Something...*happened.* It was like...I was seeing things. I don't know, it's hard to explain, I just--"

Inexplicably, the worried look slowly disappeared from River's face. He exhaled in relief, it seemed, and Tera was as puzzled at his reaction as she was frightened by what had happened to her.

"My poor baby...look, Tera, I know this is all...*new* to you; hey, I was tripping pretty hard myself when I first found out about it, but it'll be okay, honey...we'll deal with it. The worst is over, and now that we're back together, nothing can hurt us."

River's words startled Tera so much, her crying

stopped; she froze, letting his words sink in..."back together". She drew back, looking at him in amazement.

"River...*what* did you say?"

"I said it's going to be alright, woman. Everything's new to you right now, and you're probably feeling kind of strange, but you *made* the transition. *You're here now baby*, and that's all that matters! Every day, more and more will come back to you, and you'll see all this panic was for nothing. Trust me, Tee."

Tiny seeds of a new terror festered in Tera's mind. She was now totally confused, disoriented, and fighting to hold onto sanity. It was as though she'd been suddenly cast into some strange, alternate reality where everything had been changed except *her*. *'Made the transition'? 'Back' together?*

Something was terribly off-center, and Tera wondered whether the problem was with River or herself. Her fear deepened as River spoke on.

"What are you talking about, River? What are you *saying*? I...I don't understand."

"I'm talking about what's happening to you, Tee, about what's going on with you right now."

"What? You have *no idea* what's wrong! I don't even know, River, how could *you*?"

"Tell me about your dreams, Tera," he said somberly.

Tera jumped as though she'd touched fire, recoiling from River's body.

"*What??!* Oh my God...Oh, my God--did I talk in my sleep? River, what did I say?"

Another flood of tears threatened as Tera imagined the fragmented, warped passages she must have revealed while she slept. River smiled, trying to reassure her.

"Nothing, Tee. You had *plenty* to say a few hours ago," he teased, "but you slept like a log."

Tera calmed down a bit, but was still puzzled and wary.

“Then...who...*why* did you ask me about--”
“Your dream? Because I wanted your mind to be at ease, baby. Like I told you, the transition is sometimes hard, but you made it, and you’re gonna be fine in a day or two.”
“Transition? River, *what* are you talking about? You’re scaring me! And my dream--what do you know? How could you...how could you *possibly* know anything about it?”
“Because I had it for years, Tera. Until I met you.”
“What?” Tera’s voice was less than a whisper; she felt like someone had knocked the wind out of her. River sat up and swung his legs over the edge of the bed. Tera sat quietly, still dazed, as he got up and walked to the closet where matching robes hung from a hook. He handed one to Tera.
“This is yours,” he said. “I’ve been waiting for the day you’d finally wear it.”
He pulled her up from the bed, draping the robe around her shoulders.
“Let’s go in the kitchen,” he said, kissing her. “I guess I have a *lot* of explaining to do.”

CHAPTER SIX

Pieces of an impossible puzzle slowly fell into place for Tera, and some of the events of the past few months began to make *a kind of sense*...though River's explanation was too incredible to believe.

It was insanity, too far beyond the normal, reasonable, and *rational* for Tera's mind to digest right away. At face value, any rational person would have taken River's words for those of a madman, but if that were so...then that would make her just as crazy as him. And River was the most stable, sane, clear-thinking man she'd ever known. They sat at the kitchen counter sipping wine as River added details to the incredible story, and answered Tera's questions.

"So River, you're...you're *telling me* that...that...God, it feels too weird even saying it--you're telling me that my dream is some kind of breakthrough from a...*past life*?"

"Yeah, Tera. I wanted to say something so long ago, but...well, put yourself in my place. What would you have thought? Or done? I was scared you'd freak out, think I was on crack, or whatever."

"Well, something like this is *enough* to freak somebody out."

She sipped her wine without tasting it, finding a grain of humor in the whole situation. It was all so ridiculous she fought to suppress nervous laughter, but behind the laughter was the frightening thought she couldn't dismiss...*all of this just might be true.*

"You have to admit, Riv, all of this is pretty hard to swallow."

"Tell me about it! How do you think I felt when the shit started happening to me? I mean, one minute everything's fine, next minute--some straight-up, outta-nowhere drama."

"But wait a minute. If you knew this all along--as long as you've know me--seems like you could have said *something*; helped me through this so-called 'transition'," she said, the words feeling foolish as they rolled off her tongue.

River looked at her solemnly. He took her glass and held her hand, staring at her; he was dead serious.

"Tera, I know it's hard to believe, but *don't* patronize me. Don't humor me...this is *real*. If I had the most active imagination in the world, I couldn't have just cooked up a story like this!"

He got up and began pacing. Tera could see frustration darken his face. His eyes were hard.

"From the first day I saw you, I knew I wanted you...and I knew you were the one; but do you *really* think I would make up some shit like this, *just* to get next to you?," he snapped. "Do you *really* think I'm playing here? You know I'm not into games, Tera, and even if I were, *do you really believe I'd--*"

"Okay, okay, River...I'm sorry! I *want* to believe you, but...now put yourself in *my* place. Even if it's...the truth... for God's sake,
why didn't you say something?"

"That's not how it goes, baby. Telling you too soon could have caused a lot of harm. This is supposed to happen naturally without forcing or prompting from people who don't know what the hell they're doing! I couldn't chance losing you again."

"Losing me *again*? See, River--this is nuts! Man! I...!--"

"I know, I know! It's *impossible*, right?"

"Right."

"It just *couldn't be*, right?"

"Riv, I don't see how it could."

"So how do I know what you dreamed about, huh?

How do I know about escaping from that damned place, and hiding out, and crossing that river in the dead of night?"

River gripped Tera's shoulders. "Tera...*how* do I remember all that and *more*...if all I'm saying isn't true?"

Tera was agitated beyond words at River's account of her dream. Anger blinded her, and her reaction was swift and volatile.

"Dammit, River--you're lying to me! I *did* talk in my sleep, didn't I? *EVERYTHING* you just told me is something I said, isn't it?"

She jumped up from her chair, backing away from him; tears clouded her eyes and she stumbled against one of the tables.

"I don't know what your game is, but you win, baby--*you win!* You didn't have to do this, River...you already had me. I thought you were for real when you said you loved me, but all you're doing is playing games with my head! I *believed* you, River...I believed you," she cried.

River stayed where he sat, calmly watching her. He spoke softly.

"Then believe me now. I *do* love you, Tera, more than anything; more than this life we're living right now. And *everything* I just told you is the truth. When I told you before that I'd know my Ms. Right in a heartbeat, I meant that...in the deepest sense of the word. It's you, Tera. It always has been." He got up and walked toward her. She glared defiantly as he continued to speak.

"Death has separated us before, Tee. No doubt, it will again; but I'm at peace with that because I *know* that somehow, someday...we'll pass this way again. I felt just like you, but now I know the truth of what I'm saying to you...and in your heart, you know it, too."

Tera's hard expression softened as she broke into tears again, and this time River drew her close, comforting her. Her mind fled in a thousand different directions, trying to escape what rang true in River's words...but she knew that he hadn't—*no one could have*--created such an elaborate lie, just for some ulterior purpose. As her crying gradually eased, Tera regained enough composure to start thinking and questioning River coherently.

"When this happened to you...what did you do?"

"I won't say it's coincidence, 'cause I don't believe in that--everything happens for a reason. But I met someone who helped me; someone who helped me to recall, to unlock all those memories that had been buried somewhere inside me all my life."

"Who, a shrink--I mean, a therapist?," Tera sniffled.

"No," River chuckled, kissing the tip of her reddened nose. "Not a shrink. A hypnotherapist who specializes in past life regression."

"Oh, like you run into one of *those* everyday. How'd you meet this hypno-whuddycall'em?"

River walked Tera back over to their seats at the counter and handed her her wineglass.

"Well, it's funny; I was introduced to this hypnotherapist, Dr. Speller, by a doctoral candidate at Roosevelt who just happened to be specializing in the same area, past life. Me and this doctoral candidate happened to strike up a lunchtime conversation about his dissertation, and some of the stuff he mentioned just rang a bell; it reminded me too much of the crazy dreams I was having, so I ran it past him, and *boo-yah!* He hooks me up with Dr. Speller."

"And this Dr. Speller did exactly *what* for you?"

"He cleared up the muddiness, Tera. Hypnosis opened a door that had always closed on me before, just as I was on the verge of understanding my dream. Under hypnosis, I remembered a past life. Who knows? I may have had a hundred more, but *this* one chose to break through into my life now. And it was making me crazy."

Tera thought about how often she'd found herself standing right on the edge of recalling... *something*--only to have the memory snatched just beyond her grasp; *maybe Dr. Speller could help me, too.*

"Anyway," River continued, "I was a slave. I lived on a plantation in South Carolina, owned by a Mr. Walton, and I drove his carriage. My name was Mason."

Tera recognized the name immediately. She didn't know why; maybe it was because misery loves company...but it was a comfort to know that her experience wasn't isolated. Here was someone who knew exactly what she was going through.

"Mason who?," she asked, wanting to hear River say more about this man who'd filled her dreams night after night for months.

"I don't know...just *Mason*. I drove Mr. Walton's carriage, and I tended his horses. Believe it or not, it was supposed to be a position reserved for his so-called 'trustworthy nigras'. So much for his ability to pick someone trustworthy, 'cause every chance I got I'd sneak off, looking for places to hide away, just be by myself."

Tera was drawn into River's tale; it was the other side of her own dream.

"I thought about running off lots of times...*most* slaves thought about it; but I never did. I guess I didn't have a strong enough reason. I didn't even know where I might have gone, until one day when I was out wandering and ran up on a small group of Indians. *Native Americans*, that is...don't wanna be politically incorrect or anything. Anyway, I thought I was dead for sure...until I saw that one of them was black like me.

He and some other slaves had escaped years earlier, joined up with the Choctaws, and were living free."
"God...I've read about that before, Riv, how Native Americans used to let escaping folks live with them, even helped them to escape sometimes."
"That's right. Tera, that's what happened to me. After that first time running into them, I saw I had nothing to fear from them. They weren't the dangerous savages Mr. Walton had said they were; they were just men.

I went back to that place again and again, and I saw them a lot more times. And I saw more black warriors, too. And with them interpreting for me, I talked to the others...we became friends. They told me many times, *"come with us and belong to no one but yourself"*, but for reasons I couldn't even understand then, I didn't.

Sometimes I felt like a fool for not taking what was freely offered, and I used to wonder, *am I really that scared of getting caught? Do I feel some sense of loyalty to this master?* The answer to both those questions was 'no'...but I just couldn't go. Something told me that if the time came for me to run, I would know it." River paused for a long moment, lost in thought. He turned to Tera, a hint of a smile on his lips.
"Then one day while I was out to the stables mucking them out, Mr. Walton's wagon came driving up. It was the one he always used to go to town on auction day, looking to maybe buy a new servant or two. I put my pitchfork down for a minute because I saw three folks sitting in the back of the wagon. All the rest of the servants slowed up but kept on working just enough to keep the overseer off their tails; they wanted to get a look at the new people, too. The wagon stopped near a well out by the slave quarters and the people got out. One of them was a woman, oh, middle-aged; I figured she was gonna be the new cook, since old Mattie was

getting on in years. The next one was a young man in his twenties, around my own age. He had a serious expression and a scarred-up back, and I didn't figure him for one to stick around any longer than it would take to plan an escape."

River paused again, leaning close to Tera and taking her hands in his. Love lit his eyes as he stared into hers. "The last one out of the wagon was a young woman... the most beautiful girl I had ever seen. She was about eighteen or nineteen, and she jumped down out of that wagon before anybody could help her. I could tell, she just didn't want the strange men touching her. Her skin was a deep chocolate color, and she was a little bitty thing--but there was a *'don't touch me'* look on her pretty face. I didn't have to guess why Mr. Walton had bought her, though I suspected the old man would have a hell of a time trying to tame that one. When Mr. Walton started my way, I should've started back in with mucking those stalls; but I couldn't move. I couldn't take my eyes off that girl.

She walked behind him, staring back at the people in the fields. When Mr. Walton stopped in front of me, I was sure he was about to tongue-lash me about the stalls, but he didn't. You could have knocked me over with a feather when he told me he'd bought the girl for *me*; seems he'd noticed that I wasn't keeping serious company with any of the other women...in other words, he didn't like seeing me unattached--*unattached people run.* He said he thought this feisty little wench was just what I needed to get started with a new crop of pickaninnies.

Like any other slave, I seethed inside and kept my mouth shut. It was nothing new; every other servant on the place had dealt with the same disrespect on a daily basis, and I wasn't exempt--even if I was one of his trusted niggers.

At first, the girl looked up at me with the worst

scowl on her face, but in the twinkling of an eye that scowl faded, and she looked at me like I was a long-lost friend; she smiled at me. Such a pretty smile. *And I knew right then why I had never run away.* Mr. Walton's laughter was vulgar and wicked when he said something about me and this little wench getting a new sucker planted in her right away, but both of us were beyond listening to him and his foul thoughts; something sacred was happening between her and me, and nothing profane could touch it. From that moment on, Tera, that girl was life to me. Her name was...Hannah."

"Hannah Forrester," Tera whispered.

River's eyes snapped to attention, drawn back from the mists of past remembrances.

"You *do* remember!," he said excitedly. "I knew you would; I knew it when you called my name."

"Mason...?"

"Yes, yes! Oh, Tera," he sighed, "do you see? Can't you see now that I'm telling you the truth?"

An immeasurable weight lifted from Tera's shoulders as realization sank in that she truly was not alone.

"I believe you, River; I guess I always did, but...I was scared. I'm *still* scared." She wrapped her arms around his neck again, seeking the security of his embrace.

"What happens now?," she asked.

"Tomorrow we can call Dr. Speller...see about making an appointment for you to see him."

"Okay."

"And if you don't mind, I think it would be good for my doctoral friend to be in on this; I mean, if it weren't for him, I might be in a rubber room right now. He's still working on that dissertation, but I know he'll make time for this."

"You mean this man is *still* working on his dissertation? Wasn't that a few years ago when you met him?," Tera asked. River just laughed to himself.

"Yeah, yeah...he's *still* plugging away at it. He left the area for a year or two but he's back now, and going at it full force."
Realization hit Tera like ice water in the face.
"Oh, no River...*don't tell me.*"
"You guessed it, woman. It's Cam Wilson. I was worried that transition might be rough on you, and I told him about it. He's expecting our call...that is, if it's okay with you."
Tera felt drained. Like that day at the beach when River had seen her swimming nude, she thought again, '*surely, the gods must be laughing!*' Of all the people in the entire world, it was *Cameron*. She had felt an immediate rapport with him, even seriously thought about dating him...and now, to find that *he* was somehow tangled up in this whole dream, past-life, hypno-mess...*it was too much*. Everything was moving so fast!
"What do you mean, he's *expecting* us to call? Riv, how much does he know? How long has he known?"
River's patient smile broadened, but he didn't say a word.
"Oops...sorry, Riv," Tera laughed. "Obviously, he knows *everything*, has known it as long as *you* have...hell, before you even laid eyes on me. Stupid question, huh?"
"No, it's not stupid. It just takes awhile to adjust your thinking, you know? To absorb everything and get details straight in your mind--that's all. I mean, this is some *heavy shit* I just laid on you! I'm glad to see you dealing with it as well as you are."
"Hmm. I don't know about all that--how "well" I'm dealing with it. I still have a lot of questions."
"Shoot."
"Well...in all this time, I've been thinking my meeting Cameron on the train was just happenstance, a coincidence; *was it*, or was that meeting planned?"

River burst out laughing, shaking his head at how premeditated everything must have appeared to Tera. "Baby, this isn't 'Mission Impossible'. There's no way I could've planned anything like that. No, you and Cameron met on your own, I had nothing to do with it. Like I said before, '*coincidence*' is just an explanation we use to make sense out of things we don't understand, maybe weren't *meant* to understand. For whatever reasons, you and Cam met because you were *supposed* to meet."

"Maybe, but...did he know who I was when we met?"

"Initially, no. He just thought he'd met a fine woman on the train. He says he didn't make a connection until you all *both* went over to the university; from my description, he figured it must have been you I'd been talking about."

"Okay, fine...but after he *knew* who I was...*why* did he keep calling, asking me out? It was almost like he was, I don't know, trying to get me to feel comfortable around him...like he was somehow keeping tabs on me..."

"Honey, I know this is all a mystery to you, but you're reading too much into it. Nobody was trying to 'monitor' you, you weren't under *surveillance*," he said. *Damn you, Cameron!*, he thought; *man, what were you thinking?*

"I suppose he asked you out for the obvious reasons, Tera--you're a beautiful, intelligent woman that *any* man would want to go out with."

"You...knew that he was attracted to me."

"Mm-hmm. And I didn't say anything. I could have blocked with you and Cameron but it wouldn't have meant as much as it did for *you* to choose *me*."

River could see that Tera was still confused by his attitude; *at least it was a diversion from talking about Cameron's involvement.*

"And that didn't make a difference to you..."

"*Everything* concerning you makes a difference to me, Tera. But what you meant to me in the past doesn't automatically brand you as 'mine' right *now*. People still have to work at relationships, you know? Yes, we have a connection but we're not joined at the hip. You've always been free to choose--whether it's me or someone else."

"But what would've happened if Cameron and I had started seeing each other?"

"I don't know; only you and he could answer that," River said. "I won't lie and say I wouldn't have been jealous, but I wouldn't have interfered."

He caressed her cheek gently smiling that enigmatic, little-boy smile she loved so much.

"Death is only *one* of the things that can separate lovers, Tera--everybody knows that. Either one of us could've taken another route, ended up in a whole other situation in this life. You could still choose to be with someone else besides me; but I meant what I said in Jamaica: Cameron Wilson--and no one else, for that matter--can make you feel the way I can, girl. I *know it*."

Tera's face was warm with embarrassment, but she smiled; River was right about that. She *definitely* had it bad. But she knew her heart was in good hands. There were still so many loose ends, so many unanswered questions; but they'd come in due time. Some of the paralyzing fear she'd felt was finally leaving her. What River had told her was almost beyond belief; but it paralleled her own experience *too closely* for her *not* to believe.

"Listen, you wanna throw on some clothes, maybe go for a walk?"

"No, Riv...not really."

"I just thought you might want to get out, you know, get a change of scenery."

"Unh-unh. I like the scenery right here, thank you very

much," Tera smiled.
"How about over to the Bottomless Cup? You know you love their coffee, especially that rocket-fuel blend."
"Maybe tomorrow morning, River."
"O--kay...wanna go see a movie?"
"Nope."
"Ride bikes? Go rollerblading?"
"Unh-unh, River!"
"Climb Mount Everest? Swim across Lake Michigan?"
"River! *No.* What's up, you trying to get me out of here, what?"
"Okay then, let me be real here," he said. "I'm trying to give you an out, my dear--a chance to come up for air."
"Mm-hmm. Do *you* need air?" Tera's sexy smile mocked him.
"Look, woman, I'm *trying* to tell you, if we don't leave this house *right now*, I'm thinking we're gonna end up back in bed, and...well, you know..."
"I'm counting on it, cutie."

###

River and Tera slept well into the morning after making love again and again the night before. Realizing that they had to pace themselves before they *killed* each other, they finally drifted off to a peaceful sleep. They might have remained in bed until afternoon had it not been for River's phone waking them up. River fumbled around for it, his head still buried under the covers.
"Hello," he rasped. "Oh! Good morning, Mrs. Morton." Tera's wide eyes peeped over the edge of the comforter at the mention of her mother's name.
"Oh, I'm fine, Mrs. Morton. Mm-hmm...oh yeah, Tera's fine, too." He laughed politely.
"Yes ma'am, we had a very nice time. Oh, we had a little dinner, talked, watched t.v. Yep. Just a quiet evening. Uh, well...you know, I *was* gonna take her

home last night, Mrs. Morton, but...it was getting late and Tera said never mind, so I just sacked out on the couch and let her have my bed. That's right. Oh, yes ma'am, the couch is really comfortable. I slept like a rock. Oh, no, Tera's snoring didn't bother me--she had the door closed tight. Excuse me, could you hold on for just a minute?"

River looked like he was about to explode; he clamped Tera's hand over the receiver and fell back on the bed, howling with laughter. Tera snickered but quickly composed herself, placing the phone to her ear.

"Hi, Ma."

"Unh, unh, *unh*! Girl, what in the world did you do to that man? I hear him laughing."

"Nothing, Ma! What are you talking about?," she asked innocently. "He's not uh, laughing...he stubbed his toe."

She looked over her shoulder at River, who was still struggling to regain his composure.

"Liar," Mrs. Morton chuckled. "That boy is laughing his butt off. Must've spent a *good night* to wake up in such a happy mood."

"Well, yeah...we did have a good night. Dinner, t.v., conversation...just like River told you."

"Ooh, child, you lie like a rug! Your sister's got River's keys, remember? The way Mara described the whole love nest layout, I know that boy didn't go to all that trouble for y'all to sit around and parlez all evening," she laughed.

"Now, Mother...don't be nosy, it's not nice."

"Hah! I *knew* it! If nothing happened between you, then there would've been *nothing* to be nosy about, am I right? Oh, Tera Marchelle," she sighed, her voice wavering with sentiment, "oh honey, I always knew there was something there. He's a sweet boy, you know I've always liked him. Ooh, I'm so *happy* for you two!"

"Calm down now, Mama...we just started seeing each other! We're taking it slow, so don't go ordering wedding invitations and putting our names on a registry or anything, okay?"
"Don't give me any ideas, honey; you *know* it's just a matter of time! That boy *loves* you, he told Mara! You're too stubborn to admit it, but you love him, too."
Tera tried not to say too much about what she was feeling, but she couldn't help it. She glanced over at River, whose dark eyes invited her to climb back into his arms. It was hard to resist the invitation, but she continued her conversation with her mother.
"You're wrong, Ma...I'm not so stubborn after all."
"You mean...? Ohhh! Ooohhh! Aaaaahhhh! *Ohmygod*--Tera! Oh, honey that's wonderful! Oh! This is serious, child. All that mess you just said about not picking out invitations and stuff...before I know it, you two'll be walking down the aisle, settling down together--"
"Ma..."
"Oh, you two will make such beautiful babies together, I just know it! You *will* start a family right away, won't you?"
"*Ma!*"
"You know, *you* should keep *your* place and ask River to move in with you; your place is the largest, and with that big, nice yard and everything, the babies will have *plenty* of space to roam around, and--"
"Mother, you are a truly, *truly* sick woman," Tera laughed.
She handed the phone back to River, letting him catch the overflow of her mother's excitement.
"Excuse me, Mrs. Morton, I didn't mean to be rude...yes. Yes. Oh, yes ma'am, thank you. I think we're gonna be very happy, too. Mm-hmm. Yes," River chimed in--though he could barely get a word in

edgewise.
He cut his eyes in Tera's direction, winking at her. He knew how much Mrs. Morton liked him, and the feeling was mutual; he patiently listened as she chatted on and on about everything from choosing the right spot for their reception to the benefits of breast-feeding.
"Yes ma'am, you're right, but that's just a *little* premature, don't you think? Oh, no--don't misunderstand me, now. That's definitely in our future. Hopefully, our near future."
Tera's ears perked up; she looked at River quizzically, mouthing *'what in the world are you telling her?'*
"Well, Mrs. Morton, we haven't had a chance to even discuss dates yet, but give us time. Oh...that's so sweet. Yeah, I guess 'Mrs. Morton' *is* a little formal at this point... 'Mom'," he said with emphasis as Tera playfully cringed.
"River, you are *so* wicked," Tera whispered.
"It shouldn't take us long to do our running around, Mrs.--I mean, Mom--and we'll be over right after, okay? Alright, then. See you. Tell everybody 'hi' for me. Bye-bye."
"Whew," River sighed, hanging up the phone.
"See what you did, Riv? You know how my mama is. I don't know what y'all were talking about, but it sounded like something *she* might interpret as wedding plans."
"Well," he asked, "isn't that the next logical step?"
"River, you're as exasperating as my mother." Tera cuddled up behind him and hugged his waist, resting her chin on his shoulder.
"I love you, River Jordan Bennett. Strange as it still seems to me, I'm realizing that I've loved you for a long, long time. But let's not rush."
Her arms moved up to encircle his broad shoulders and she rubbed her cheek against his soft, wooly locks.
"When I think about being with you, one day marrying

you...nothing makes me happier. But I'm caught up right now, my head is spinning from everything that's already happened...I don't know if I can stand even *thinking* about anything more right now. Do you understand?"

River pulled her around in front of him and sat her on his lap, wrapping her in his arms.

"Yeah, baby, I understand. And you're right...we've got nothing but time. But don't get upset if it seems like I'm moving too fast; you gotta remember now, that I've been moving *slow*, almost at a stand-still waiting for this to happen. Have patience with my *im*patience, okay?"

"Okay. Let's get on up; let's get out of here, right now."

"Huh?"

"If we don't," she murmured, kissing his neck, "*I'm* thinking we might end up back in bed, and...well, you know..."

"Yeah, I know. You'd better shower first, 'cause if we go in together...well, you know."

"I *know!!*"

CHAPTER SEVEN

River and Tera went to Tera's place before visiting her folks. She wanted to drop off her things, check and answer any messages--generally reacquaint herself with her place after being gone for two weeks. It was surprising to Tera, how new everything seemed after such a short absence. There was a message on the answering machine from Cameron, and River raised an eyebrow in mock-suspicion as they listened to it.

"Hey, Miss Tera...just called to say 'hi', thought you'd be back by now, but...I guess not. Anyway, hope you had a real good time on vacation, gimme a call later if you get time, okay? Talk to you."

"Hmm," River said, "trying to put on that old innocent, big-brother front, eh? I got his number."

"River, you're a *nut*. I'm about the furthest thing from that man's mind. He's too wrapped up in that late-freight dissertation to be thinking about much else. Matter of fact, that's probably what he wants to bend my ear about...that, or the things *you* told me."

"Yeah-yeah, sure-sure...tell *me* anything."

"I'm serious, River," Tera said, playfully punching him. "You know what's up; there was just nothing in the cards for me and him...except the 'friend' thing."

"If memory serves me correctly, woman, that's the *same* thing you thought about me and you," he teased. Tera made a face.

"Okay, so I was wrong *that* time. I'm not wrong about Cameron, though. And even if I were, it wouldn't matter," she said, wrapping her arms around him. "You're looking at a woman in love."

"So does this mean I don't have to worry about you running off to Timbuktu with this dude?"

"Hmm...let me think on that...I hear Timbuktu is pretty

nice, especially this time of year..."
"Ooh, Tera--that's cold, baby."

###

Visiting her folks felt...strange...wonderful...*both*. It felt good being part of the everyday, inner workings of her family; it reminded Tera just how much she could depend on their strength and stability, and how grateful she was to have them. But now, being around them made her feel off-center, as though she no longer knew her place within the family structure. She was surrounded by loved ones...*but the same story that had helped unlock her dream had shut down and isolated her in the waking world...*

When she and River walked through the door of the Morton house, Mama Morton greeted them with a strong bear-hug that neither of them had thought possible from such a petite woman.
"Ooh, you two! *Mm-wah!*", she planted a lipstick kiss on Tera's cheek; "*mm-wah!*", and River's cheek bore an identical imprint. Reluctantly, Tera allowed herself to be steered into the living room where she knew she'd see her dad sitting in his recliner with the remote control.

She was surprised to see that Mara was also back in town, with her husband and child. The aroma of home cooking filled the air, a rare occurrence anymore around the Morton household since none of the kids lived at home and Tera's parents spent so much of their free time traveling. Tera was overwhelmed.
Everything felt the same...except her. Everyone hugged and kissed, talked, laughed, ate together--even cheered along with Daddy when his favorite baseball team scored; and through it all, poor Tera muddled along enough to pass the scrutiny of her mother...her mask of a smile firmly in place. But River could read her like a book and knew what was troubling her. He said nothing, not wanting to hover too much or decide for

her exactly how much she could handle; he'd learned long ago from Dr. Speller and his own experience that it was best to let people in transition find their own balance point between reconciling past and present--without outside interference. Mara wasn't fooled by Tera's mega-watt smile, either.

"Hey, Tee," she called, "come on and help me clear these plates and stuff outta here."

"Okay." Tera was grateful for the chance to get away from the animated living room chatter. As soon as they got to the kitchen, Mara turned to her sister with a questioning look.

"Tera...girl, what's wrong with you?"

"Huh?...nothing, Mara. I'm cool."

"Unh-unh, Tee...no you're *not*. You're slinking around in there like a cat or something.

I'm surprised Mama ain't checked it out yet."

"You're imagining things, Mara. Besides, Mama's so pumped about me and River getting together, she probably wouldn't notice if I was bouncing off the walls."

"Hell, you almost are! And River sees it too; the way *he* was looking at you is what made me notice in the first place."

"No Mara, really...I'm just tired, that's all; nothing a good night's rest won't take care of."

Mara smiled at her little sister; she knew something was bothering her, but she also knew Tera wasn't about to speak on it. Mara knew that either *she* or the awkward vibes in the room would have to go; she chose to stay.

"A good night's rest, huh? Well, I don't see how you're gonna get *that*, not with that fine man hanging around!"

"Ooh, Mara...you are wicked."

"I ain't lying! Look at you, girl--you're *glowing* from all that good stuff he's putting on you, but your eyes are a dead giveaway--no sleep!"

"Mara girl, you have the *dirtiest* mind--"
"In the *world*, baby! In the *world*!," Mara laughed. "What, 'cause I can see that you and Dread Man been knockin' it out real tough? Don't be shame, girl...get you some stuff."
Mara was too amused, watching her sister squirm. "Tera?...ain't this a--girl, you really *are* embarrassed, aren't you?"
"I'm just not as...open as you, I guess."
"Hmph. Ain't *no* shame in my game, baby--I'm *real* well acquainted with gettin' down... me and sex are on a *first-name basis*. And from the looks of thangs, I'd say you kinda renewed *your* acquaintance, too."
"Mara, Mara, Mara...I don't know what to say about you, girl."
"Say I call 'em like I see 'em. And I see *your* ass is whipped--like butter, baby!," Mara teased. "And he ain't no better!--dreads all wild-looking and everything--you all better slow it down. You don't have to get it all today, save some for tomorrow."
Mara's joking toned down; her voice softened.
"Tee...is he good to you? Do you love him?"
"Mara...oh, Mara..! Words don't even say enough."
Mara's eyes widened; the joker had returned.
"Well, *damn*, Tee, I knew you had a vibe for that man, even when you didn't know it, and him? He's been sprung on you for a *minute*, but...damn! This is deep."
"Yeah...it is."
"Look honey, you know I wish you all the best; I've always *loved* me some River and thought y'all would make a good couple. Now, I *know* something is bothering you—something besides 'plain old tired'. And I'm not gonna ask again what it is...just take care of yourself, okay? Handle your business."
"Okay, Mara. And thanks."
"For what?"
"For always seeing what's underneath; like seeing the

cake under the frosting."
"Or the dog doo-doo in the grass? Or the broccoli in the teeth? The *ashy leg* under the run in the stocking? The--"
"See, your ass is totally foul, you know that? Here I am, thinking we're doing that 'bonding' thing, and you go and blow it up. You're a trip, girl."
"Mm-hmm, and you wouldn't have me any other way, would you? Gotta luh me!," she squealed, giving Tera a reassuring hug. "Now let's get back out there before Mama sends in the militia."

It required more than River's and Mara's best arguments to convince Tera's mother that she and River needed to leave soon; that Tera needed her rest.
"Oh, don't be *silly*," she said. "I thought it might be nice if Tera, Mara, and I went over to the mall for awhile to shop, have lunch, shop some *more*--you know? I haven't seen my baby girl in over two weeks, and Mara even longer than that. I'm sure River and Nate and Little Man wouldn't mind staying here with Daddy while we go."
It had seemed like a plan the hapless daughters would have to live with--or hurt their mother's feelings--until a wild card suddenly popped up: their father.
"Olivia," he said to his wife, "leave those kids alone! They don't wanna go to no *mall*... buying up a lot of stuff they don't need *or* want."
"Well...Hector! You make it sound like I'm twisting their arms or something."
"You are, honey. Them kids *ain't* interested! Now, you *know* Mara Nicole don't care nothing about shopping--just look at how she dresses."
Mara smiled dryly, looking down at her long, seventies-style dress. "Thank you, Daddy," she laughed as he continued.
"And Tera's standing here, looking like a couple o' miles of bad road, she's so tired." Tera and Mara shot

each other knowing looks, trying to hold in their laughter; Daddy was gruff, but he'd gotten them off the hook.

"Well, excuse me for *living*," Mrs. Morton said; "all I had wanted was to do something nice with my girls...is that so bad?"

Hector Morton felt his rough edges trying to smooth out; his wife's sad, little-girl look and plaintive voice never failed to melt his heart...just as Olivia Morton knew it would.

"Woman, you are impossible," he grumbled, "but if it means *that* much to you...*I'll* go to that stupid mall with you--even buy you that dress you were looking at--but you let these kids go on about their business."

"Anything you say, Hector darling," she smiled sweetly. She hugged her daughters tightly; "maybe next time, girls."

After a lingering goodbye at the front door, River and Tera were at last on their way back to Tera's. She could feel herself slowly unwinding as River eased the car out of her folks' driveway and headed up the street.

She would be glad to see this Dr. Speller and get it over with, if it meant that life could return to normal...whatever '*normal*' is.

Anxious thoughts about all she'd been told by River returned to plague her at the most unexpected times. She wondered what the doc would be like. Would he really be able to help. She closed her eyes, her thoughts absorbed in what River had said about hers being a relatively 'easy' transition...and wondered what fate had befallen those folks who'd had a rough time of it. *She couldn't imagine a more confusing and disturbing experience than her own.* And she was having trouble understanding why it was so important for Cameron to be involved. He wasn't a therapist...exactly what was *his* connection? She continued to relax, gradually, and concluded that it would all be revealed soon enough.

River looked over at Tera, relieved to see that she seemed to be coming around from the agitated state she was in at her mother's house. There was still so much she didn't know; and there was a limit on how much he was at liberty to say. Without a doubt, he needed to tell her more...but he had to be careful, speaking of only the basics. Maybe after they'd gotten settled in, they could talk some more; *better yet*, he thought, *she won't want to talk about anything having to do with it.* That would be fine with him. She would know all that she needed to know very soon. Some of it would be painful--heavy doses of truth often are--but River was hopeful, still optimistic that Tera would come through safe and whole, and ready to begin their life together...again.

###

Tera whirled around and around, doing a little dance before sinking down to the sofa in her living room.

"Whew, am I glad to be back *here!*," she said.

River sat next to her, massaging her shoulders to relieve some of her stress.

"Listen, Tera--why don't you go on in and take a nice, warm shower...and while you're in there, I'll make those calls to Dr. Speller and Cam, okay?"

"Okay, Riv."

Tera was still skittish about the session, but eager to try anything that might help her to get beyond her present state.

She could feel the tension draining from her body as she stood under the cascading water, and Tera almost hated to come out of the relaxing shower. The familiarity of her own surroundings was exactly what she'd needed. Finally, she came out of the shower and walked to the living room. Her eyes were drawn to the shelf where she'd put the mirror from Mara--*Hannah's mirror*. She went over and got it off the shelf, fingering it delicately; *strange*, she thought, *how it no longer feels unfamiliar*. Even more strange the circumstances that had caused her to reclaim it. She replaced it, finally able to appreciate its beauty.

She looked at River lying outside on the grass, propped on his elbows and looking out over the lagoon. She smiled, shaking off the fantasy image of River chasing one little child around the yard, with another one happily clinging to his back. Her mother had planted that thought, but Tera knew there were things in her life that badly needed repair before she and River could even consider parenthood. She quickly threw on shorts and a shirt and joined River out by the lagoon. She lay next to him, looking up at the clouds passing overhead.

"River...finish your story."

"Huh? What'd you say?"

"I said, finish your story, the one you started before we went to my folks'; what else happened?"

River sat up and gazed out over the placid waters, thoughtfully considering Tera's request; again, he concluded it would be best to stick to the basics. He spoke.

"Well, it's like I was telling you...something just clicked between me and Hannah, and it was like we'd known each other forever. We spent every spare moment together, and every chance we got, we'd go off together. I shared my world with her, showing her the things I'd seen, letting her meet the folks I'd met...teaching her what I knew, and vice versa. Early in the morning--in the wee hours before the sun came up--we'd slip away and meet each other at the oak tree on the old Tollie farm. Old man Tollie had died years before and his land went up for sale; matter of fact, old Walton had thought about buying it, since it bordered his land. In the meantime, though, the farm just sat, and there was nothing there but the old house and that gigantic oak tree. With nobody else around, Hannah and I could have our privacy. Before dawn, we'd slip away to the quarters, unnoticed. It was like...like...how can I put this? Being with Hannah made being in bondage...*bearable*".

"Riv, if everything seemed...well, *bearable*...then why did you two run away?"

"We had no choice...one day while I was out in the stables, old man Walton walked by with another white man. I heard Walton say he was ready to *'sell off some of his stock'*, and my ears immediately perked up; they hadn't seen me, so I bent down and hid, listening. I wanted to know who the old man was thinking of unloading. The other man said he was willing to buy all Walton had to sell...but asked was he certain he wanted to sell that wench he'd bought for his driver, Mason? Him and that wench Hannah had got pretty close, he said--might old man Walton have second thoughts about busting those two up? Well...Mr. Walton told the man yes, he was sure--that his servants had *no* say-so about anything because they were *his* property, not the other way around. And if that uppity nigger of his, Mason, dared to say anything about it ...he'd have his black hide lashed to pieces. I waited until the coast was clear, but I knew what I had to do. I didn't stop to tell Hannah what I had heard, I just headed for the woods hoping to run across Tall Bear or some of his men. When I did find Black Sky, I told him what had happened. Black Sky... *he* was in favor of slipping onto Walton's place at night and killing the old bastard while he slept, but that would've caused too much trouble for too many innocent people; a lot of people would've been hurt while patrollers searched for the one responsible for giving the old man what he deserved.

"Anyway, we came up with a plan, a very good plan

on such short notice; and I was so thankful to have already known the surrounding land and found hideaways, shortcuts, and whatever...that knowledge came in handy. I went back to the stables, just like nothing was wrong...and when Hannah came in to bring me some food from the kitchen, I told her everything. She was so scared; didn't know what to do. She wondered if it might do any good to plead with Mr. Walton not to sell her."

It was beyond Tera's comprehension, how it must have felt to *be* a slave...and then, *to have to beg someone not to sell you.* It was painful to even think about.

"Well...*why* did he want to sell her in the first place?"

The fire of anger blazed in River's eyes for a moment at the remembrance of past wrongs done against him, against Hannah; he sat for a moment, thoughtfully twirling a blade of grass between his fingers. *This was dangerous ground...*still, he would rather be vague than to outright lie to Tera.

"What reason did he need? *Any* reason was good enough for a master to sell his 'property'...and there wasn't a damn thing any of us slaves could do about it. *Except run.*

I had figured we had a few days at least, maybe even a whole week to secretly prepare what we'd need. We went over our plans very carefully, and I told her *"be ready to go at a moment's notice"*; we just didn't know when we'd be forced to leave. We let things blow over the next day, acting normally--but we were quickly putting away things we'd need: blankets, clothes, socks, food. And that mirror Hannah loved so much," he smiled.

Tera thought of the little mirror, now resting on a shelf in her living room.

"Her mother had given it to her, and she'd somehow managed to keep it hidden, sewn into the hem of her skirt, so that no one would take it when she was sold.

The day after I'd heard Walton and the other man went by okay--we were ready, and we'd managed to do what we needed to do without raising suspicion. We were prepared to wait a few more days, but the next day, all hell broke loose."

"What happened?," Tera asked; River had her full attention.

"That boy, Lucky--the one who old Walton had bought along with the cook and Hannah--he ran away. I don't know, maybe *he* was in the stable and overheard just like me; anyway, I knew from the first time I'd seen him that sooner or later, he would run. I only regretted that he hadn't done it much, much sooner.

As it was, his running brought a lot of heat, a lot of local patrollers who were keeping an even closer watch on the roads and surrounding properties; you see, Lucky got away clean--and those white folk didn't want any of us other niggers getting the idea we could do the same."

River paused again, deeply focused on the story and its tragic ending. A look of profound sadness clouded his face.

"After it was dark and everybody had gone to bed, Hannah met me at the stable. When we were certain that no one else was around...she stole out across the fields. When she'd reached the far edge, she signaled to me--the call of a wild bird. That let me know she hadn't been seen; I knew she'd wait for me at the oak tree over at Tollie's. It was pitch black. I listened for the sound of any patrollers, but there was nothing. They'd passed by earlier, and would likely fan out much further and then circle back around to Walton's. Hannah and I would be long gone by then; they didn't really think anybody would have the nerve to leave so soon after Lucky. When I reached our meeting place, Hannah and I took off into the forest. We hid out during the next day in a cave, and then that night we crossed the river in a canoe that Tall Bear's men had hidden for us near the bank. When we reached the clearing where his men waited with horses...I thought we were home free."

"We rode all night, and just before daylight we could see the base of the hills where Tall Bear was waiting for us. Hannah was so nervous and excited...I could tell, she wanted to just ride hard for the safety of the trees, but...we walked the horses instead. I thought everything would be fine; a couple of the men riding with us had even gone back to cover tracks. Suddenly, we heard shots being fired. The gunfire spooked Hannah's horse, and it threw her. I was riding just ahead, and when I wheeled around to come back and get her...I saw the patrollers; and old man Walton was with them! I don't know...he must have gone by the stables and, not finding me there, went over to the quarters and found me gone. It wouldn't take a genius to figure that if I was gone, so was Hannah. Fast as possible, I cleared the short distance to where Hannah had fallen...and just as I...reached for her hand to pull her up on the horse with me, I...I heard a..."

River had to stop again, this time to control his quavering voice; he clasped his hands together to stop their shaking.

"I heard a...rifle blast...and Hannah was shot," he said quietly.

"The force of the blast threw her forward, and she landed right at my horse's feet. I jumped down, cradled her in my arms; my clothes were covered with her blood. Then I heard more gunfire coming from the direction of the trees; it was Tall Bear, riding down on the patrollers. He must have had nearly a hundred men. And not one of those patrollers escaped with his life, including old Walton. Tall Bear's gunfire gave me the cover I needed, and I was able to get Hannah up on my horse. We rode straight for the trees, and Hannah held on as tight as she could...but when we reached the trees I could feel her weaken and start to slip. Black Sky, one of the men who rode with us, caught her."

River sat in silence for a moment, watching sunlight fade above the tops of the trees.

"My heart was breaking, Tera...after escaping from that awful place; after having so much hope for the future; after planning to spend the rest of our lives together...I could see that my Hannah was dying. I held her, pleading with her not to leave me...but when you hear that call, you have to answer...*she* had to answer. I could see the light in her eyes slowly fading; and with her last breath, she told me she'd love me forever. And I promised her, Tera--promised *you*--I would always love her...and that someday, we'd be together again."

River rolled over onto his stomach, looking at Tera thoughtfully.

"And so it is, Tee...here we are today...together... again."

Even before River had finished his story, even before Tera had any insight into the possible meaning of her dream, a feeling inside had told her that there are some things which can't be explained, can't be measured against what is considered 'the norm'...and that her dream was one of those things. So River's story had not sounded as incredible as it might have months or even weeks ago; and even in its completeness, Tera could feel that there were some missing parts. And she realized that the missing parts were a combination of things she hadn't yet remembered...and things River apparently chose *not* to tell her. River said that she would finally meet and talk with Dr. Speller on Friday; then, maybe the fragmented pieces of this puzzle would make sense. Tera still got a strange feeling each time she thought about Cameron Wilson being there too.

Why did he need to be there? What was his angle? Instinct told her that his involvement ran deeper than mere academic interest, and there were quite a few unanswered questions about him. She hadn't been mistaken about his initial interest in her, even after realizing who she was; but she was still puzzled about why he'd backed off. *Maybe*, Tera reasoned, *it was a conflict of interest, pure and simple.* After all, he and River knew each other, and he knew how River felt about Tera. *But why hadn't he backed off sooner, as soon as he found out who she was?*

According to Riv, Cameron had known who she was since that first day when they'd walked over to Roosevelt together...yet he'd still asked her out the following day. He'd called her a few times since, they'd even gone out on another date--though it was obvious that he'd pulled back quite a bit; he was decidedly more detached than he'd been the *first* time they went out together. Still, River had insisted that Cameron's interest was exactly what it seemed to be, rather than an attempt to gain her confidence. *Whatever.* It was a little confusing to Tera, and she decided to find out what it was all about--from Cameron, *before* Friday.

In the meantime, there were other, equally pressing things on Tera's mind. She looked at River; they were in the first flush of an exciting new relationship she'd never before believed possible. She had always admired him and treasured their friendship, but now...everything was so different between them. His name conjured images of peaceful, flowing waters that appeared tranquil yet swirled with an irresistible power and depth just below the surface. She touched his arm, and it was like a low-voltage current running across her fingertips. She remembered his kiss in Jamaica; the heat that had passed between them was an incredible rush that left her breathless. When he smiled at her, it occurred to Tera that she was holding her breath again. River's face was only inches from hers...and suddenly the thought of talking to Cameron or anyone else at that moment was the furthest thing from Tera's mind. Shadows were deepening, and the clouds glowed with the warm orange and gold of sunset. One kiss, and Tera could feel herself again drawn into River's powerful undercurrent...again wanting to drown in it.

"Tera," he whispered,".....let's go inside."

###

"What exactly happened, Tera?," River asked.

"I...I don't *know*," she answered," but nobody will be happier to see Friday come than *me*! This...this whole thing is really starting to work my nerves."

"Tell me what you saw, Tee. Tell me what you remember."

Tera collected her thoughts for a moment, then started telling River as much as she could recall. There was, of course, the darkness, the oak tree barely outlined in purplish-black
against the night sky, the desperate flight through the forest to the cave at dawn; and there was the meeting with their Native American allies and the grueling ride across the plain to a place of refuge, the foothills where Tall Bear and the others awaited them.

The fateful shot again rang out, and Tera felt the blinding pain and heat with its impact...she could still feel the swift, inevitable flow of the life force ebbing from her body. She had again seen herself lying in her man's arms, slipping away despite her strongest efforts to linger; she clearly remembered their mutual promise of love everlasting...and there, again, was the void. The first time Tera's dream had taken her there, she'd felt nothingness, but this time *something*, *someone* lurked in the ethereal darkness. This time, she drifted away from the sunlit, forested hills into the absolute blackness and quietude of the void. Tera had felt alone yet unafraid; and suddenly, she was aware of another's presence...*the sorrowful presence of a soul not at peace.*

Soundlessly, it reached out to her, pleading for... *something*--but Tera didn't know what...and then, as it had dozens of times before, the dream had wrenched Tera into wakefulness, reaching out to make contact with an answer...*a reality just beyond her reach.*

"That's as much as I can remember, River...what could it possibly mean?," she whispered.

River sat in silence, pondering Tera's question... *knowing there was no more he could tell her.* If everything went as planned, Tera would soon understand the meaning of this latest revelation.

"Dr. Speller should be able to help you find the answers you need, Tee," he answered.

He couldn't lie...*wouldn't* speculate. *He knew, but could say nothing*...his input might have an effect on the outcome of Tera's meeting with Dr. Speller and Cameron, and he would not risk the consequences of revealing more than Tera was ready to handle. A slightly mischievous half-smile flashed across Tera's face for a moment.

"So...in other words, *you're* not going to tell me what it means."

"It's not my place."

"So you know!"

"I didn't say that--I just said it wasn't my place."

"Right--and if you *hadn't* known what it was, you would've said 'I don't know'. But you didn't say that, did you Mr. Bennett?"

"No...I guess I didn't."

"So that means you *do* know...River, please tell me--"

"Unh-unh, Tera--forget it!"

"River...*please*, pretty please..."

River swung his legs over the edge of the bed; a look Tera had never seen before clouded his handsome face, and the tone of his voice was chilling in its seriousness. "Look, honey," he said, "I'm being straight-up with you, no jokes...I want you to understand that this is nothing to play with."

Tera's playful smile waned, and she listened to River intently.

"If I thought telling you more would help you through this period, you know I would--in a heartbeat! But...there are some things that just have to be done in a certain way--I don't know why, but that's just the way it is. And there's nothing any of us *can* or *should* do about it. This is one of those things, Tera. Dr. Speller can help you find the answers--not me. Maybe it sounds strange, but...you'll just have to trust me on this, baby."

"Alright. I'm sorry...I didn't mean to--"

"You don't have to apologize to *me*; I should be making amends with you for...well, for the way everything's gone up to this point. But I promise you, Tee...the day will come when all this is behind us...and our life together is gonna be better than either of us could have imagined; I promise you that."

"Promise me one thing more, River."

"What's that?"

"That you'll be with me through this; that you won't let me be alone on Friday."

River wrapped his arms around her, burying his face in the curve of her neck.

"You won't be alone on Friday, or any *other* day, unless you want to be. If you need me and I'm not *already* around...all you have to do is call me. For anything. Oh, Tera," he murmured, sprinkling her with feather-light kisses, "*Don't you know* anything you want from me...is already yours?"

"I do...I guess I just needed to hear you say it...right here, right now."

"Mm-hmm...is there anything else you need--right here,

right now?," he asked.
"I'll give you three guesses."

CHAPTER EIGHT

By Thursday morning both Tera and River clearly understood each other's need for privacy. They'd been locked in marathon togetherness ever since coming back from Jamaica, but now there were a number of reasons to pry themselves apart. It was still too early in the game for them to have grown tired or restless with each other's company; on the contrary, both of them needed rest--to *slow it down*, as Mara had cautioned. Aside from that most obvious fact, both of the also had personal business to attend to at their respective residences like laundry, phone calls, housekeeping--all the things they'd neglected while wrapped in each other's arms.

As River had expected, Tera wanted to talk to Cameron. And he wanted to talk with Dr. Speller...he could certainly use the last-minute encouragement; the affirmation that everything would be alright. River kissed Tera goodbye at her front door, promising to call later in the evening after 'some of the dust had settled'. Tera watched him bundle his things into the back seat of his car and drive off.

She went into the kitchen, bypassing the stereo in the living room; this particular morning the quiet was enough. She opened the patio doors and enjoyed the cool breeze and morning song of crickets and birds. For awhile Tera just sat, basking in the glow of love and the sudden flush of warm feelings she experienced whenever River crossed her mind. He'd only been gone a short while but she already missed the heat of his skin against hers...the gentle brush of his locks against her cheek...his solid weight pressed against her body. She hugged herself tightly, catching a faint scent of him, and was reminded of how completely he'd become a part of her. *This was the kind of feeling she'd always imagined when she thought of what it meant to "be in love", and she could still hardly believe it was happening to her.* Of course, she could hardly believe any of what had happened to her recently, and looked forward to uncovering the final secrets of this mystery that had ultimately brought her and River together. She had no idea of what obstacles lay ahead for them, but she could sense River's uneasiness that something might happen to upset their newfound happiness...and Tera was determined to meet it, head on. Now that they'd found each other, she wouldn't allow anything to separate them! She looked at the clock above the refrigerator; it was just after 9:00, and she decided it was time to call Mr. Cameron Wilson.

Hesitantly, she reached for the phone and dialed his number. Though she didn't look forward to their conversation, if there was even the slightest chance that he might be able to shed some light on this whole situation, well...

"Hello."

"Hi, Cameron...it's Tera." After a long silence he spoke.

"Well...hey, Miss Lady. How are you, how was your vacation?"

"It was good, Cameron...but you know that's not why I called."

There was an expected, uncomfortable pause.

"Yeah, I know. River called me. I guess I have a lot of explaining to do, huh?"

"...Yeah, Cameron. You *do* owe me that much."

"Listen Tera, I never meant to...to be--"

"Deceptive? Misleading? Or a combination of both?"

"Now, hold on. Whatever else I did or didn't do, I never lied to you, not about anything."

"Did you and River go to the same training class? That's the same thing *he* told me. Fine. *You didn't lie to me*...you just weren't straight with me. I don't know what I expected from you, but it wasn't this."

"Look, believe it or not, I'm struggling with this just like you are. *Just like River, too.* And believe me, all I'm trying to do is help straighten things out, once and for all."

"*You're* struggling? What's all this got to do with *you*, other than it fits in with your study?"

Cameron sighed heavily; *the time was fast approaching.* He hadn't handled things well, and deeply regretted that he hadn't gotten to know Tera better before this moment. She liked him, but her trust was questionable. *And if she didn't trust him...it could ruin any chance of making things right.*

"Cameron, are you still there?"

"Yeah, Tera--I'm here."

"So, what's the deal? Tell me what's going on...at least, what's going on with *you*."

"All right. But we need to talk face-to-face."

Tera hesitated; she knew he was right, but felt funny about either inviting him over, or going to his place to talk.

"I realize this is kind of awkward, so maybe we ought to meet on neutral ground, say, at the same place we went before over on the lakefront?"

Tera was instantly more at ease with Cameron's suggestion. It was both sensitive and perceptive.

"That sounds fine, Cameron. But we really don't need to go all the way into Chicago just to talk. How about if...if we meet at the Bottomless Cup, grab some coffee and donuts, and walk the nature trail?" Tera made a face, thinking *how squishy and sentimental is that?* She and River had done that exact same thing before she went to Jamaica; maybe the good vibes they'd had made her feel it would be a safe choice with Cameron as well.

"Are you sure, Tera? I just want you to be comfortable."

"I will be. Look, Cameron...you're right, this *is* kind of

awkward, but...last time we saw each other, we were getting to be friends, right? I have some things to ask you, and you have some things to explain, but this isn't an inquisition. This is two friends--*two new friends*--clearing the air. What do you think?"

"I think that's why I liked you the first time I saw you, Miss Tera Morton," he said. "Okay, the Bottomless Cup it is. What time?"

"How much time do you need?"

"I could meet you there in about, oh...half an hour?"

"I'll be there."

###

At her first sight of Cameron, a lot of Tera's suspicions evaporated like mists at sunrise. He waved and smiled as he walked up the street, and Tera saw the same man with whom she'd fallen into such an easy friendship--not a mysterious stranger whose motives she mistrusted. He kissed her on the cheek, guiding her into the quiet coffee bar. After getting large Styrofoam containers of coffee and an assortment of donuts, they headed across the road to the nature trail.

Their first few minutes walking along the shaded trail were spent getting up to speed on each others' lives. It seemed a likely way to begin, since neither of them really wanted to rush right into talking about the dream, Dr. Speller, or any of that stuff yet. Cameron proudly announced that he'd finally pulled the last few pages of his dissertation together, and was ready to deliver it to the printers. Tera expressed the appropriate congratulations, but was more than a little puzzled; *if his dissertation was already finished...then why did he need to be at her session with Dr. Speller? If not for research purposes, what was his involvement?*

"Cameron, that's great," she said, patting him on the back, "it's the best feeling in the world to have all that behind you, I know."

"Yep. Just a few loose ends left, that's all."

"Well, there's always a 'loose end' or two with research, right?," she asked. "Something that might lead into a whole new area or different slant on the area you've explored?" *Yeah,* she thought, *that's it...he must be planning on using info he gets from me for a different study.*

"Yeah...but I'm about ready to give *this* field a rest, at least for the time being."

"Why? I mean, I could tell when we first talked about this that you really love it; when you find a research project you enjoy, you should press further with it--you know that."

"I also know that you have to step back from things, Tera, when you find you can't be objective about them anymore," Cameron replied, a deeply contemplative look in his eyes. Tera sensed where he was going next; it was time to *really* talk. She let him lead the conversation.

"Come on...let's sit down over there, " Cameron said, gesturing toward a shaded bench near a quiet creek. They sat in silence for a few moments just listening to the swiftly moving, shallow water as it ran past them. Finally, he spoke.

"You know, Tera...it was years ago--*too* many years ago--that I started this research; and no one could have told me it would have led to...all this."

Tera remained silent, though unanswered questions burned in her mind like stones baking in the desert sun. Cameron continued.

"When I met Dr. Mullins at that conference in Atlanta, I had only a seed of the study I wanted to do...hey, I wasn't even sure *why* I wanted to do it...but when Dr. Mullins invited me to come to Roosevelt and introduced me around in the Department of Philosophy and Religion...I was on top of the world."

"Of course...that was a great opportunity; a great honor."

"Yes...but with any honor there's also great responsibility attached; the responsibility of always acting with integrity, Tera...and making sure you do right by other people who might be involved in what you're doing."
"People like...who?"
"People whose lives are touched by what you do; in my case, my research participants. When they entrust their fears, and their secrets, and their confusion to me...I have the responsibility of treating that information with respect. And where our lives overlap, where our lives affect each other because of what *I've* uncovered...it's my job to help *them* first, rather than serve my own ends. Or there'll be hell to pay."
"Cameron...*what are you talking about?*" She had thought at first that he was just rambling about how he'd become a doctoral candidate...but this was much more.
"Ever heard of 'karma', Tera?"
"Yeah. That's the idea that what you put out into the universe returns to you."
"Exactly. But it's more than an idea; it's reality. And when you put something bad out there, that evil will return again and again...until you finally learn from it, and do something to change the karma."
Tera felt uneasy; something about the direction of Cameron's conversation didn't sit well with her. *But she had come to find out the truth...she had to know where he was leading.*
"So...do you have...bad karma, something you need to change?"
Cameron chuckled softly to himself.
"Of course I do, Tera. Most of us do. That's one of the reasons we return...if you don't correct it in *this* life, you have to set things right in a life to come."
"Does your karma involve me? Or River?"
Cameron toyed with his empty coffee cup, a faraway

look in his eyes; he turned to Tera and smiled.
"Everybody I know or have ever known is involved in my karma in one way or another. That's true for everyone."
"Now you're being mysterious."
"I know. And I'm sorry. But yes, you and River are involved."
"How?"
"Let's just say for now that...it has to do with forgiveness."
Knowing what response she'd likely get, Tera still asked the obvious.
"Who needs to forgive who, and for what?"
"Tera...you really need to wait until tomorrow, when you meet with Dr. Speller--"
"Dammit, Cameron!," she exploded. She wondered which was creepier--the actual dream, or the way Cameron and River were acting *about* the dream.
"I've already had that same speech from River, and now from you! *Why* can't anybody just give me a straight answer for once?"
She got up from the bench, pacing impatiently. At the same instant she began to feel that meeting Cameron was a mistake, fear nagged at her like a splinter under a fingernail. *What could be so terrible that it had to be cloaked in such secrecy?* Cameron could see her anxiety. He had to say something; some explaining was definitely called for, and he wanted to show her there was nothing to fear...not any more.
"Tera...did River tell you that I...I've known who you were since the day we met?"
Tera stopped pacing, looking at him strangely.
"Yes...yeah, he did. I wondered about that; about why you never said anything."
"What was there to say? You didn't know about any of this stuff, not even how River felt about you. I had to wait, at least until after Riv spoke to you...and after

that, well...*you* know the rest. You and River have been kicking it so tough...you and I just never saw or talked to each other. Until now."
"Yeah. Forgive me if I seem to be back-tracking over things that shouldn't make a difference any more, but...I just wanna understand. About *you*, I mean. Correct me if I'm wrong, but...when we met, it seemed like...like--"
"Like I was hitting on you. I was," Cameron smiled self-consciously.
"I could understand that, at the point we *first* met; but why after? When you *knew* my connection to River...why?"
"Why does anyone try to get or hold onto something or someone that's not for them, Tera? It was selfishness. I was interested, and....at the time, that was all that seemed to matter."
Tera listened, her mind forming a question she knew she'd never ask. *If that's true, then why did you back off?* And, as if in response to her unspoken query, he answered.
"Believe me, it wasn't easy to change my way of thinking," he said taking one of her small hands in his. "But I *have* learned a couple of things: one, that *every* attraction between two people doesn't have to be expressed through sex, and two, *sometimes*, no matter what you might be feeling, you just have to do what's right."
Tera again felt that inexplicable closeness with Cameron so strongly it made her next question unnecessary; she already knew the answer.
"You're someone from my past, aren't you? That's why it feels like we already know each other....isn't it?"
"Yes, Tera."
"I *knew* it! I knew there was more to it than just our paths crossing because of your research."
A fleeting, sad smile crossed Cameron's lips; *Tera had*

no idea how much more there was to it. He released her hand.
"Tell me...how well did we know each other?," she pressed. "Were we relatives? Friends? Just acquaintances?"
She was excited that some of her questions seemed to be getting answers at last; but Cameron's cryptic comment put the brakes on her enthusiasm to know more.
"Tera...sometimes our roles in past lives were very different from what they are now; I mean, a brother today could have been your mother in another life...a friend today could have once been your worst enemy."
It sounded ominous.....
"Not exactly a comforting thought, is it? I mean...if that's true, then...how do you know who to trust, Cameron? What if you're *loving* somebody you should beware of? Or *trusting* in somebody you shouldn't...?" Her own questions brought fear rising into her throat in a rush that nearly choked her. *Oh, God,* she thought...*River!* River had said something similar, something about having no guarantee that their relationship in the present would be the same as it was in the past. *What if...what if River was someone she should not fully trust? What if Cameron, the man sitting right next to her, was somebody she should fear?* It took everything in Tera to subdue her paranoid fantasies of River and Cameron delivering her bound and gagged to this Dr. Speller, who would then cart her off to the nearest MHI. Her thoughts must have drifted momentarily, because when Cameron touched her shoulder, she almost leapt out of her skin. He apologized for scaring her; but by then--in fact, long before then--Tera had gotten tired of the mysterious half-answers and double apologies she kept getting from him, from River..."sorry" just wasn't good enough.

"Well Cameron, if you didn't *mean* to scare me, what did you mean? How did you *think* I was gonna feel?"
"I guess...I didn't. *Think*, that is. I was just talking; that's my whole problem sometimes. Remember a while back when I told you that opening my mouth and just letting things jump out comes real easy for me...but when it's time to be serious, it's hard for me *not* to beat around the bush...say things that don't help. That is all this is; I shouldn't have said what I said, especially since it's making you think and draw conclusions that...well, that just aren't true."
"And you just <u>know</u> what I'm thinking, right?"
"It doesn't take a genius to know you're thinking I don't mean you any good; or that you're not sure whether to trust me, or Dr. Speller...maybe even River, for that matter."
Tera's eyes widened in surprise.
"River loves you, Tera...and you don't have anything to fear from me or Dr. Speller."
Cameron's words were so sincere she couldn't help but be convinced he told the truth. Still, she was ready to go; this fact-finding mission of hers had left her with more questions than she'd started with.
"I believe that, Cameron; but I think this whole thing was a mistake. I came here with some questions...but now I'm not sure I want them answered--not by you, not by River...not by Dr. Speller, either."
"But that's just it, Tera--you *do* want answers. And you know what? *You already know what those answers are*; deep inside you know, but you're afraid."
"Afraid of what?"
"You're scared of how reconciling the past might affect the present; that your ties to the past might hold you back and keep you from making peace with your life today."
The truth of Cameron's words struck a chord somewhere inside her; she was agitated without

realizing why. She felt as though she'd been wedged into a hot, dark corner. Reflexively, she struck out at the source of her discomfort--Cameron.

"What are you scared of, huh?," she countered.

Cameron just looked at her and smiled.

"I'm afraid of the same things you are: that the past won't let me move forward...that I won't have the chance to make things right...that I might have to do this all over again if past wrongs can't be corrected."

"Whew," Tera exhaled deeply, running her hands through her tightly-curled hair. She still didn't understand Cameron's involvement; strangely, her wariness of him had lessened even though he'd given her *more* reason for suspicion. Still, she couldn't deny the connection she felt with him; she could no more mistrust him than her own little brother Xavier.

Maybe he and River were right; maybe the help and guidance of someone like Dr. Speller was needed to get through this.

"Well," she whispered, "I won't say I need more to be explained--you already know that. But I guess I have to accept...finding the explanations when it's time. And with Dr. Speller's help. So...so now, I just..."

"You just *wait*, Tera. Until tomorrow. And you *trust*, too--trust that all of us want what's best for you."

Cameron gave her a quick, reassuring hug as they headed back up the trail to their starting point.

"I'd be lying if I said it was gonna be easy for you tomorrow...but you don't have to fear what you might find, Tera."

"Just your *saying* that makes me scared," she answered.

It was so strange; her mind had an awareness of danger, but her body wouldn't respond accordingly. The whole situation *should* have sent her running and screaming and tearing out her hair--but instead she was calm...as though she'd been sedated against fear.

"That's not my intent...", he mumbled.

He couldn't say another word. There had been a number of times when Cameron had wanted to say more, so much more; he'd wanted to tell her everything. But he clearly understood that it was not the way things should happen. Telling her *his* version of what had happened rather than allowing her own memory to reconstruct the event--in its entirety--would have been wrong.

He couldn't cheat karma by influencing Tera's reaction to what she found. He knew River had also told her everything he could *admit* to knowing; all he could do now was hope that, when Tera recalled everything, when *every detail* came back clearly to her troubled mind...her choice would free them all, instead of damning them to repeat the past.

"Cameron," Tera said softly, shaking him out of his deep thoughts. "What's going to happen tomorrow?"

"I don't know, Tera...but once you know *everything*...you'll know what to do."

###

When Tera got back home she was greeted with the sight of River leaning against his car in her driveway. He was a most welcome sight, too; when he saw her, a dazzling smile replaced the thoughtful, concerned look he'd worn before. Tera rushed into his arms as though she hadn't seen him in weeks instead of just hours ago. The time she'd just spent with Cameron had added more confusion than it had cleared up; *a good dose of River was just what she needed.*

"Hey, baby," she murmured against his cheek.

"Hey. I know I said I'd call later; but when I called you were out, and I...well, I assumed you had gone to see--"

"Cameron. You assumed right."

"So...you talked."

"Mm-hmm."

"And?"

"And nothing. Let's go inside."

River flashed a quick smile as they walked together up to the house. *Damn*, he thought; he could have kicked himself for starting right in, quizzing her about Cameron. Patience had been the key up to that point--he'd just have to exercise more of it, let Tera handle things in her own way...and talk when *she* felt like it. Once inside, he drew her into a close, loving embrace.

"I'm sorry, Tee. I shouldn't be sweating you about this; it's just that I...baby, I just want everything to be alright with you...with us."

"I know, River. Me too," she whispered. "But you know what? I'm not scared like I was before."

"No? I'm glad... but what happened? Was it something Cameron said--"

"No, it wasn't; and it's not like he gave me any more answers than I already had, either. I don't know...but I feel like...like it's going to be fine."

She buried her face in River's thick hair, letting a feeling of peace descend on her.

What she'd told him hadn't been exactly the truth--she *was* a little frightened. Still, she felt the conviction of her words: somehow, everything would be fine. She didn't know what the next twenty-four hours would bring; but she knew that it would include an end to the confusion and anxiety and fear...and a new beginning. River held onto her, breathing a sigh of relief. He wanted to confirm her belief that everything would turn out fine, and tell her that she was in good hands with Dr. Speller; he wanted to tell her that when the time came for her to decide what to do, he would be there to guide her. *But that's not the way it would go. He could not tell her what to feel or to do; all he or Dr. Speller or Cameron could do was bear witness...and hope for the best.*

They spent the rest of the afternoon and early evening doing 'normal' things. Tera buzzed around cleaning up the place while River put on some music

and started in trying to sort Tera's mountain of laundry.
"Hey, woman,"he teased, "what do you do, just buy new clothes when the old ones get dirty?"
"Ha, ha, Mr. Funny-Man. For your information, my laundry *never* piles up...that is, unless something distracts me from keeping it up."
"Hmm. And just *what* might that 'something' be?"
"Oh, I don't know, let's see...it's a feeling I get sometimes; and I've been getting this feeling a lot lately, you know?"
"A feeling?"
"Mm-hmm. Makes me feel like my arms and legs just turn to Jell-O. Can't do a thing about it, either."
"Sounds serious."
"It is, it is! When it hits me, I'm just...out for the count; helpless, know what I mean?"
"Definitely. Same thing happens to me, too."
"Really? Well, what do you think causes it, Riv?"
"This," he whispered, covering her mouth with a soul-melting kiss. Tera was glad she'd just finished tidying up, because River's moist lips on hers made her forget about dishes and mop buckets.
"Mmm," she purred, "I think you're right, 'cause it just happened to me."
"Man, it's even worse that I thought, Tee--*it's catching*!"
"I know, it's terrible. What can we do about it?," she asked mock-seriously.
"You know, sometimes the *cause* of this affliction is also the *cure*..."
"You think so?," she asked innocently, reaching under his shirt and running her slim fingers across the hairs on his taut stomach.
"*Ahhh....I'm almost sure of it*," he sighed, tightening his arms around her.
"I don't know, baby...what if it's the opposite, and the cure is the cause?"
"Tell you what," River said, scooping her up into his

arms, "let's go find out which is which."
"What if we never find out?"
"That's alright, baby...it's the *effort* that counts; and I'm willing to really work at it...even if it takes all night."

###

It took as much restraint as Tera possessed to stifle a cry of fright as she passed from dream-horror into wakefulness. Her tightly-clenched body was as taut as the skin on a drum, and her heart sped as though she'd been running a forty-meter dash. When she woke up and realized she was in the safety of her own bedroom, tears of gratitude pooled in the corners of her eyes and coursed slowly down her face. She had never been more frightened in her life; the latest occurrences of the dream had gripped her in a terror she'd never known. Almost afraid to move, she slowly turned to River and was thankful beyond words that her trembling hadn't awakened him. She couldn't have dealt with him seeing her in such a state. She watched him for a few moments. Satisfied that he was still asleep, she turned away and stuffed a corner of her pillow into her mouth and cried; *Dear God,* she prayed, *let this end! Please let this Dr. Speller, or Cameron, or somebody be able to help.* Tera was nauseous. The taste of fear was sharp on her tongue...and the events of the dream came back to taunt again...and again....and again.

Hannah struggled with the heavy buckets of water she'd drawn from the well to carry to the kitchen for Mercy Lee, the cook. She'd stopped often to set them down and rub her aching hands together where the bucket handles had cut painfully into her palms. Hannah finally reached the back door and set the buckets on the porch, relieved to have finished that task. There was no one to help her with it, since old Mattie wasn't able to carry anything heavier than Master Walton's hot toddy tray, and the new cook

Mercy Lee was too busy cooking for the household.

Hannah looked in the window and saw that Mercy was nowhere around; she was just about to lift the heavy buckets one last time to haul them into the kitchen when she turned to see old Walton coming up the porch steps. He smiled, taking one of the buckets from her, and carried it in. He always seemed to be doing something nice like that; still, his kindness made Hannah somewhat wary. She had learned early to mistrust seemingly kind deeds from the whites. Overall, though, Hannah had considered herself relatively lucky to have been bought by this white man. After discovering that she had not been bought for his bed wench, and then meeting Mason, she realized that her lot as a slave could have been much, much worse--though freedom, of course, would have been much, much better.

Walton was certainly not the worst master Hannah had seen. But something about the way he looked at her sometimes made her flesh crawl. As quickly as she'd had that thought, Hannah dismissed it, reasoning that Walton was probably too old to still be trying to sleep with all the slave women on his plantation--he must have been fifty-five, maybe even sixty. Besides, he had given her to Mason. None of that really mattered, though. Hannah knew she would rather endure a beating than have that old white man touch her. She calmed her anxious feelings, telling herself that she was safe from any advances from him.

It was a complete surprise when she felt his hands reach around from behind her and grab her breasts, squeezing them roughly. She'd been taught all her life to obey the whims of her master, but when it came to unwelcome demands placed on her body, Hannah reacted as she had many times in the past: she wrenched free, turned, and slapped the man's leering face. As soon as she did it, she knew it was a mistake;

old Walton would surely have her beaten for it. He just stood looking at her, an evil, lustful look clouding his beady, gray eyes.
"I like a gal that fights me," he breathed raggedly. "More fun that way!"
Hannah managed to control her disgust enough to speak civilly.
"Please, Mr. Walton sir," she said evenly, "let me be! I didn't mean to hit you sir, it's just I... I got my moon time, and you don't want no gal who's having her moon time, and--"
"Stop lying, gal! I know that ain't true, 'cause I have old Hester down at the quarters report to me about stuff like that, so I can know what wenches are knocked up," he hissed, moving closer to the retreating girl. "She told me just the other day that you and Lily and Ellie Jean been done with that business a week or more, so don't go lying to me."
Hannah stared at the floor, fighting to control her growing anger and hatred.
"What's the matter, gal, savin' it all up for that black boy o' yours? Think you too good for the one what bought-ya?"
He stepped to her, trying to grab her hands but Hannah slipped easily from his grasp, keeping the kitchen table between them. Each time Hannah had been bought and sold, she'd lived in fear of days such as this, and knew the routine all too well: some white man would buy her, then try to possess her body--and when she resisted, she risked being beaten, or sold, or both. A couple of her former masters had succeeded in getting what they'd wanted from her; but both had decided that bedding her wasn't worth the scratches and battle scars she'd leave for their wives to find. Fighting back had earned her a few scars too, but her beatings had never been severe enough to lower her 'purchase price'; and each former owner would quietly sell her off to the next without

letting him know <u>*why*</u> *he wanted to get rid of her. She cautiously circled the table, wondering which would be her fate this time. Somehow, her foot became entangled in her long skirts and she tumbled, giving old Walton the advantage he needed; he pinned her flailing arms to the floor as she fought viciously to escape. Her strongest efforts weren't enough to overpower him, leaving her only one weapon with which to fight: a strong knee to the groin. Hannah pulled away quickly and regained her feet as Walton lay crumpled on the kitchen floor, doubled over in pain.*

"You little black bitch!," he screamed, "who the hell you think you are? You won this round, wench, but you won't win the war…and I'm gonna enjoy makin' you holler!"

The damage was already done; Hannah had nothing to lose by unleashing her anger and telling him just how much she despised him.

"You nasty old man!," she cried, "you ain't got enough to make <u>*no*</u> *woman holler! Why don't you get you a wife, somebody who wants you, and leave me alone?"*

"What? I can do what I damn well please with you! You ain't no different than any other wench."

"Yes sir, you <u>*do*</u> *own me; but sir, you ain't* <u>*never*</u> *gonna make me. No matter how hard you try, I'll fight you."*

"What??!," he sputtered. "Why, you uppity little slut! I'll have Tiny string you up and I'll whip all the meat off your bones myself, gal!"

"Go'on and beat me, then," Hannah said, fearful yet determined. "Won't be my first time."

She dreaded the lash but knew that she was too valuable for this old man to have her beaten to death. No...he was too shrewd a businessman to throw away his 'investment' just like that. She mentally prepared herself for the beating to come, thankful at least that he'd said nothing about selling her.

"Alright then, you smart-mouthed little whore. You'll be

sorry you had so much to say when my whip lays your back open," he hissed. Even as he lay there on the floor incapacitated, he was still as frightening as a viper coiled to strike.

"Get the hell out of here!," he shouted, and Hannah ran out of the house and back to the women's quarters as quickly as her legs would carry her. Safe on her own rough mattress and winded from running, she thought about what had happened...and she was afraid. Not of the beating itself, for she suffered a few of them in her lifetime; she feared how deeply it might affect Mason. There was no way she could avoid telling him about it.

Even if she said nothing, he would see her tied to the whipping post whenever that fateful day came. What would he do? What <u>*could*</u> *he do, besides hurt inside from helplessness to stop it? Why couldn't she have held her tongue, maybe just...gave in like the others?*

"No!," she whispered vehemently; <u>*why*</u> *couldn't that old bastard have just kept his hands to himself? He already owned her as though she were a horse, or a dog, or a cow--and he used her and the others to do his work, like they were mere farm animals. What gave him the right to violate her body, too?*

Things looked bad, and Hannah's mind turned over with fear of what might happen. Once she'd managed to calm down, she decided not to say anything to Mason until the day Tiny came to take her to the whipping post; that way, she reasoned she could make up a story that Mason would believe, something about broken dishes or a burnt meal--anything but the real reason why the old man was having her whipped. Every man had his threshold, and Hannah feared Mason would reach his if he knew that Walton wanted her beaten because she wouldn't let him touch her. As it was, she was still afraid of what Mason might do to old Walton if he hurt her. Hannah lay on her bed, fighting a growing sense of foreboding as she realized that, no matter what, the incident with Walton would have a terrible outcome.

The frightening recollections from before had been bad enough; the ugly reality of old Walton's attempt to rape Hannah only made things worse...and the returning memories rushed in like flood waters.

Hannah's nerves stayed on edge as one day, then two, then a week passed without anyone coming to the women's quarters to drag her away to be whipped.

She went about her daily routine as usual--as though she could have done otherwise--and said nothing to Mason. Each day that passed without incident only increased her anxiety, but she told herself that perhaps the worst was over; maybe the old man had just decided to let it go. She remembered the rank odor of liquor on his breath. Maybe the old fool had even forgotten what happened! She'd tried to stay out of his way after that, but still saw him in passing, and he seemed like his old self. He never singled her out or so much as glared at her, nothing...but Hannah knew that he had not forgotten. Not by a long shot. If anything, his bleary gray eyes still glittered with longing, just as before. But he didn't say or do anything...and that was what counted, she supposed. As the days stretched into another week, Hannah had reluctantly convinced herself that the ordeal was over...until Mason shattered her hopes with the news that he'd overheard their master's plan to sell her!

Hannah's heart sank at the thought of being sold away from Mason. He was her love, her life...much of her existence had seemed meaningless before the day they met; what would she do without him? Either of them could live alone--they had up until the day she came to Walton's plantation--but why did they have to part, just because she had fought against that old man's desire to ravage her body?

Tera could feel Hannah's turmoil and her fear as she and Mason plotted together, then escaped into the night; the fervent hope that she and her love would actually evade their pursuers was dashed as the men overtook them near the foothills. And in the end, when she relived the sensation of Hannah being shattered by the rifle blast and her spirit drifting free of her lifeless, torn body...Tera felt the presence again--insistent, sorrowful, anguished. This time, it had enveloped her with such sadness, such a feeling of regret...what did it mean? *What did it want of her?* The violent swirl of emotions exhausted Tera.
At last, her breathing slowed and she was able to control and stop the constant flow of tears; she would count the hours until time to see Dr. Speller.

River lay quietly, fighting to keep up his pretense of sleep. He'd spent part of the early morning watching his darling Tera sleep; loving the way her nostrils flared as she breathed, and the fluttering of her eyelids as she chased sweet dream images. Suddenly, her eyebrows had creased with fear, her breath becoming ragged and irregular...and River knew that it was the dream again. At first he'd held her, hoping the closeness of his body might comfort her, but she wouldn't wake up; she lay in the grip of frightening, surreal visions that set her trembling and struggling against his embrace. It broke River's heart to see her in such distress, but there was little he could do...except feign sleep, and preserve her dignity. River knew Tera would feel even worse knowing he'd seen her at her weakest.

It was getting harder to keep still. He shifted his weight and moaned as though coming out of a deep sleep. Tera eased away from him and was off to the shower before he'd opened his eyes. The minutes Tera spent in the shower gave them both a chance to

unwind from the stress the dream had caused and recharge their energy for the final ordeal to come. When Tera came out of the bathroom, she saw River lying in bed with his palms tucked behind his head, watching her; he smiled.
"Good morning, beautiful," he whispered.
"Good morning," she answered. She knew that even in the semi-darkened room, River could see the puffiness of her eyes and know that she'd been crying. And more than she could ever say, she was grateful that he never said a word about it. River got up and walked to her; his arms around her chased away the night's terror...she felt safe. His tenderness and understanding almost made her cry again, but the feeling was too comforting, too welcoming for tears.
"In just a few hours, Tee, all this is gonna be like a dim memory; trust me, I know."

CHAPTER NINE

Mercifully, 4:00 finally came, and it was time to take the drive into the city to see Dr. Speller. Since it was such a warm and humid day, Tera had showered again before dressing. It was just her woman's pride, Tera supposed; but when she thought of those pictures she'd seen of people under hypnosis, lying limp and shining with perspiration, well...she'd decided *she* wasn't gonna go out like that. No way. There was probably nothing she could do about the 'limp' part, but she was *not* going to be limp *and* sweaty. She was dressed comfortably in her long sundress with the cris-crossed straps and white seams. Her freshly trimmed hair lay in soft, crisp waves. She was just about to put on a trace of lipstick and blush, then stopped. *Idiot*, she chided herself, *this ain't no photo shoot! You're going to get your head screwed on straight, not pose for Essence.* Tera's laughter released a lot of pent-up tension, and brought River into the room to see what was happening. He smiled, watching her change large gold hoop earrings for tiny rhinestone studs.
"Hey, woman, you look *good*...is everything alright?"
"Yep," she chuckled, "it is now."

###

Tera gladly accepted River's offer to drive, and settled back behind her ever-present sunglasses, watching the fast Dan Ryan expressway traffic zoom past them. River was doing about 70mph, but traffic in the fast lane still passed them as thought they were standing still. As they took the Garfield exit and began to drive east to Dr. Speller's house in Hyde Park, Tera pulled out her pack of Marlboros. If ever there was a time she felt like smoking a cigarette, *this* was it. She lit up without so much as glancing in River's direction. She knew he didn't like her smoking.

"Hey, Tee--give me one of those," he said.
"Huh?" Tera was incredulous. "Give you one of what?"
"Gimme one of those smokes."
"You're kidding, right?"
"Nope. Can I have one, please?"
Reluctantly, Tera tapped one out of the pack and passed it to him. It looked so funny perched between his tight lips, she almost laughed.
"Light, please?," he asked in a muffled voice.
Tera held the lighter to the end of his cigarette as he took a serious drag, and then coughed.
"Thanks," he wheezed, barely able to get the word out. "Ah, yeah...nothing like a good smoke to quiet your nerves, right?"
"River...what in the world are you doing?"
"Just trying to unwind, baby...just trying to unwind."
"River Jordan Bennett...this is nuts! What are you trying to prove? Do you know how crazy you look?"
"Yep," he hacked before throwing the cigarette out the open window. "That's exactly my point. As crazy as I look to you, *that's* how crazy you look to me. I know there are some things riding you and you're not over the hump yet, but cigarettes aren't gonna get you there, baby; that's not you. If you were already a serious smoker, well...I'd *still* be trying to encourage you to quit, but I'd understand. *This* I don't understand. Anybody who can smoke once every two or three weeks can stop altogether."
Tera smiled self-consciously, crushing out her cigarette in the ashtray.
"That's better," River said gently. "Now just relax; all of this will be behind you soon."
It can't be soon enough, Tera thought as she settled deeply into the seat, staring out the window.

###

Dr. Speller's ivy-covered house sat on the corner of the block next to a dead-end street, giving it an air of seclusion even for Hyde Park which was one of the quieter Chicago neighborhoods. The tree-lined street was shady and tranquil; had it not been for all the occupied parking spaces, one might have gotten the impression that no one lived around there at all. Fortunately, Dr. Speller had a small driveway, and River pulled up next to the house.

"There's no car here, Riv," Tera noted, "maybe he isn't home." *She wished.*

"He's there. Dr. Speller doesn't own a car, doesn't drive," he said. "He says he never cared to learn...didn't need the hassle, especially since public transportation is so available."

They got out of the car and started up the steps.

"Not that I'm complaining--it saved us some steps--but why the driveway if he doesn't drive?"

"It came with the house!," Dr. Speller chuckled, standing on the porch.

Tera was startled; she hadn't noticed him there and was a little embarrassed that he'd heard her question.

"Oh...hello."

"Hello, Tera. I'm Dr. Abraham Speller," he smiled, reaching for her hand.

"Hi, Dr. Speller," River said. "Well, here she is."

"Indeed. And you didn't exaggerate, River; she *is* lovely."

Tera smiled nervously, but felt strangely at ease upon meeting this man whose very name had conjured up big-time anxiety.

"Come on inside, dear. Let's talk for awhile first," he said. He led them in, walking slowly and steadily with the help of an intricately carved, gilt-handled mahogany cane.

Dr. Speller was a slight man, no taller than Tera.

His soft hair was pulled back and braided into a long silvery plait that reached well below his shoulders. The old man's piercing eyes, long, sharp nose, and walnut-brown complexion spoke to his Native American and African heritage. Though delicately built, he didn't seem at all fragile and walked confidently with the help of his cane.

Once in the living room, he gestured for Tera and River to sit. River placed a restraining hand over Tera's when he saw her about to stand and help the proud old man pull his heavy oak armchair closer to the couch where they sat. Dr. Speller settled into the chair and faced Tera; a gentle smile spread slowly across his handsome, weathered face.

"Do you know me, child?," he asked.

"No...no sir, I don't."

"Good! Good. There's absolutely no reason why you *should*; just making sure there are
no confused identities or anything," he said.

A skittish smile remained plastered on Tera's face; *at least he's a pleasant-looking weirdo*, she thought. She looked around the room.

There were entire walls of bookshelves, lined from floor to ceiling with an amazing collection of books. Her eyes were drawn to the mantle, which was decorated with an unusual assortment of artifacts and framed photographs; one picture in particular held her attention. It was a very, very old daguerreotype--the kind that looked like it belonged in a museum exhibit--of an old Native American man in traditional tribal dress. His brow and cheeks were lined with age; deep crow's feet etched the corners of his sharp, knowing eyes. In his right hand he clutched a staff adorned with long feathers. He appeared to be even older than the man who sat facing her, but there was a decided resemblance between them. Maybe that's why he looked so familiar to Tera, but...no; there was

something else. Behind the camouflage of age, Tera still recognized the strong, proud features of the man in the daguerreotype... he had once fought to save her life.
"Tall Bear," she whispered.
"Yes," Dr. Speller smiled; "my great, great, great-grandfather."
"That's amazing," Tera smiled. "I can see the resemblance."
"He and I have a lot in common, it seems," Dr. Speller continued, "long ago, he led the way for you; now it is my duty to help you free yourself."
The doorbell rang, and Tera jumped; it was Cameron. Dr. Speller rose from his seat, motioning for River and Tera to stay put, and walked slowly to the door. Cameron entered the room following the old man. Tera thought he looked ill-at-ease, which made her even more nervous. Cameron smiled wanly, which did nothing to calm Tera's anxiety, either. She didn't know why, but something about his being there was slightly menacing. Dr. Speller sensed the change in her; he spoke.
"It's good to see you again, Cameron. Have a seat with us...and stop looking like the world's coming to an end. Don't be afraid; you either," he said gently, returning his attention to Tera. "Open your heart...and I promise you, this is the day that will set you free." Tera nodded in agreement, like she'd been spoken to in a foreign language. She didn't have the slightest idea what Dr. Speller referred to, but was hopeful that it wouldn't be much longer before the whole ordeal was over. She no longer questioned Cameron's involvement; she was ready for *whatever* it might take to clarify this mystery and rid her of the dream's torment. Dr. Speller took her hand.
"Come, child. It's time."
River smiled at her and nodded, gesturing for her to follow the old man into the next room. The four of

them proceeded into a spacious room which was semi-darkened by heavy drapes at the windows. Dr. Speller led her over to a large sofa done in earth hues and sat her down. She looked up at River and Cameron; their faces were as somber as she felt. Dr. Speller smiled once more, staring at the two men from behind hooded eyes.

"Light those three candles on that table there," he said, pointing to the fresh white tapers in brass candle holders. He chuckled softly at the mystified look on their faces.

"There's nothing mystical about those candles...I just *like* them! And I wanted to give you something to do, you look like you're about to jump out of your skin. After you light them, have a seat on that other couch there; I'll call you when it's time." He turned his attention to Tera.

"Lie back, child. Trust me, and don't be afraid."

Tera did as he'd instructed. She did trust him, but couldn't help the surge of fear that coursed through her limbs. It was all she could do to settle back on the couch instead of leaping to her feet and running out of the house. The old man's kind face carried the spirit of the man she'd once entrusted with her life many lifetimes ago; this distant son of Tall Bear gave Tera the courage she needed to cross the final bridge between past and present, and bind the loose threads of her life together.

Dr. Speller's clear, sharp eyes immobilized her; it was as though Tera had been sedated. Slowly, Dr. Speller lifted a small, shiny object before Tera. Reflected light from the candles glinted off its edges, making it appear that he held a palm full of stars.

Tera was fascinated; she wanted to reach out for the sparkling object...but her relaxed muscles would not obey. Dr. Speller brought it closer...closer... The light intensified, changed color, and branched off into slender beams that opened the center of the glowing object.

Suddenly, Tera saw her face reflected in the center surrounded by the shards of light; with a shock of realization, she saw that it was her mirror, *Hannah's mirror*, that Dr. Speller held. *How did he get it?*, she wondered momentarily; but her relaxed state wouldn't allow her thoughts to drift toward anything too puzzling. The woman in the mirror returned her dreamy smile.

"Do you see her?," Dr. Speller asked gently. "Look closely, child; tell me who you see."

Tera focused on the mirror, wondering why he would ask so obvious a question; it was her reflection, of course. She was seeing *herself*.

"Look very closely, Tera...look beneath the surface."

She obeyed, staring at the light-framed reflection. The dark brown eyes staring back were her own. Her questioning face stared back at her like an image shimmering off the surface of a lake; and as she continued to concentrate on the image, it rippled, dispersed, changed.

Tera no longer saw a disembodied face, rather, she saw a full-length view of a woman, as though she watched an event on a small-screen television. Even without the long, rough skirt and bodice, Tera would have recognized the woman in the mirror; it was Hannah Forrester. The image grew larger and larger still...until Tera no longer just *looked* into the mirror--*she was inside it.* She was no longer *close* to Hannah, she *was* Hannah. She wanted to be afraid of what was happening to her, wanted to cry out, to react in some way...but she could feel Dr. Speller's hand wrapped protectively around her own...and she knew that she was not alone. The dream she now walked through--the same dream that had shadowed her for months on end--no longer seemed as confusing and frightening; she had someone with her, and she held onto his hand, hoping that this journey they took across the surreal dream scape would be the last.

It was as though Tera wore Hannah's body like a cloak; she moved around seeing Hannah's world through her own eyes...recounted the terrible memories.

Tera moaned in agitation and fear as she saw, through Hannah's eyes, Mason's back as he guided his horse toward the foothills where they'd believed they would be safe from their hated pursuers; the morning of death grew steadily brighter on the barren plain.

She felt the gentle walking motion of her horse, a calming movement that belied the violence that would follow.

Dr. Speller had long since released her hand; he would be there for her if she needed him, but for her own sake, he could not lead her through the memories step-by-step. She had to recall them herself...unaided.

As Hannah had known they would, the shots rang out. There was nothing she could do to calm the terrified horse as the beast reared and tossed her to the ground like a pitiful rag doll. Mason had wheeled around on his horse, reacting as quickly as he could...a heartbeat too slow to save Hannah from the bullets that cruelly pierced her when she reached for Mason's hand to pull her onto his skittish horse's back. Each pulling stride of the frightened horse caused Hannah's blood and her life to seep slowly away as she clung to Mason's rough jacket; and even in accepting the inevitability of her death on the dusty plain, she wondered why it must be so. She wondered what kind of hatred motivated old Walton to follow and destroy, rather than allow her and Mason the smallest shred of happiness together.

Triumphantly, Hannah realized that she and Mason had indeed made it to the freedom of the foothills where Tall Bear and his men fought to protect

them and, in the end, to avenge her mortal wounding.
Tears rolled down Tera's cheeks as she lay on the couch in the cool interior of Dr. Speller's home. Things were coming to her slowly, and clearly...
and she could feel her heart turn over with pain and outrage at the terrible injustice done to her and the one man she had loved forever. As long as possible, Hannah hung onto life, hearing Mason's promises and offering her own pledge of love everlasting, until the dizzying, irresistible pull of the spirit lifted her from Mason's arms, above the grass where she lay with her head resting on his knees, above the pines, above the hills, far from the world...into the void.

She reached out for Mason once, wanting to draw on his strength to bring her back, but it was no use, she was too far from him; with resignation and with a dull pain she could only feel from afar, she accepted the void's embrace...and all was blackness. And in that infinitely quiet place, there was time to ponder what had happened...time to lament...time to accept and move on toward the light, toward the peace. But it was not to be! Hannah was not alone; another was there, one who had recently left earthly life, as she had. One whose anguish and remorse wrapped around her like a shroud, allowing her no rest...who was it?
"Who...who are you?," Tera mumbled, "what do you want?"
The dark void brightened, but not with the tranquil light of daybreak or the perfect, beautiful light of heavenly presence. And what this light revealed was loathsome; it was old Walton. Hannah felt a wave of revulsion pass over her. Why was it that, even in death, she could not escape him? Instead of a deepening of the peace she had felt since the moment of slipping away from her flesh, Hannah could feel anger building inside her spirit...and she knew that she must reckon with old Walton this last time--if she truly wanted to end the cycle

that had caused their paths to cross time and again, life after life, without resolve.

"What is it, you have to tell me! *What do you want?! Who are you??,*" Tera moaned. She was perspiring heavily, despite the coolness of the room. Dr. Speller motioned for River and Cameron to come closer; and he gave a final directive, one neither River nor Cameron was in a hurry to complete.

"Tell her, Cameron," Dr. Speller urged. "Tell her who you are...she needs to know."

Cameron lifted one of Tera's limp hands and felt her stiffen as though she'd been doused with cold water; her eyes snapped open, staring at him ominously.

Dear God, Cameron thought, *she remembers!*

Suddenly, everything was clear to Hannah...everything. She had been given to Mason out of no generosity on Walton's part; he had only wanted to increase his slave population. Seeing her with Mason week after week, though, in a life that should have been only toil and misery--for they were slaves--had stirred envy and lust in the old man's heart. He wanted whatever it was that made them happy despite their servitude while he, despite his wealth and freedom, was not. He wanted Hannah. The greater her rejection, the more determined he was to possess her.

Every effort had proven fruitless, and there was no forcing her unless he intended to kill her...and he didn't want to hurt her. Walton had decided to sell her away from Mason to a neighboring plantation to separate them--and give Walton the bargaining leverage of using promises to see Mason in exchange for what he desired from the girl. Any hope of coercing Hannah in that way was destroyed when she and Mason ran away together, and old Walton had been overcome with jealousy and anger...and fear that they might actually escape.

Madness drove him on in pursuit of the slaves

with one objective in mind: to capture the object of his obsession--Hannah--and kill the one who stood in the way of having her--Mason.

Hannah felt again the impact of the high-caliber rifle bullets as they tore into her, realizing this time that they were not meant for her, but for Mason. She felt again the clinging, begging presence of Walton's spirit as he too was killed by Tall Bear for his vengeful act...and even though she could feel the power of his regret for what he had done, her own spirit was overcome with but one emotion--revenge. Not forgiveness!

She shook off the cloying touch of Walton's spirit, her own vengeance surrounding and smothering him like the ever-tightening coils of a python. Here was the one who had killed her, the one who had robbed her of her precious life with her beloved Mason! Here was the one who had intended to kill Mason...take him away from her, just as his accidental shooting had taken her away from Mason. Hatred boiled over in her spirit; she wanted nothing more than to crush the old, evil one into oblivion.

Adding to the white-heat of Hannah's anger was her realization of the last, pathetic piece of the maddening puzzle. Just as the obsessed old slave master had pursued her to her death, so had he pursued her, life after life...and he was still after her, still seeking forgiveness she would never give!

The beauty he now cloaked himself in didn't change her feelings or inspire any sympathy in Hannah, nor would it sway her from her determination to utterly destroy him, as his obsessive madness had destroyed her many lifetimes ago. He had taken on the form of an angel, but what did that matter? He would not fool her this time.

*Her hatred pressed in on him like a living thing; her spirit gripped his...*just as the semi-conscious Tera gripped Cameron's arm. Tera stared into Cameron's

face, her eyes glittering with hate; despite the handsome countenance, she recognized her adversary...her murderer. *All this time you've stolen from me*, she thought; *but no more...it ends today, when you die...*
"Tera, no!," Cameron shouted, his face contorted in pain. He tried to pull away, but was as helpless as a child trying to pull free. There was something there, some kind of energy in the room...he felt a great weight pressing him from all sides, cutting off his breath. "Tera...*please don't*," he gasped; his lungs felt as though they might burst, and his heart lapsed into an unsteady rhythm.

This was the moment Cameron had feared ever since meeting Tera. Even before Tera told him who she was, there had been an undeniable attraction; when he knew the reason why, he'd done his best to remain at arm's length with her...tried not to impose his will or his feelings on her...something he had failed to do lifetimes before. There had been many chances for reconciliation, but for one reason or another it had never happened.

In lives past, he had obsessively pursued her, even been responsible for her death; on two different occasions, she had killed him; in a few past lives, their paths had never crossed at all, and they'd lived their lives never knowing what was wrong, but feeling that something was left undone; and now, here they were again...a few minutes more, and she would surely kill him, and doom them to repeat this scene again and again...until they arrived at the place that would bring ultimate peace to them both: forgiveness.

It was the one outcome they had never achieved. It was the one outcome they must achieve, or play out this tragic repetition of violent death over and over and over...
As Cameron felt himself slipping from consciousness, he could only pray that this time would be different.

Tera's unblinking eyes stared dispassionately as he slumped to the floor, barely breathing. The crushing energy pressed relentlessly...Cameron's pulse and heartbeat slowed...slowed...Hannah wanted it to stop completely. But in the final moments, when Cameron's life force had diminished to a tiny, flickering flame that could be extinguished in one breath, Hannah found that she could not do it. She wanted to...but she could not kill. Even though hatred and resentment were a bitter brew rising in her throat; even though the sweet taste of revenge would have choked back some of the bitterness...Hannah realized that Cameron's death would do nothing to replace the years she and Mason had lost.

The smothering grasp of her hatred eased, replaced by a deep despair that left Hannah empty. What would happen now? There was no more anger. There was no feeling of revenge. No retribution. Nothing, but the despair of having no driving emotion to motivate her, nor any knowledge of what she should do next.

"Help me," she whispered. "Help me."

Tera was unaware of Cameron's limp body sprawled on the floor beside the couch where she lay. She had no idea how close to death Cameron had hovered, nor that her own hatred and need for revenge had brought him to that brink. All she felt was the pain and desperation of Hannah's soul searching to find its way out of the accursed cycle that had wrought this tragedy for them all, time after time... "help me," Tera moaned; she stared into the mirror in Dr. Speller's hand once again...and felt herself drifting away.

Resting on Mason's knee, looking up into the pines as threads of sunlight glistened through their rough, spiky leaves... Hannah slipped the shackles of her earthly existence.

This time, when she entered the quietude of the

void, everything was different...when Hannah felt the mournful, insistent presence surrounding her, she embraced it rather than resisting or trying to exact revenge. Suddenly, the darkness of the void shifted from absolute blackness to deep midnight, from violet to fuschia, from orange to burnished gold, growing steadily brighter. The illumination was like a new day dawning in her soul.

This time, Instead of the consuming hate that had overtaken her spirit, she felt the conviction of one who does what is right...even when emotion would dictate something different. Her spirit was not dominated by the presence of the other, nor did she submit her will to it...this time, her spirit was calm as she accepted what must be. Revenge and destruction could not bring back even one moment she and Mason had lost. Anger and hatred could not restore the love they had once shared; all of that was in the past...just as old Walton and his cruel acts were in the past.

But Tera and River were in the *present*; what they had found together could be strengthened or torn apart by *her* choices--their choices--in the here and now. Tera's eyes fluttered closed once again and her breathing was peaceful and even.

Hannah saw the broad, grassy field before her with its ancient, weathered oak tree; it was the field where she and Mason used to steal away to be together. Her heart leapt with the joy of recognition as she made out Mason's silhouette against the glowing horizon.

For the first time, he was coming to meet her as the dawn broke--not running back to the quarters before the old master discovered him gone. For the first time, she could see his beautiful face as he smiled and waved to her, stepping across the flower-strewn field. And for the first time, he was not alone. Walking with him was an old man; his proud and stately bearing reminded Hannah of someone...of Tall Bear. And again she felt happiness; just seeing Mason and this companion of his gave Hannah a feeling of well-being...everything was going to be alright, she could feel it.

She ran across the field, mindless of damp grass and pebbles under her bare feet. When she reached Mason, she clung to him fiercely. There was nothing furtive or anxious about this meeting. They were not running from something, rather, they were on their way to something. Mason gently released her, beckoning for her to pick up her belongings and come with him.

Where were they going? Neither Hannah nor Mason knew. Each past attempt to find their way to each other had been thwarted; the road they would finally walk together was new, and neither of them knew the way. But it didn't matter. Somehow, they knew that this time, they would find their common destiny. Hannah picked up the small burlap parcel and stood by Mason's side. The old one, Mason's companion reached out his hand to Hannah.

"Come, my child," he said. "It is time. Let us leave this place."

Together, the three of them began walking across the field, moving in the direction of the rising sun. Hannah paused for a moment, taking a last look over her shoulder. Instinctively, she knew that this would be the last time she'd ever see this place, and she wanted to take something of it with her in memory.

In the darkness, she had never before noticed how generously the purples and the oranges and the buttercup-yellows of the field flowers were scattered. She hadn't ever seen the way butterflies floated and danced in the morning sun. More than ever before, the giant oak seemed to her like a protective grandfather, watching over and providing a place of rest for his weary children.

A mist of unshed tears clouded her eyes as she waved goodbye to the old tree under whose sheltering limbs she had passed many a night. As she turned to rejoin Mason and the old one, Hannah suddenly stopped; something was missing.

"What's wrong, Hannah? I thought you'd be more than ready to leave from here; what you waiting for?," Mason asked.

Hannah's sharp eyes scanned the grassy slope. She patted her bundle of belongings, even searched the pockets of her apron, but she couldn't find it. It had been with her since her sixteenth birthday, a special gift from her mother. Through the worst of times, she had managed to make it through and hold onto it...she was not about to give up on it now.

"Hannah, what is it? It's time to go, honey...we got to go."

Hannah looked away into the distance beyond the old oak. The darkness of a storm was closing in behind them, while the brilliance of morning opened a path in front of them. It was a clear sign, and Hannah knew that she needed to move away from the darkness that had already shrouded too much of her life. She knew that she must leave...but could not. Not without something so precious to her. She dropped her bundle, heading back to the tree...

"No, Hannah, no! We've come too far...don't go back.!"

Mason's words were a distant echo as she walked toward the oak, unmindful of his voice or the approaching storm or anything else as she searched.

"Hannah, please! Whatever it is can't be that important, can it? You and me, we're free now. We can move on now...ain't that the most important thing?," Mason pleaded.

Hannah turned to see Mason and his old companion standing at the top of a small ridge. Dazzling sunlight silhouetted them as they stood waiting for her. Mason was right; she was finally free. They could have what

they'd risked everything for--a life together. And it was what she wanted...but she couldn't leave behind something that had been such an important part of her life for so long. The storm swirled closer and closer, threatening to envelop her, but Hannah stood where she was. And then the old one slowly raised his hand.
"Is this what you seek, child?," he asked.
Hannah could barely hear his voice above the wind. She strained to see beyond the dust and gloom that had suddenly surrounded her. Sunlight glinted off the shiny object in his palm; instantly, Hannah recognized the gift given to her on her sixteenth birthday by her beloved mother...the silver filigreed mirror. Hurriedly, she gathered up her bundle again into her skirt and moved toward the ridge where the two men stood. The high winds whipped around her and dirt stung her eyes; Hannah reached out toward the voice that directed her.
"Come back, child...come back toward the light! Here is my hand...take it."
Hannah groped forward blindly. She was closer, almost close enough to reach the old one's hand...
"Hurry up, Hannah! Hurry up!," Mason shouted over the roaring wind. "We gotta get out of here! This is our last chance!"
Hannah stumbled the last few yards up the ridge; sharp winds whipped at her, finally knocking her to the ground near the old one's feet. She reached out for him.
"Come, child," he said, helping her regain her footing. "It's time for us to leave this place."
Once again, sunlight beamed ahead of them, just on the other side of the ridge. Behind them, the storm swelled and moved, battering at the old oak tree.
"Are you ready to go home?," the old man asked.
Hannah looked back and forth between him and Mason.
"Home?"
"Yes, child...home."

"But I...I don't know the way, I--"
"Don't worry. I know the way. Just take my hand, and follow."
"Mason?"
"It's alright, Hannah," Mason assured her, "I'm right here with you."
Hannah reached out and took the old one's extended hand; suddenly, an unbearable brightness exploded around her, bathing everything in a surreal, blinding light.
"Mason!," she cried, "I'm afraid! I can't see!" Her grip was like iron as she held onto the old man's hand.
"Hannah, you're home," a voice whispered gently. "Open your eyes."
Even before opening her eyes, Tera recognized Dr. Speller's soothing voice. As she slowly opened her eyes, Dr. Speller smiled. He didn't try to disguise the concern and relief in his own eyes as he tried to ease his hand from Tera's painful grip.
"Oh, Dr. Speller...I'm *so* sorry, I--"
"No need to apologize, my dear," he said, massaging his fingers. "I've had worse things happen than a beautiful girl squeezing my hand," he smiled. "How are you feeling?"
"Groggy...but okay, I guess," she answered.
The drapes had been reopened and the light was blinding as Tera looked around for River and Cameron. At first, she was unable to focus clearly on what she saw. She tried to sit up, but Dr. Speller motioned for her to lie still.
"Where's Riv, Dr. Speller? And Cameron?," she whispered. Her eyes followed Dr. Speller's as he glanced across the room to the sofa where she'd last seen them. As her eyes adjusted to the light and shadow in the room, she made out River's form; he was bending over the couch with a towel in his hand, a slightly concerned look on his face. Tera was so happy

to see him, she hadn't focused on anything else until she heard a low moan coming from the area where River stood.

It was then that she saw Cameron laid out on the couch, sweating profusely as River applied the damp towel to his forehead. *What happened?*, Tera wondered. And almost as soon as she'd wondered why River hadn't been right there at her side when she came around, or why he was attending to Cameron, or why she wasn't worried that Cameron might not be alright... *she remembered again*. She recalled the intense struggle between their spirits, and the death grip she'd held on him. She recalled the moment when she could have easily snuffed his life, like a candle flame between thumb and forefinger. *With relief*, she recalled that she hadn't made that choice... and that after reaching the same turning point they'd reached time and again, forgiveness had finally spared life instead of allowing vengeance to take it away.

River looked up at her and smiled. Even through the tears forming in her eyes, Tera could see River's love, and his reassurance, and the little-boy smile that let her know everything would be alright. Cameron was finally coming around, and Dr. Speller remained by her side as she continued to rest on the couch.

"You're still very tired, my dear," Dr. Speller said. "If you need to rest, do it; when you get up, you'll be fine."

For the first time in months, Tera was able to drift off to sleep with the assurance that she would rest undisturbed. Something, some undefined feeling told her that it was over...that the past was truly behind her now. Her eyelids became heavier and heavier, and the last image she saw before closing her eyes was River's mouth forming the words '*I love you*'.

"I love you, too," she whispered.

EPILOGUE

The day was, as they say, 'picture perfect'. Tera couldn't recall a day when the sky had been more vibrant, or the breeze had rustled the willows more gently, or the sun's kiss had been more loving.

It had been only a year since she and River had gone to see Dr. Speller; it was hard to remember what life had been like before he helped her break free of the tormenting dreams that had eventually taken over her nights *and* her days. It was hard to recall the emptiness in her life before she and River had gotten together...it all seemed so long ago, a lifetime away.

And now she stood in her bedroom looking out across the lawn, which was lined with neat rows of folding chairs. She looked at the silver and white bows decorating each row, and the flowered arch with its silver bells. She watched as her brother, Xavier, and her mother showed guests to their seats and then helped straighten Little Nate's bow tie. Tera smiled, thinking what a handsome little ring bearer her nephew was. Her heart overflowed as the reality of the occasion set in...*I'm getting married!*

"Hey, Tee," Mara said, "come *back*, girl! You're a million miles away."

"Unh-uh, Mara. I'm right here. I *still* can't believe it's really happening...but I'm *definitely* here!"

"Okay then, since you *are* 'here', how 'bout taking this package I been trying to give you for the past five minutes?," Mara teased. "It's got your stuff in it: you know, 'old, new, borrowed, blue' and all that jazz."

She handed Tera a small, delicate pouch purse which was decorated with fine embroidery and tiny seed pearls. Tera looked at it closely, admiring the scalloped design around the opening. Once again, Mara had found just the perfect accent. She hugged her sister, thanking her for the beautiful gift.

"Oh, honey, you ain't getting off *that* easy. We getting ready to open this right now, so you'll know what's what." Mara opened the pouch and reached inside. Well," Mara said, pulling out a neatly folded twenty dollar bill, "*this* is something new. It's one of those ones with the big ol' face. Now, don't you and Dread Man spend this all in one place," she laughed.

"And this," she continued, "is my cowrie shell pendant; put it on now, it'll look nice against the color of your gown."

Tera unhooked the clasp and put the necklace on. It *did* look beautiful against the cream lace of her West African *grand boubou.* Tera stood for a moment admiring it, and the *gelee* headwrap she wore; *River will love this,* she thought.

"Yeah, Tee...girl, that looks *good.* So now, that's your something borrowed--and *don't* forget where you got it from!--and here's your something blue," Mara said, taking out a lapis ring. Tera slipped it onto her right pinkie.

"Everything is perfect, Mara...but where's my something old?"

"It's outside, Tee. Don't worry girl, you'll see it," Mara answered. "Now let's finish getting you together...I bet River's about ready to storm in and carry you up out of here!"

"I'm ready," Tera said, taking a final appraisal of herself.

The music of the ensemble playing on the lawn drifted through the open window, and Tera heard each instrument clearly as they blended in perfect harmony: acoustic bass, cello, harp, flute, clarinet, drums. She looked out the window at the rows of guests, and saw

River standing near the flowered arch with his father. The music changed, cuing her that it was time...time to meet River at the arch...time to stand before God, family, and friends and proclaim their love and commitment to each other; and, as River had often said to her, it was time for them to start their life together...*again*.

Mara followed Tera as she walked to the open patio doors. The two of them stood there looking out over the group of people until Mara kissed Tera's cheek. "Lot of luck, lot of love to both of y'all, baby sis," Mara whispered, then began her slow march up the aisle, signaling the imminent arrival of the bride.

The music changed again, and this time all heads turned to see Tera walk out onto the patio where her father, Hector, waited to escort her down the aisle. "You look beautiful, Tera," he told her. "And I'm so proud of you."

"Thank you Daddy, and... Daddy?...Daddy, you're not...crying, are you?," Tera asked, trying to keep her own tears from bubbling over.

"Me? Crying? 'Course not, Tera! It's just *allergies*, girl...you know about my allergies. So, are you ready?," Hector asked.

Tera looked up and saw her groom, her soulmate; the love in River's eyes was a magnet drawing her to him. "Yes, Daddy...I'm ready."

###

"...before God, and in the presence of these people, I now proclaim that they are husband and wife," Reverend Bennett said, as he officiated over the ceremony uniting his son and daughter-in-law. Even before he could finish the traditional ending, *"you may now kiss your bride..."*, Tera had found her home in River's arms and claimed his warm lips, much to the amusement of their guests. The couple's closed eyes and locked lips couldn't block out the sounds of laughter, or cheering, or Olivia Morton's voice wailing, "*my baby, my baby*", though they certainly seemed to be in their own world until Reverend Bennett tapped his son on the shoulder, whispering that the honeymoon didn't start until later.

"I don't know if I can wait that long," Tera whispered, softly kissing River's neck.

"Me neither, but let's at least *try*, woman. That means *leave my neck alone*, or I can't be responsible, you hear?"

###

At last, the time of evening came when food had been served; the wedding cake had been cut; champagne toasts had been made; gifts had been opened, cards read; hands shaken and cheeks kissed on the receiving line. It was time for the guests to say goodbye to the departing honeymooners. It had taken all of Tera's control to stay in her own room, away from the room where River had gone to change into his travel clothes. In a way, though, she appreciated the time alone with her own thoughts.

She was filled with happiness, just being with her friends and family on the most wonderful day of her life. If there was any disappointment at all, there was only the tiniest twinge that Cameron hadn't been able to attend the wedding. In the past year, he had--at last!--completed his Ph.D., moved back to Decatur, and started work on a new aspect of his research. Tera smiled as she read the card he'd sent:

Dear Tera & River,

So you finally did it, eh? That's beautiful. I'm sorry that I can't be there, but you know I'm with you in spirit [no pun intended]. You two are a sure shot to make it through any situation, that's a fact. May you always have each other, may your lives be filled with new and exciting things, and may you always be surrounded by people who love you, the 'old souls' who have been with you always--just look around you, they're everywhere! Best Wishes, Cameron Wilson. p.s.--Tera, you were right. There is always another 'loose end' worth exploring when you research something that's interesting to you. Thanks for reminding me of that. C.W.

Tera folded the card up and placed it with the others; she and River could read through them all again later. *So he understood what I was talking about with the research,* Tera thought; *I wish I knew what he meant by 'old souls' being everywhere. Who were they? How was she supposed to recognize them?*

Even after her experience of a year earlier, the idea of being around folks--those whose paths may have crossed hers in another lifetime--was still mind-boggling. A knock on the door shook her out of her thoughts.

"Tera, are you ready?," River asked. "I'll be back for you in about five minutes."

She was on her way out the bedroom door when she ran into River, who was about to knock again...and she was *very* glad they'd met up at the door. If he'd come inside, the two of them might not have been seen until the next day. River kissed her cheek and took the heaviest of their two suitcases. The guests were lined up outside, ready to shower them with bubbles and send them off with congratulations and love. "Come on, woman," River said, "let's go."

When they came out of the house to say goodbye to everyone, River and Tera were met with a barrage of bubbles being pumped from a couple of contraptions strategically placed on either side of the patio. Guessing that her crazy sister had something to do with it, Tera grabbed Mara's hand and pulled her from the crowd of well-wishers.

"This is your doing, isn't it Mara?," she asked.

"You could tell? I guess game recognizes game. Anyway, I thought it was better than all that messy rice and everything."
"Mara, I didn't know anybody even *dealt* with these many bubbles...not since the Lawrence Welk Show, anyway. Lawrence Welk...oh, I get it! So, this must be my 'something old', the thing you said would be outside, huh?"
"Nope. *Good guess*, but unh-uh," Mara said before giving her sister and River a final kiss on the cheek. "You two run on, you got a plane to catch, right? Have a beautiful time," Mara said.
"Oh, it's like *that*? You're not even gonna *tell* me where it is...*what* it is? That's cold."
Oh, quit whining, Tee. I said it's out here, it's out here...don't worry, you'll definitely see it".
Mara took her younger sister by the shoulders, giving her a look Tera couldn't quite define. It was sentimental, yes...but there was something more, something...? Tera gave up; Mara was emotional, she was a philosopher, she was a visionary, and she was a *nut*, a real joker--so it could have been almost *anything* Tera saw in her eyes. Mara spoke.
"When you see it, Tera...well, just remember that you have people around you who love you; and we'll always be here for you."
Mara smiled through eyes that had suddenly brimmed with tears.
"Oh, Mara," Tera said, surprised by her sister's unexpected mushiness and tears which seemed to be contagious. "Oh, sweetie, I didn't know you were such a big softie."
Mara wiped her eyes quickly.
"Oh, sweetie my *ass*, okay? Look, you all just get on, don't miss your plane standing around talking to me--I'll be here when you get *back*. Love y'all."
Tera and River ran over to their car, which had been

decorated with all the silly odds and ends that might be expected to adorn a newlyweds' vehicle. A '*just married*' sign. Ribbons. Streamers and flowers. Tin cans on a string. Old shoes. They stood in front of the car for a moment, just laughing; and again suspected that Mara had something to do with it.

"Your sister," River chuckled. "Hey, Tera...look at this." He removed the small leather pouch from where it had been taped to the passenger's side window. The attached note said "*Something Old*". Hannah's mirror was inside the pouch, and Tera smiled, looking for Mara's face in the crowd as she opened and read the note:

Dear Sis,

Well, here's the 'old' thing I was supposed to give you. Yes, I know I already gave it to you before; but that was before you knew what it once meant to you.

For years after Hannah's death, Mason held onto this mirror, and when the day came that he decided to leave us and head further north into Canada, he gave it to me as a token of our friendship. It has been in our family for generations, though I understood that one day you and I would meet again, and this mirror would return to you, its rightful owner. Sorry I lied to you and said I'd gotten it from that antique shop! And if you've ever wondered how Dr. Speller got hold of it for your hypnosis session, it was me who gave it to him—I've got keys to your place, remember? He said that it would help the session to have something of yours that was meaningful to you. I guess he was right!

In any case, our lives have come full circle. You once accepted this mirror as an unusual gift from your sister. Now, accept it from me as your friend--one who has known and cared for you and River both...for a very long time. The circle is now complete, and I am happy for the wondrous change it has brought.

You have made it this time, Hannah and Mason, so live and love in peace; and when you have children, pass along the mirror as an heirloom, just as it was passed to you. Blessings now and always,
Mara
[once known as Black Sky]

The note in Tera's hand trembled slightly. She looked across the lawn in time to see Mara standing at the patio door, carrying a tray of food into the kitchen; when their eyes met, Mara winked. Now she understood what Cameron meant...they were surrounded by people who loved them; people who always had been there, always would be...

"Come on, Tera. It's time," River said.

--the end--